One Night with a Millionaire

Daring Divorcees

Book 1

Shannyn Schroeder

Chapter 1

Tess shimmied into her silk navy dress, knowing it wasn't quite as fancy or formal as some women would wear, but it would do. Her life rarely called for formal wear.

She checked the time and realized Nina would be arriving any minute. Trevor said he'd stop by to help as well. When her ex bailed on taking the kids for the weekend, her friends had stepped up.

The night was important to the hospital because it raised so much money, but for Tess, it was the only night of the year when she wasn't taking care of anyone. She wasn't a nurse or a mom. She was just a woman out for a good time. And with the kids home for the summer, she needed a real night off.

The doorbell chimed just as she slipped on her heels.

Opening her bedroom door, she heard the cacophony of her home. The boys fought over something in their room, and Zoe yelled from her position on the couch.

"Someone's at the door!" Zoe called for the second time.

Walking past, she tapped her daughter's head. "You could've answered it."

"You always taught me not to open the door for strangers."

Tess rolled her eyes. "Nina and Trevor aren't strangers."

"But they're babysitters. As if I need one."

She ignored Zoe and opened the door to see Nina standing on the porch with a huge smile.

"You look hot!" Nina told her.

"Eww," Zoe called from the couch.

"You should be thrilled your mom can pull this off. This is your future," Nina said and gave Tess a quick hug. She swept a hand down the length of Tess's body. "This is amazing. Don't listen to the cranky teenager."

"Thank you."

Nina narrowed her eyes. "But it needs something..." She pointed a finger at Tess's neck and then rummaged in her overnight bag. A moment later, she held a sparkly necklace in her hand. "I know you don't do much jewelry, so I brought this. It'll look fabulous."

"That's so thoughtful, but I can't wear that."

"Yes, you can. Turn around." She twirled her finger. "It looks incredible for an expensive fake."

She had no idea when Nina had become so bossy. They'd been friends for years, but it had taken Nina months of coffee dates with the group of divorcees before she'd engaged in conversation. Now she was telling Tess what to do.

Tess lifted her hair to let Nina clasp the necklace. As it dropped into place in the deep V neckline of her dress, Tess touched the cool stones. Adding glitter made her feel a little like a princess.

As if reading her mind, Nina said, "Okay, Cinderella, let me see."

The doorbell sounded again, and Billy and Andrew tore into the room screaming, "Trevor!"

It was like they had radar for finding a guy who was fun. They both ran to the door and fought over who would answer it. When they finally yanked it open, they launched themselves at Trevor.

"Hey, guys. Way to make me feel welcome," Nina said.

The boys pulled Trevor into the living

room. He looked like the Jolly Green Giant being tugged by munchkins.

"Wow," Trevor said when he saw Tess.

She smiled. "I know that's a compliment, but I can't help but wonder what you think of me every other time I see you."

"Aww, you're always beautiful. But this... this is wow."

"Gross," Billy said. "That's my mom."

"I know. And she's my friend. Don't you know any girls at school who are pretty?"

"Yeah, but..." He looked at Tess with his whole face scrunched. "She's Mom."

"Yeah, I love you, too, buddy. Go to the kitchen and wash up. Pizza should be here soon."

Andrew started to follow Billy, but he turned back and whispered, "I think Trevor's right." Then he took off to the kitchen. Tess turned to Zoe. "In bed by ten thirty."

"It's the weekend."

"You still need sleep, and you're not staying in bed until noon. Chores tomorrow."

"Gawd. Does it ever end?" Zoe shoved off the couch, tucking her phone in her pocket.

"Sure. As soon as you turn eighteen and move out." Zoe heaved that teenager sigh Tess despised and walked to the kitchen. Tess focused on not grinding her teeth, which would cause tension to build, which would lead to a migraine.

"Go. Get out of here. Have an amazing time," Nina prompted.

Tess inhaled deeply and released the breath.

"Thanks. Thank you, too, Trevor. Don't spoil the boys or let them stay up too late."

"You mean no *Walking Dead* marathon fueled by greasy food and sugar? What the hell am I here for?"

Tess laughed. "You guys are awesome. I totally owe you."

"I'll stay until the boys are settled in bed

and then head out," he said. "Have a great time."

Giving Nina another hug, she whispered, "My bed is made. Get comfortable there. I'm not sure when or if I'll be home."

"Stay out, have fun, get laid. We'll be fine."

She grabbed her clutch purse and shoved her lipstick and phone in beside two condoms. With her keys in hand, she rushed through the kitchen to give the kids a quick hug and kiss and a final warning to behave.

The pizza delivery guy pulled up as she walked toward her minivan. Nina stood in the doorway and waved her off. It was one night. They'd be fine. She knew it, but she still got a sinking feeling every time she left the kids.

Mom guilt sucked.

When she went to work, she usually took the train, but traveling on the El in a party dress didn't seem wise, so she drove into downtown Chicago. The city skyline was beautiful. At least that's what she told herself as she fought with the cabs in the gridlock of the city.

By the time she turned the corner toward the Peninsula, she'd had enough. Even though it went against her nature, she forked over the exorbitant valet parking fee for the night. She didn't care how many extra hours she'd have to work to make it up. Not having to drive around and look for parking was worth it.

She stepped from her mom-mobile and smiled at the valet, who was classy enough not to laugh at her and the picture she made—elegant dress, high heels, perfectly curled hair, climbing from a minivan that reeked of French fries. Yeah, she was ready for a drink.

Inside the lobby, she texted her friend and coworker Angie to let her know she'd arrived. They'd made plans to have a drink together and scope out the crowd. Their boss thought they were there solely to help fill the coffers for their department.

Tess usually put in her hours for the hospital and then went to the hotel bar to find company for the remainder of her night. If nothing else, she might be able to talk Angie into hitting another hotel or club.

Miles Prescott sat on the edge of his bed, careful not to wrinkle his tuxedo. The mere thought of listening to his mother nag that he looked like he'd just rolled out of bed was enough to keep him neatly pressed. The St. Mark's Hospital gala would be his third event this week. His second black-tie of the month.

Normally, he didn't care about the fundraising and charity events he was expected to attend as the face of his family. While his siblings did the "real" work of running the family software company, he mostly dictated where they should send charitable contributions. But tonight, he was tired.

In fact, since his dad had died, this had begun to take its toll. When his father had been alive, Miles had been able to do his work in his office and at board meetings. His parents had been the face of the family. He'd attended only a handful of events. Now, the bulk of such affairs fell to him.

And he hated it.

Of all the Prescotts, he was definitely the partygoer. Hell, everyone loved a good party. Except these weren't parties. They were *events*. All polite conversation, shameless flirting with older women who always went home with their husbands, and superficial smiles with people he rarely wanted to see again.

Part of him would kill to go back to being in college. To drink beer at a party. To meet women who actually wanted to talk to him, not just to get a contribution.

Shoving off the bed, he smiled as he thought of what his mother's reaction would be if he ordered a beer tonight. A knock let him know she was ready to go downstairs. At least with the gala being held at the Peninsula, he had an awesome view of the city and excellent food for the night. It was almost enough to make up for everything else.

Another sharp rap had him moving faster. He opened the door with an apology on his lips.

"What are you doing?" his mom asked before he had a chance to say anything.

"Getting ready. It's a big suite. Long walk from one end to the other." His sarcasm was lost on her.

"Are you ready?"

"Just about." He looked at her for a moment. Something was off. Stella Prescott was always formal, but tonight she looked stiff. "What's wrong?"

She swept into the room, lips pressed tightly. "It's the gala. I thought I could do it."

"What do you mean?"

"This one was always your father's favorite. I didn't make it last year..."

She didn't finish the thought. Miles knew she hated admitting how lost she'd been when Dad had died. She was slowly coming back to herself. It was part of the reason why Miles kept agreeing to attend these things.

"It'll be fine, Mom." He walked across the room and gathered his wallet and key card. "Why did Dad like this one?"

Her face softened. "Because, like you, he hated formal high-society gatherings."

Miles laughed and pointed at the tuxedo he wore.

"Well, let's not get carried away, Miles. Of course, if you want to raise any real money, the event has to be black-tie, but this gala is open to so many more people. He loved talking to guests from all walks of life. Many of the hospital employees attend. Mostly, I think it's an attempt to draw in more funds. They plead their case directly to benefactors."

Interesting. If his dad had liked this event, maybe Miles's night wouldn't be a total loss. He found it funny his mother managed to think doctors were of a different class. He highly doubted the maintenance staff would be joining them for the evening.

He held out his arm for her to take. "Shall we?"

She looped her hand through his crooked elbow. "Keep in mind not all of the guests will be who you're used to. Try not to comment on off-the-rack gowns and rented tuxedos. Not everyone is as privileged as we are."

"First, have I ever embarrassed you by looking down on anyone?"

"Well, I didn't mean that."

"Yes, you did. And second, do you think I would be able to tell an off-the-rack dress from a designer one? I'm too busy imagining the dress on my floor to think about something like that."

His joke had the desired effect. She lightly smacked his arm. "That is exactly the type of talk to which I'm referring. My friends find you simply scandalous."

He led her to the elevator.

"While my peers know you are playing games, not all the women here will understand."

His night was looking better by the minute. While it wasn't a kegger, he might have the chance to actually enjoy himself.

The elevator arrived with a swish and a subtle ding. Inside, his mom rested her head against his shoulder as the doors closed. "Thank you for doing this, Miles. It means a lot to me."

Moments like these were exactly the

reason he continued to agree. He could fight his brother and sister about always being the one to go. They could just as easily make appearances, but he couldn't fight his mom. He liked knowing she could lean on him.

Never one to show any kind of weakness for long, she straightened and put on her game face before they reached the ballroom.

Miles waded through the throngs of people to reach the bar. While his mother was content to sip champagne all night, he wanted something a little stronger. At least she'd been right about the crowd being different than the guests at the usual events they attended.

At the bar, he ordered a scotch, and while he waited, he eavesdropped on conversations happening behind him.

"Are you saying the work you do is more important than the cancer wing?"

"Of course not. We're all working our ass— really hard to save lives every day."

Hearing a woman nearly slip and swear at prospective donors made Miles turn to watch the interaction. The couple behind him he recognized. The Baldwins were generous but loved to make a recipient work for it.

Mrs. Baldwin reached out and laid a hand on the woman's arm. "Really, dear. How do you do it without becoming severely depressed every day?"

The woman stood with her back to Miles, so he couldn't see her face, but her voice carried clearly. "Many days break my heart. I work with sick babies. When a newborn is so small she can fit into the palm of my hand"—she held her hand out, palm up to demonstrate—"and I hold and care for that baby daily, nothing in the world feels as satisfying as the day I get to see her go home."

Miles's gaze followed the line of her arm from her hand to her shoulder. Her brown hair fell in waves down her back. The dress she wore hugged her but wasn't tight. It also wasn't too revealing, which sucked for him. He didn't want to have to imagine her body. His eyes landed on the curve of her ass and down the length of her long legs, which were bare. The toned muscles made him ache to touch them.

Mr. Baldwin chimed in, "Why should we fund such a small department? Wouldn't our money have a greater effect at a hospital like Lurie's or even St. Jude's, where children are their sole focus?"

"Those hospitals are phenomenal, of course. But not every family can or will go to either of those places. Yes, St. Mark's is small, but we do amazing things in our tiny department. Our families come to us for help. We're close to home for them. They have extended family nearby for support. They don't have to disrupt the lives of their other children in order to save the newest member of the family. At St. Mark's, we care for the entire family, not just sick children."

"Are you sure you're a nurse, Theresa?" Mr. Baldwin asked.

"Absolutely. Why do you ask?"

"You talk like someone who has a lot of experience reaching into deep pockets and wringing them for all they're worth."

She chuckled, and the low sound shot straight through Miles. The bartender set his scotch at his elbow, but Miles was afraid to turn away. He wanted to see the woman who had caught Carter Baldwin's attention.

"I assure you, I work the floor every week. The only fundraising I do is attend this gala every year."

"If you're half as good at being a nurse as you are at talking about how good the hospital is, you should be running the gala."

Another gentle laugh. "Thank you for the high praise, Mr. Baldwin, but I love my job.

I'm not looking to run anything. It was very nice to meet you."

Baldwin sipped his drink and nodded at her. "I'm sure we'll be meeting again."

She shook his hand, and Miles leaned forward, hoping she'd turn enough for him to see her face. As she moved, her long brown waves fell back from her shoulder, and Miles leaned to the side to see her. Then she turned completely around and faced him. Her eyes widened when she caught him staring at her. She inched her left eyebrow up a fraction as if to ask for an explanation, but she smiled.

"Can I help you?"

For a moment, Miles was dumbstruck. She was beautiful, with creamy skin sprinkled with freckles. But it was the smile that got him.

"Busted." He stepped forward with a hand extended. "Hi, I'm Miles Prescott. I'm sorry. I was eavesdropping on your conversation with the Baldwins."

"Why not join in?"

"I was intrigued by any woman who could capture Carter Baldwin's attention like that, but I prefer my conversations one-on-one."

She shook his hand. "So, you know the Baldwins?"

He nodded. "They're good friends with my parents." He released her hand. "Can I get you a drink...Theresa, was it?"

She nodded. "I'd love some champagne. Thank you."

Instead of stepping back to the bar, he waved a waiter over, snagged a glass from the tray, and handed it to her. She raised the glass, and Miles watched her lips settle on the edge as she sipped. Her head tilted back a little, allowing him to watch her throat work.

"So, tell me your secret. How did you captivate Mr. Baldwin so easily?"

She lifted a shoulder. "He asked what I do for a living. Personally, I don't think it's all that captivating."

"You might not think so, but I've been to functions with Baldwin, and I've been in board meetings with him. If he spares you more than a passing glance, you've caught him. Not an easy thing to do."

"Board meetings, huh? So what do you do, Mr. Prescott?"

He flinched. "Miles, please. I'm a numbers man."

"An accountant?"

"Not really. I help my family's business allocate funds." He retrieved his scotch from the edge of the bar and sipped.

"Well, now that is interesting."

"It's not like I save the lives of premature babies."

"No, but you're the man who can make my job easier. It seems as though you're the person I should've been using all my charm on instead of Mr. Baldwin." She took another drink of her champagne with a smile.

"I'm pretty sure that's unnecessary, but I

would love to hear more about your work. Do you have a seat saved for dinner?"

"Are you asking if I'm here with a date?"

"That obvious?"

"A little." She finished her champagne.

"Does that mean you won't tell me?"

"I'm alone, except for my friend Angie."

"Excellent. Then the two of you can join me at my table."

She pursed her lips. "We'll see." She reached past him and set her empty glass on the bar. "Pleasure to meet you, Miles. I'm off to mingle."

Miles knocked back the rest of his drink and stared at Theresa retreating through the crowd. She walked with confidence and the alluring sway of her hips wasn't lost on him. As she stopped to speak with various people, he kept an eye on her.

His gut told him that spending dinner with Theresa would be an excellent way to pass the night.

Chapter 2

Tess smiled as she bowed out of another conversation with a guest. She couldn't even remember the woman's name because she was distracted by Miles staring at her. His attention was appreciative, not creepy. And it had been a hell of a long time since she'd felt a man look at her like that.

Of course, it had been equally as long since she'd been dressed like this. Her everyday wear consisted of scrubs while on duty, and jeans and T-shirts at home. She wandered to the tables of silent-auction items. Sliding a glance over her shoulder, she took another peek at Miles.

He stood with an air of confidence as he spoke to people. His face was too pretty. One that belonged to someone who didn't have worries. He had a neatly trimmed close-cut beard, a little scruffy—definitely added to his sex appeal.

And his tuxedo. Obviously made for him. He could give James Bond a run for his money.

Just then, Miles raised his glass in her direction. What had he said? *Busted*. She straightened her shoulders. Well, it was only fitting since he'd been staring at her. She winked and turned her attention to the basket in front of her. It was filled with some fancy French soap. Nothing interesting.

Behind her, a couple of women were chatting, and when she overheard them mention Miles's name, she slowed her progress down the aisle.

"I wouldn't mind another evening with him. I thoroughly enjoyed myself, and it's been a couple of years."

"Sorry, Anastasia, I've heard he's being far more discreet with whom he chooses to spend time."

Anastasia giggled. "Whoever you're using for information is wrong. I've seen him with three new women this month. Really, you need to get on social media. It's far more reliable than the old rumor mill."

Tess moved down the line to check out the other items, refusing to look behind her to check out Anastasia. She tried not to let the sting of disappointment get to her. Of course someone as good-looking as Miles had his pick of women. For a brief moment, his attention had made her feel special. In reality, he was exactly what she was looking for. But messing with a possible donor probably wasn't the brightest idea. Especially if he wasn't truly discreet. She'd never slept with a guest from the gala. It was a little too much like sleeping with someone from work, which was a line she would never cross.

She continued to check out baskets and gift certificates for the auction. Every year, she bid on a couple of things but never actually won. Her bids mostly prompted others to bid more, and they quickly exceeded her budget. As she neared the end of the first table, a glass of champagne appeared in front of her.

Turning, she saw Miles standing beside her.

"You look thirsty."

She accepted the glass. "Thoughtful, but I am capable of getting my own drink."

"I used the champagne as a reason to accept your invitation."

"Invitation?" He stood close, and her skin

flushed with his proximity. This guy knew how to get to a woman.

"You winked at me."

"What? I did no such thing." *Since when do I play coy?*

He lowered his mouth, closer to her ear. "Sure you did. When I caught you staring at me."

"I'm sure I have no idea what you're talking about," she responded, not hiding her smile.

"My mother always told me I had a wild imagination and was given to fantasies." He brushed her hair off her shoulder, barely skimming his fingers over her neck and causing a ripple of pleasure to race across her skin.

Tess wondered what fantasies he might have. Flirting with Miles was fun. "Have you bid on anything?"

"Hmmm?" He stared at her, his eyes never wavering or wandering.

She tilted her head toward the table. "The silent auction."

"I haven't even looked yet. Mind if I join you?"

"By all means. Anything for a good cause." She turned to head back to where she'd started, looking over her shoulder to make sure he followed.

"We should start from the beginning. Wouldn't want to miss anything."

"There's a specific path to take?"

"Not officially, but if you start in the middle of one table, you'll lose track of what you've seen and what you haven't. What if you give up, thinking you've already looked at a table, and you miss out on the one item that would complete your life?" she teased.

Miles crowded into her space and spoke softly. "You're telling me the answers to all of life's problems can be found right here at this auction table?"

"You never know," she answered with a

smile. "In this fine basket, we have fancy soap. From France," she said with a flourish of her hand.

Miles bent over and peered into the basket. "It's soap."

"That's what I just said."

He pointed to the bid sheet below the basket. "People are bidding a ton of money for soap."

"To each his own?" she offered.

"For that price, I'd expect the soap to jump up and rub itself on me."

Tess snickered at the image he provided. *I wouldn't mind being part of that shower.*

"Sorry. That was probably inappropriate."

She laid a hand on his arm. "I spend a good portion of my day cleaning up bodily fluids. It'll take much more than that to bother me."

"Good to know."

They moved down the table, and Tess found herself having a great time. She and

Miles made jokes about some of the baskets and questioned the contents of others. Miles began putting in bids on many of them simply because they made him laugh.

"What are you going to do if you win a whole bunch of these?"

"Go home with a smile on my face."

She couldn't imagine handing over that kind of money—charity or not. She paused in front of the next item. She had no jokes for this one. She'd had her eye on it since first thing tonight. It was a spa retreat. She had made the first bid, which had since been totally blown out of the water.

"What's this one?"

"A spa day." She turned her face to his. "Not something someone like you needs."

"What's that supposed to mean?"

"Your skin is flawless. You don't need a rejuvenating skin peel." Damn. She wasn't being any more subtle than he'd been when he'd fished for her date status.

"Good genes," he answered. But he picked up the card that described all of the spa services included.

Tess held in her sigh at the thought of her loss. That was the problem with pretending, even for one night, that her life was different than it was. She started to long for things. Things like a spa package she'd never be able to afford.

Moving away from the gift certificate, she turned the corner to the final table before realizing Miles hadn't followed. When she looked back, he was speaking to another woman. It appeared he'd found something more interesting than their jokes.

She shook her head. Miles was promising. He was flirty and probably likely to accept a single night of fun without asking too many questions. Plus, he obviously had a reputation for one-and-done. She left the auction tables and wound back through the crowd.

The event tended to draw couples, so it

wasn't exactly a singles mixer. After dinner and maybe a dance or two, if she were lucky, she would go upstairs to the Shanghai Terrace for a drink. There, she always had luck in finding companionship for her night out.

Dinner would start soon, so Tess began looking for Angie so they could sit together. They found each other walking from opposite ends of the bar.

"Here," Angie said, pushing a glass of champagne toward her. "I snagged an extra because they never reopen the bar fast enough after dinner. Where do you want to sit?"

Tess immediately thought of Miles's offer to sit with him. "I'm not sure."

"Table five," a low voice said behind her.

She spun to find Miles. "You're making a habit of sneaking up on me."

"Is that a problem?"

"Maybe announce yourself as you get near so my heart doesn't forget to beat."

"Introduce me to your friend?"

"Angie, this is Miles. We met at the bar and shared a few laughs at the auction table."

"Where you abandoned me," he joked as he extended a hand to Angie. "Nice to meet you."

"I did not abandon you. You were caught up in conversation with someone." She hated that someone came out more like an accusation.

"I was asking a question before placing a bid." He turned back to Angie. "You're both invited to sit at my table. Do you work at the hospital as well?"

"I'm a nurse, too." Angie nodded and smiled appreciatively at him.

"Shall we?" Miles asked, extending his arm toward the banquet tables.

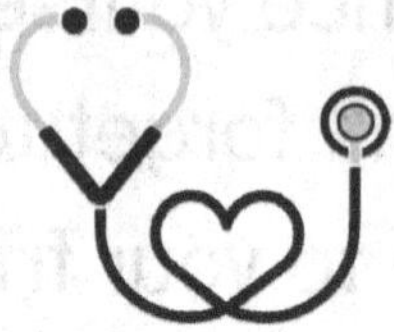

Miles owed his mother a gift for making him attend the hospital benefit. Of all the events he'd participated in over the years, he couldn't remember ever having such a good time. Dinner breezed by faster than he'd wanted it to.

After he introduced the nurses to everyone at the table, including his mother, Theresa and Angie kept him engaged in conversation the entire time. They were probably rude to the others at their table, given the looks his mother had shot his way repeatedly.

But even she had enjoyed talking with the nurses. The emcee announced the closing of bids for the auction and that winners would be posted shortly after the speakers were finished.

Theresa leaned close. "Sure you don't want to run over there and up your bid? Someone else might walk away with the fancy French soap."

"I think I can pass."

As they settled in to listen to the speakers address the audience, Miles went to the bar and got another round of drinks for the women. Thankfully, the speeches were short. That meant dancing would start soon, and he had plans for the dance floor and Theresa.

When the list of auction winners went up, he followed Angie, who hoped to win one. Theresa declined, saying she hadn't bid. Much to his surprise, he won three of the items he'd bid on, including the one he wanted most. Tucking two envelopes into his jacket pocket, he picked up the remaining basket—a Chicago sports team theme.

Back at the table, Theresa's face lit up. "What'd you get?"

He set the basket down.

She gave him an exaggerated frown. "I really hoped to be able to try out the fancy soap."

"What are the two of you going on about with the soap?" his mother asked.

"Nothing." There was no point in trying to explain it to his mother. "I bid on this because I thought Sabrina would like it." He spun the basket to his mother.

She narrowed her eyes as she took in the contents. "I'm sure she will like that. It was very thoughtful of you."

"Sabrina?" Theresa asked.

"My older sister. She's a sports nut. My dad was a season ticket holder for the Bears, and she used to go to all the games with him."

His mom leaned forward. "Sabrina's my oldest. My husband had hoped for a boy. Even though Bradley came along only two years later, as soon as Sabrina was old enough to sit through an entire game, it became their time together. By the time she reached junior high, she was involved with every sport imaginable.”

“Much to my mother's dismay. She never got to treat Sabrina like a Barbie doll.”

“I have never acted as though my daughter was a doll.”

“That's not what Sabrina says.”

Mom *humphed* at him. “As if asking her to dress appropriately, in a gown, was asking too much.” She leaned even closer to Theresa. “Not even for her prom. I had to fight to get her into a dress. She almost didn't go.”

Mom spoke like it was unfathomable to not attend your prom. Miles guessed to someone whose life depended on being out in society, not going to something as momentous as prom probably felt like a death knell.

“Did you attend your prom, Theresa?”

“Yes, I did. I loved it. Dressing up, feeling

like a princess." She took a sip of her water. "It's why I come to this benefit every year. I spend my days wearing scrubs, but here, I get to be beautiful."

"I bet you're beautiful regardless of what you wear," he said.

Theresa's cheeks grew pink. Before either of them said anything else, Angie returned carrying a small basket.

"I got it!"

"What?" Theresa asked.

"Check it out." She set the basket on the table.

"How did I miss this one?" She poked at the cellophane to move an item inside.

"Your method of following a specific path didn't work out after all, huh?" Miles leaned closer to see what the excitement was all about.

"I guess I was distracted and missed out, which proves my point."

"Your loss, my gain," Angie said.

"You'll share, though."

Miles peered into the basket. "Coffee? That's what's got you ramped up?" It was almost as bad as soap.

Theresa rolled her eyes. "Coffee is the lifeblood of the nurse who works twelve-hour shifts, sometimes without being able to stop to eat. Our time is fueled by caffeine."

"And in case you didn't know, the hospital coffee is awful. This is special." Angie petted the basket.

The band had set up and began playing music, and a few couples took to the dance floor.

"Would you like to dance?" he asked.

"I shouldn't leave Angie."

Angie shoved her. "Go dance. I'm going home anyway."

"What? It's early."

"I'm on at six tomorrow morning."

"That sucks. I thought you were off."

"Nope, but at least I'll have my new friend

to comfort me in the morning." Again, she stroked the basket.

These women were strange. They stood and hugged briefly. Miles stood as well and offered to walk Angie out, just so he could prove to his mother that she had raised him right. Even though Angie waved him off, his mother gave him a nod of approval.

Miles held out his arm for Theresa. "Shall we?"

She wasn't shy at all about getting close to him and letting him hold her. The music was nothing contemporary, but Miles didn't care. For a change, he was enjoying being at a fundraising event, and his night was only getting better.

"Have you come to this gala before?" Theresa asked.

"No. My parents always attended together. This is the first time my mom has come since my dad died."

"I'm sorry to hear that."

She quieted again and allowed him to guide her closer to his body. While she didn't rest her head on his shoulder, his cheek brushed her temple. He wanted to kiss her. But not here on a dance floor full of people, with his mother nearby to witness.

No, he wanted her all to himself.

More than anything, he wanted to invite her upstairs, but he was afraid of offending her. He wasn't thinking about sleeping with her. Well, he was, but it wasn't the reason for the invitation. He wanted to get to know her, and if that led to kissing and touching, all the better.

They stayed on the dance floor for three songs before she pulled away. "You're a really good dancer, but my feet are killing me. I'm not used to walking around in heels."

Back at the table, his mom stood. "I'm tired, Miles, so I'm going up to my room."

"Hold on a minute. I'll walk you." He

turned to Theresa. "I'll be right back. Will you wait for me?"

She nodded, but his mother said, "I do not need a chaperone."

Miles nodded, even though he wanted to laugh.

"You young people have a good time." She grabbed the basket he'd won for Sabrina. "I'll take this so you won't forget it."

He kissed his mother's cheek, and Theresa reached over and shook her hand. "It was nice to meet you, Mrs. Prescott."

"I look forward to hearing what your department will do with the donations."

"I'm not sure they'll give me a full report since I'm just a floor nurse."

His mother scoffed. "We both know it's the floor nurses who keep things running."

Theresa smiled. As his mom walked away, Miles realized Theresa was shorter because she'd kicked off her shoes. When she sat again, she stretched her legs out and placed her feet on an adjacent chair.

"I guess that's a no to more dancing, huh?" he asked, looking at her bare feet. "I hope that doesn't mean you're planning on leaving."

"Not if I get a better offer." A wicked little smile played on her mouth.

"What constitutes a better offer?"

She tilted her head, and he watched her hair flow to the side. The desire to tangle his hands in it struck him hard. "Maybe a drink up at the Terrace. I love the amazing view of the city."

Now it was Miles's turn to smile. The Asian-inspired restaurant in the hotel was great, but he had a better idea. "If it's a view you're looking for, I can do one better and offer privacy."

"Really?"

"I have a corner room with a panoramic view of the skyline. And since I didn't attack the minibar before coming down here tonight, it should be well stocked."

"You have a room here?"

He nodded in the direction of where his mother had gone. "Not sharing with my mother. I haven't done that for many, many years."

She laughed at his joke. "I'd love a private viewing of the skyline. Lead the way."

Chapter 3

Tess's heart thumped in her chest. She hadn't expected things to turn so quickly. She'd thought she'd need to finesse the situation with Miles. While she wouldn't have suggested getting a room here—she'd never expect someone to spend more than her night's pay on a room—it was certainly convenient. She held on to Miles's hand as she slipped back into her shoes. Her feet were not happy about being squished again, but she mentally told them they'd be free in one short elevator ride.

Miles continued to hold her hand as they walked to the elevator. When they stepped inside and the doors closed, he said, "You're sure you're okay with coming to my room? I'd like to get to know you better. No expectations."

"What if I have expectations?" she asked, trailing a finger down the front of his shirt.

Pleasure zipped through her as she watched his throat work at her suggestion. She withheld a laugh. Surely he'd been with women who'd asked for what they wanted.

"I've never done this with a man I've met at the gala. And here's the thing, Miles. I don't get to go out and have fun all that often. I really, really want to have a good time tonight. Think you can help me?"

The elevator finally dinged, and she stepped out without waiting for an answer. When she turned, she noticed they were at the top floor.

"Mine's this one," he said, leading her to the door on the left.

There were only two rooms on this floor, which meant it wasn't a room, but a suite— and not a simple living-room-kitchen combo. This was like an apartment. *Holy crap*. Forget what she'd thought about losing a night's pay for a room. This was a paycheck's worth. He opened the door and held it for her to enter.

As he hung up his jacket, Tess sent a quick text to Nina letting her know where she was and who she was with.

"Problem?" he asked as he came up behind her.

"Not at all. Letting a friend know where I am." She tucked her phone away again and turned.

"I've been waiting for this moment all night," he whispered and laid his hands on her hips.

That was all the warning she got before his mouth descended on hers. For as taken aback as he'd seemed in the elevator, he was completely sure of himself now. He kissed like a man confident he'd have her naked soon enough.

And she sure as hell wasn't complaining.

His beard tickled her lips as he moved, sending licks of pleasure through her body. It had been much too long since she'd done this. Miles moved his hands over her, palming her ass and bringing her flush against his body, his hard-on pressing against her belly. A moan slipped past her lips and into his mouth.

He pulled away and stared into her eyes. "Having fun yet?"

"That was a pretty good beginning, and if it's a preview of what's to come, I'm on board."

"I promised you a drink and a view."

Seriously? He wants to stop for a drink now? Her face must've revealed her thoughts.

He smiled and patted her ass. "The

room's mine. For the entire night. I don't have anywhere else to be. Do you?"

She shook her head, not wanting to admit that her real life was waiting for her a few miles away.

"Then we have time, and there's no hurry. Make yourself comfortable." He moved away to pour drinks.

The only light filtered in from the street outside and the adjacent room, which she assumed was the bedroom. The living room was still dark, and she liked it. She kicked off her heels and dug her toes into the deep plush carpet. Walking to the corner of the room, she stared out the bank of windows, taking in the cityscape.

"Do you want some more light?" Miles asked when he returned with their drinks.

"No. This is perfect."

"I think so, too."

From the corner of her eye, she saw him

looking at her and not out the windows. He handed her a glass of whiskey.

"I can order up a bottle of champagne if you'd like."

"I'm good." She sipped even though she didn't really like whiskey. She didn't plan on drinking much anyway. "Before I forget. This is for you." He held out an envelope.

She eyed it suspiciously as her gut churned. This was like a scene from a movie, where the guy thought he was with a hooker.

"What's this?" She set her glass on the table near the window.

"Open it."

The excitement in his eyes made her believe he didn't think he was paying a hooker, so she opened it. Inside was a card for the spa day she'd wanted.

"I saw you wanted this, but you didn't bid on it, so I did. That's why I was talking to the woman at the table. I asked her what kind of bid would ensure I'd get it."

Tess's head spun. When she'd left the table, the price had been more than she would ever consider paying for any kind of spa day, luxurious or not. "I can't accept this."

"Why not?"

"You don't even know me. And this cost a lot of money."

"As you pointed out downstairs, it's for a good cause. I don't need to know more than what I overheard you telling Baldwin. You save lives. You work twelve hours at a time with the most defenseless of patients. Who deserves a break more than you?"

Tess didn't have any words. The gesture was incredibly sweet. And, yes, she wanted it more than she would admit, but she also knew such gifts came with strings. As much as she was enjoying her night with Miles, that's all it would be—one night. Accepting such an expensive gift might come with the expectation of more time together.

But she knew trying to explain any of that to Miles would make her sound ungrateful, so she set the envelope on the table beside her glass, wrapped her arms around Miles's neck, and whispered, "Thank you."

They kissed, and while their tongues tangled, Tess began unbuttoning his shirt. She pulled it from the waistband of his pants and stepped back. His entire torso was sculpted muscle. She ran her hands over him and raised her gaze to his. She flicked the button on his pants open and shoved him back into the chair positioned in front of the window.

Kneeling in front of him, she took off his shoes and then peeled off his socks. She kissed her way up his body from his waist to his neck before crawling into his lap and straddling him. Her dress rode high, sliding almost to her hips. He brought his fingers up into her hair and brushed her scalp before he tightened his grip and took her mouth in a hungry kiss. His left hand kept his hold, while his right gripped her ass and brought her tightly against him.

Within moments, they were both moving and grinding, and the kisses devolved into a clashing of lips and tongues and teeth.

Miles ripped his mouth away from hers. "You're wearing too much. Get up."

As much as she enjoyed the contact with his body, she wanted to be naked with him, so she followed his direction and stood. She reached up to unclasp Nina's necklace, but Miles was in a hurry. He had her dress unzipped and falling off her body in seconds. A chill coasted across her bare skin, and she shivered. Miles stepped close, the heat from his body warming her.

From behind, he moved his hands across her breasts and down her stomach. Just as she started to feel self-conscious about her much-softer-than-his body, he trailed his tongue down the side of her neck and slid one of his hands past the edge of her panties. If her squishy stomach didn't turn him off, she could ignore it. Reaching behind her head, she held on to his neck and rocked her hips against his hand.

For someone who'd complained about the amount of clothing she was wearing, he was still mostly dressed. Her rocking motion caused her to bump into his hips, colliding with his hard dick. The movement pulled a grunt from his lips.

"Just when I thought you were immune to my advances," she said.

"I'm anything but immune. Turn around. I need to touch more of you."

She turned in his arms. He reached for the clasp on her bra as she shoved his pants and underwear off. His dick bobbed for attention, so she wrapped her hand around him. A hiss whistled from his lips as he palmed her breasts and tweaked her nipples.

He walked forward, forcing her to retreat

until her back pressed against the cold glass of the window. His chocolate brown eyes darkened with desire. "Stay there."

His command caused a warm flush to course through her and compete with the chill at her back.

Miles dropped his shirt, allowing her to see his entire body, which was a damn fine sight. He skimmed his hands down her sides and caught the waistband of her panties on the way down. He lowered himself, feathering kisses on her skin, causing another shiver.

Once his knees hit the floor, he nudged her legs wider and buried his face between them, licking and sucking her until she was ready to climb the window behind her like Spider-Man. He brought her to the edge of release and stood up, holding his pants in his hands.

Tess tried not to glare at him for stopping, because she knew he must be searching for a condom—thank God for the man who always assumed he might get laid—but she really wanted to come. He ripped open the condom, rolled it on, and then began kissing her neck again.

His dick slid between her legs, rubbing against her, and she practically jumped. She spread her thighs wide, inviting him in. They both thrust their hips, and while it felt great, it wouldn't be enough to get her off.

"Miles." His name was barely more than a gasp.

"Uh-huh."

"Get inside me. Now."

"Getting there."

She dug her nails into his shoulders as he nipped her neck and then sucked a nipple into his mouth. "Now."

He pulled away with a smirk. "I believe I promised you a view of the city." As he spoke, he continued to stroke and caress her all over. "Turn around."

She turned with his hands still touching

her. It was like he didn't want to leave an inch of skin unexplored.

"Put your hands on the glass."

Completely turned on, she did as he said, her hands trembling with desire. Leaning forward a bit, she kept her legs spread wide. Cool air kissed her bare skin now as Miles looked at her. She made quite the picture, enough that she should be embarrassed, but she wasn't. His eyes on her only stoked her passion.

He stepped close with his dick in his hand, guiding it to her. With one hand on her hip, he thrust into her. She closed her eyes and pressed her forehead against the cool glass. God, he felt so good. Her body quickly adjusted to the intrusion, and she pressed against him, wanting—no, needing— movement, friction, release.

Again, he fisted his hand in her hair and tugged. "Can't see the beautiful scenery with your eyes closed."

His breath coasted across her cheek. She heard the barely restrained control in his voice, another turn-on.

"Open your eyes and watch, Theresa."

She dragged her eyes open as she pulled her forehead from the glass. Of course, the skyline was beautiful, but more staggering was their reflection in the window. Miles's gaze focused clearly on hers, and he began thrusting. Slowly. One long stroke out and then back in to the hilt. He dug his fingers into the soft flesh of her hips to keep her in place, preventing her from controlling his penetration. When he picked up the pace, rolling his hips to hit all of her favorite spots, she was brought back to the edge again.

Their eyes never parted, staring at each other in their erotic reflection. This was the freedom she'd been looking for—to be the woman she used to be, not the one buried under scrubs and mommy responsibilities.

Thankfully, she didn't have to say

anything. Miles curved an arm around her body and toyed with her, not losing the rhythm of his thrusts. She came apart in his arms, and his pace slowed until he came.

Miles lay in bed with Theresa snuggled on his chest. Just as he'd begun cursing himself for only having one condom, Theresa countered with two of her own. They'd exhausted their bodies, and Miles had been lucky enough to call down to room service before they closed for the night.

After two more very satisfying orgasms, they'd gorged on ice cream and cake. Then they'd shared a shower, where they'd indulged in pleasure without penetration. In between kissing and coming, they'd talked and joked, and Miles thought he might've just experienced one of the best nights of his life. Theresa played things close to the vest, though, and he had no way to read her.

"When can I see you again?" he finally asked as she started to doze.

"I dunno. I work a lot."

"So do I, but everyone needs some time off. Even if we just meet for drinks." He stroked her shoulder and down her arm, hoping for agreement.

She rolled over, taking the whole blanket with her, and mumbled, "Talk tomorrow."

He settled for her answer even though she hadn't agreed to see him again. He'd had more than his fair share of one-night stands, especially after being forced to wear a tux and play nice all night. But more often than not, it had been all about the sex.

Being with Theresa was the first time in a long time that it had been more. Of course, the sex was at the top of his list, but he enjoyed every minute they'd been together. He trailed his fingers down her back.

Usually, at this point in the evening, he was itching to leave. Or expecting her to. Theresa sighed into sleep beside him. He waited for the itch that didn't come.

More disturbing was that it didn't bother him.

Tess rolled over, and her muscles protested as she reached for the bedside clock. *Shit. Five a.m. How the hell did that happen so fast?* Miles's arm was draped across her hip. She'd forgotten how nice it was to simply share a bed with a man, have his arms around her in the middle of the night.

She sighed and slipped out from his light grasp. She stood next to the bed and took a moment to admire him. He was sexy and funny and had given her everything she'd wanted for her night. Part of her felt bad about sneaking out now, but after their night together, and despite his reputation, Miles hadn't said, "Thanks for the good time. See you around."

He wanted to see her again. She didn't even know what to do with that. She didn't know how to date. How would he react when he found out she had three kids? That alone was enough to send most guys running. She'd learned that little tidbit when she'd first dipped her toes in the dating pool after the divorce.

She'd rather be a good memory for him, let them have this night, than ruin whatever image he'd created in his head about where this might go. After quickly gathering her clothes, she pulled them on and carried her shoes. She yanked her hair into a messy ponytail. Hopefully, no one would look at her like she'd just spent the night being thoroughly ravaged.

She slid quietly from the room and put her shoes on as she waited for the elevator. It wasn't until she walked through the lobby that she realized she'd left Nina's necklace by the table where she'd taken it off last night. *Damn*. There was no going back now. She'd have to buy Nina a new one.

Overall, not a horrible price to pay. The memories of this night would be enough to fuel her fantasies for a good long time. She turned in her valet ticket and didn't inhale deeply until she was in the safety of her van. This early on a Sunday meant traffic was nonexistent, especially going away from downtown.

At home, she snuck quietly into the house. Nina slept soundly on the couch. While the couch was fine for watching TV, it was nowhere near comfortable enough for sleeping, which was why Tess had left her bed ready. Yet, here Nina was, dead to the world.

Tess was torn. Go back to bed and try to sleep or just make a pot of coffee and enjoy the quiet of her house for an hour or so until the kids woke up. Coffee won. An hour of sleep wouldn't make up for what she'd lost last night, so it wasn't worth the attempt. She'd just go to bed extra early tonight.

She started the coffeemaker and then ran upstairs to shower and change. When she returned to the kitchen, Nina was awake.

"I'm sorry," Tess said. "I was trying to be quiet."

"It wasn't you. I mean, I knew you were here when the shower went on, but the smell of coffee woke me. I have mine on a timer at home so the smell is better than any alarm clock." Nina poured two mugs and sat at the table. "So how was it?"

Tess picked up her cup and joined Nina. "Oh my God. It was amazing."

"Tell me about Miles. Your text only gave me a name and a room number. Very smart, by the way."

"I met him at the gala. He comes from money. He had a suite at the hotel. Can you believe that? A room costs hundreds a night. A suite? I can't imagine."

"Yeah, yeah, so he has money. Get to the good part."

"He's gorgeous. The abs. I don't have words. But he's funny, too. Excellent stamina."

"Still not many details."

Tess lifted a shoulder. She'd never been one to run to girlfriends to rehash every moment of a date. She hit the highlights, and that should be enough. Then she remembered the necklace.

"I have some bad news though. I left your necklace at the hotel."

"So call Miles and get it."

"I'd rather just replace it." Tess took a

drink of coffee and looked at Nina over the rim.

"Seriously?" Nina leaned across the table and lowered her voice. "You finally get a guy who's funny, great in bed, and has a job, and you don't even get his number? What is wrong with you?"

Tess set her cup down. "It was a great night, but that's all I expected. My life is messy. I don't have time for this. He doesn't know anything about me. The kids. Nothing."

"And how is he going to if you don't have a way to reach him? I assume that means you didn't give him your number, either?"

Tess shook her head.

"I can't believe you."

"I got what I wanted. That's enough." "You keep telling yourself that."

Tess took a deep breath. "Any problems last night?" "Nope. The kids were great. Trevor kept the boys occupied with video games. I gave Zoe a mani-pedi, and we had some girl talk."

Tess arched an eyebrow. "Did you get any good information out of her? She tells me nothing these days."

Nina got quiet and sipped coffee. "I don't want to break her confidence. But I will say she's really nervous about starting high school."

Tess waved a hand. "I know. I was hoping for the scoop on boys."

"Oh, we talked boys." Nina reached over and covered Tess's hand with hers. "There's no one special yet. No dates, no pretend boyfriends, no blowjobs in the alleys."

The last part made Tess's heart stop. She hadn't even thought about that. While she'd tried to be very open and honest with Zoe about sex, the child never wanted to talk about anything, never asked questions. Her daughter took whatever information Tess gave her and filed it away.

"She's too young," Tess finally pushed out.

"Kids are doing everything. They don't think. And Lord knows, they're not getting it right. I pray for the future generations of girls who are with clueless and selfish boys. 'Cause you know they'll get their own in that alley, and it's not being reciprocated."

Tess made a mental note to talk to Zoe again about having respect for herself and expecting it from boys as well. When she'd brought newborn Zoe home from the hospital, all she'd imagined was having a beautiful, smart girl who would grow up and be her friend. She hadn't considered all of the traps involved in getting her to adulthood.

Right now, it was damn frightening.

They finished their coffee in silence, and when she heard noise upstairs, Tess set her cup aside and rose to make breakfast.

"You have his name. You can probably track him down if you want," Nina whispered on her way out.

She watched Nina leave and only thought about how she shouldn't want to find Miles.

Chapter 4

Two days later, Miles was still furious. Without a last name, he had very little recourse to find Theresa. So he'd stewed all day on Sunday, but now that Monday had arrived, he knew where to find her. He went to St. Mark's pediatric intensive care unit and stopped at the nurses' station.

"Hi. I'm looking for Theresa."

"Last name?" she asked without looking up.

"Um...I'm not sure. I know this sounds weird, but I met her Saturday night."

That got the woman's attention. "You're looking for a patient you met Saturday night?"

He smiled. "No. A nurse. We met at the gala to benefit the hospital."

"Huh." She sat back in her chair and the wheels rolled farther. "I don't know a Theresa. Are you sure you have the right department?"

He swallowed his frustration. "I'm positive."

She shrugged. "Sorry. I don't know how to help you."

Miles leaned against the counter and offered a full-wattage smile. "Come on. Can't you check a schedule or something? I'm sure she's working today because she was off Saturday and Sunday. I'm not some lunatic. I want to say hi and return something she lost Saturday."

"I wish I could help." Another careless shrug.

Damn. What was he supposed to do—

show up here every few hours to find her? He *would* look like a lunatic stalker. He turned to head back to the elevators, his mind racing to think of who he might know at the hospital who could help him when he saw Theresa's friend Angie.

"Angie," he called.

"Miles?" She walked up beside him and set a file on the counter. "What are you doing here?"

"Looking for Theresa."

"Oh."

"Oh," the nurse behind the counter yelled. "You're looking for Tess. I'm sorry I didn't pick up on that the first time. She's not on today."

Miles smiled at the woman and turned his attention to Angie. So much for Theresa working so much she wouldn't have time to go on a date. "Do me a favor?" He reached into his pocket and pulled out a card. He scribbled his cell number on the back. "Give this to Theresa—Tess. Tell her I have her necklace."

Angie took the card. "Okay. Is there anything I can do?"

Her eyes were filled with sympathy, as if she was well aware of how her friend had played him.

"Why didn't she give me her real name?" Angie stepped back and tilted her head to get him to follow. They moved down the hallway a little, and she leaned against the wall. "Theresa is her real name. She goes by Tess. Very few people call her by her full name."

"Can you tell me why she snuck out of my hotel room in the middle of the night without a word?"

Angie gave him a sad smile. "That's for her to tell. Just understand that it's complicated." Something started beeping at her waist. "I have to go. I'll make sure she gets the message."

"Thanks." Miles stared as she hurried away. Angie's words didn't make him feel any better. Theresa's life was *complicated?* Hell of a code. With his luck, she was married.

He'd been down that road before, learned his lesson. The scandal had nearly killed his mother. His siblings still gave him grief over getting involved with a married woman. At the beginning, everything had been simple and easy. They'd messed around and had a good time. He'd thought he'd landed the perfect relationship—a steady woman in his bed who didn't expect anything more from him. She'd failed to mention she was married. He should've suspected when she never wanted to have *the talk* about where they were headed.

Of course, it had all changed when she wanted to leave her husband for him. As in to settle down with him and start a family, so she could have what her husband wouldn't give her. That was when he realized the relationship had become complicated.

He preferred simple.

Miles left the hospital and went to the office, still cranky about Theresa. Tess. Not that what name he used mattered, because he simply had to return her necklace and then they'd be done. But that would be a face-to-face interaction so he could ask why she lied and left. If all she'd wanted was to fuck, she could've said so.

As he neared his office, his secretary Eleanor stood. "Mr. Prescott, your sister would like to see you before lunch. Your other messages are on your desk."

"Did Sabrina say what she wanted?"

Eleanor leveled a look at him. His sister never left specifics. She just expected everyone to jump when she called. So although her message said to see her before lunch, what she meant was for him to come up as soon as he walked in. He set his briefcase on his desk, leafed through his messages, and then went to see Sabrina.

Outside her office, her secretary Lilah smiled at him. "Is she busy?" he asked.

"She said that as soon as you arrived you should go right in. Can I get you anything? Coffee? Water?"

If drinks were being offered this wasn't going to be a quick meeting. "Coffee, please."

He strode through his sister's office door. It still felt weird to walk in here and see Sabrina instead of their father. It had been his office. Miles had spent quite a bit of time here when he was younger. He'd so desperately wanted his dad's approval that he'd tried to learn everything he could about software, but his heart was never in it.

The only thing he liked about computers was games, and his family wouldn't consider the gaming business. They were all about being productive.

"What's up, Sabrina?"

She looked up from her computer and gestured to a chair in front of her desk. "How was your weekend?"

"Fine." No way did she call him in here to chitchat.

"Mom says you met someone."

"Mom was wrong."

Sabrina arched a brow. "Do you ever plan on growing up?"

"Did you summon me just to give me a lecture?"

"No. I wanted to talk to you about a new project."

Miles rolled his eyes. His family had tried for years to get him to take on projects. Each one was designed to bring him deeper into the business. After the first two, he'd caught on and botched every one since. He'd thought at some point they'd learn.

"Don't you get it, Bree? I'm not like you and Brad. I don't want to run this empire. Isn't it enough that I have an office here? I do all of my work from this building even though I could do it from home."

"We both know you have that office because Dad made it a stipulation of you getting the job. Otherwise, you'd stay in your pajamas all day."

"Hah. Shows what you know. I don't sleep in pajamas."

She grimaced. "Not an image I need."

Lilah came in with his coffee. "Anything for you Ms. Prescott?"

"No, thank you, Lilah. Please hold all my calls."

"Don't bother, Lilah. We're about done." He didn't need to spend any more time being reminded that his dad forced him to work for the family or he'd be cut off. He'd been lucky to carve out a position he actually enjoyed.

"No we're not."

Lilah's gaze bounced back and forth between them. But, being the smart girl that she was, she backed quickly out of the room. Miles knew no calls would be saving him from this.

"You haven't even listened to what the project is."

"I'm not interested in working on the next round of office productivity software. I don't care how to make an office manager's life easy."

Sabrina laughed. "That's one way to sum up what we do."

"I've listened to it often enough."

"Remind me not to put you on the marketing team." She stood and came around her desk. "This is something totally unrelated to the office." She sat next to him. "Kind of."

That was enough to grab his attention. Sabrina had lived and breathed nothing but

Prescott Workspace for as long as he could remember. She never did anything different.

"I want to start something new."

"You're leaving here?"

"Hell, no. Why would I do that? I run everything."

The look she gave him was so purely Sabrina that he laughed. "Then what is this something new you want to talk to me about?"

"I know you've worked hard over the past few years, figuring out how to spend our money."

He clenched his jaw. They never saw him as anything but a joke. As if he didn't hold the same college degree they had. The difference was that he'd enjoyed his college years while earning his degree instead of burying himself in becoming the next Warren Buffet.

"Lighten up. I'm kidding. I think you've done a great job, but I think we can do better."

"I can only work with the budget you give me."

"It's not the amount of money, it's how we utilize it. I'd like to start a charitable foundation in dad's name. Something of a legacy."

Miles almost let loose another laugh. Their dad had insisted Miles work for him, but it had been Miles's idea to handle the finances for the family's charitable contributions. His father hadn't been that philanthropic. Not until Miles had explained the tax benefits.

"You already have organizations coming to you routinely looking for a handout, right?"

He nodded. He probably spent a couple of hours a day returning phone calls and emails to hopeful groups.

"I want to take the money for the next couple of years, invest, and establish a foundation. Then set up grants and scholarships with formal processes for application."

"So now my word and my vetting of an organization isn't enough?"

"That's not what I'm saying at all. When you and Dad came up with this idea five years ago, it was his way of trying to keep you in line. No one actually expected you to be good at it."

He loved the rousing praise he received from his family. Made a person's heart swell.

"But you *are* good at it, Miles. That's my point. I think we're wasting you as a resource."

"Starting a charitable foundation isn't some easy task. You can't just hang a shingle and make it so."

"I know that. It's an idea. A damn good one, but not one I can execute. It would be all you."

He didn't like the sound of that. He enjoyed not being in charge of anything.

Right now, there was no real way he could fuck up. He mostly wrote checks. Being in charge of a foundation was no different than running a corporation.

"I'll think about it." Having Sabrina's vote of confidence felt good.

"Don't take too long. I want to move on this as soon as possible. It'd be nice to be able to announce at the thirtieth-anniversary celebration."

And there was the catch. He should've known that Sabrina wouldn't just offer an opportunity for him to consider. It *always* came back to making Prescott Workspace look good.

"Give me some time."

He stood and left his sister's office thinking about Sabrina's offer. It was a huge task, one that would give him real responsibility.

The problem was he didn't know if he wanted it.

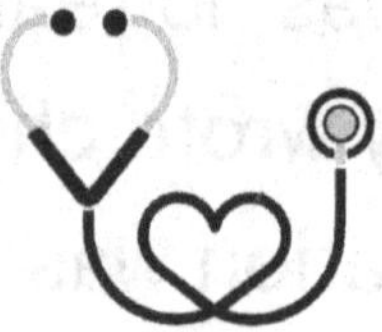

Tess stared at the business card in her hand. She couldn't believe Miles had come to the hospital to look for her. Angie had texted her Monday morning to let her know, and Tess had stopped by to grab the card and then kept it tucked in her purse for the last three days. She didn't know what to do.

That wasn't true. She needed to call him back so she could get Nina's necklace. But she didn't want to have the awkward conversation about why she'd left. Bottom line, he wasn't supposed to care.

Finally, she sucked it up and dialed, quietly praying for his voicemail.

"Hello?"

"Hi, Miles, it's Tess—Theresa. From last Saturday at St. Mark's gala?" She already felt foolish.

"I wondered if you were going to call."

"I had to work up to it."

An awkward silence hung between them.

"So, you have my necklace? It actually belongs to a friend."

"I do. It's quite beautiful. I also have the gift certificate I gave you."

"I told you that was too much."

"Why didn't you tell me your real name?"

"I introduced myself to Mr. Baldwin as Theresa, which is my name. I just never corrected you. I go by Tess because it's short and simple." She flipped his business card between her fingers.

"If all you wanted was a one-night stand, why not say so? Sneaking out is pretty immature," he teased.

Tess swallowed hard. Being called out stung, even if he was joking. "I had a great time. I really did. I thought it would be awkward to explain."

"Explain what? That you're married?"

"God, no. My life is very full and busy right now." She paused with a guilty thought. "Are you?"

"I've never been married. Totally single. You're so busy that when I came to the hospital on Monday, they told me you weren't working. So you had Saturday, Sunday, and Monday off."

Did he expect her to explain her whole life right now? Their night together was supposed to have been complication-free. "The hospital isn't my only job. Would you like me to pick up the necklace?"

"I think you owe me a real explanation. Face-to-face."

"I just said I'm busy. You're treating me like I'm a jerk, which maybe I am because I snuck out of your room without saying goodbye. So why would you want to spend more time with me?"

"Because I don't think you want to be a

jerk. And I had a great time, too. I'll bring you the necklace if you have coffee with me."

His bargaining raised her hackles. It was too reminiscent of her ex. "I'm supposed to let you blackmail me into a coffee date? Over some knock-off necklace I could just replace?"

"Blackmail is harsh. If the lure of coffee and time with me isn't enough, I'm not going to force it. And while I'm no expert, I've spent enough time around the real thing to know that your friend's necklace is no fake."

She was going to kill Nina for lying to her. Unless Miles was lying to get her to agree. Crap. Now her brain hurt. She needed to get this over with. She ran her schedule through her head. Between her regular shifts and the extra home healthcare hours she took on, her week was full. "I'm working tomorrow night. Stop by the hospital around nine, and maybe I can have coffee."

"No maybes. I'll bring some magical coffee so you won't be able to refuse."

"It's not about the coffee. And I'm not looking for a reason not to meet. I can usually take a break. But I can't dictate when shit's going to hit the fan. It's not like I can look at a baby and say, 'Sorry I know you're not breathing right now, but I'm on break.'"

He chuckled, which just infuriated her.

"What is so funny?"

"Us. This whole crappy conversation is the exact opposite of everything we had Saturday night. I want to talk. Okay, Tess?"

Her regular name sounded foreign coming from him. She liked being Theresa to him. As Theresa, she could be open and fun and forward. As Tess, she was her usual, guarded, safe self.

"I'm sorry I snapped at you. I'll see you tomorrow."

She disconnected and couldn't put her finger on how she felt. Messed up was the best way to describe it. She'd spent days thinking about him and what a good time she'd had. And it hadn't just been the sex. She'd been able to talk with him, and the conversation had had nothing to do with her kids or work. They'd talked about movies and books and wine, of all things. Of course, that had been a short-lived conversation because she drank the cheap stuff and he didn't really like wine.

But it had been adult conversation. With Miles, she could pretend her baggage didn't exist.

Until now. Tomorrow night, she'd lay out that baggage so he would understand why she'd snuck out—in order to preserve what the night had been.

Then he'd get it and move on back to his normal life.

Tess did her best to put Miles out of her mind, but she couldn't. While making sure the kids had their stuff packed for William's house for the weekend and getting them to day camp that morning, Miles had lurked in the back of her thoughts. She was now into her ninth hour of work, and all she could think about was that in three hours she would see him again.

The thought made her a little nauseated. She had never been good at letting a guy down. Not that she'd had tons of experience. And coming face-to-face with a guy she'd blown off was horrible. She didn't know what to say to him. They'd had a fabulous night together. What guy wasn't happy with that?

She stood at the nurses' station, letting her thoughts get away from her. For once, when she wanted work to be crazy, it was an utterly quiet night. Angie rolled her chair over from the other side of the desk. "Why are you letting this guy twist you up? What's the big deal?" Angie asked.

Tess took a deep breath and released it slowly. "I don't know how to do this. I tried telling him my life is too busy for dating, and he wanted to have coffee anyway. I don't want to be a bitch, but what do I say?"

Angie leaned her elbows on the desk. "Why exactly can't you date?"

"I have three kids who require a ton of supervision and chauffeuring. I have to cook and clean and help with homework. And I work two jobs, one of which involves twelve-hour shifts."

"You make yourself sound like a cross between a martyr and an old woman. You get off work by ten tonight. You could go for drinks. On your home healthcare days, you make time to meet your friends at Sunny's for coffee. You could do that for a guy. And what happens if you skip mopping your floor one week in order to have a real date? Will the world fall apart?"

Angie didn't get it. "It's just so much all the time. I don't know how to fit something else in."

"Bullshit."

"What?"

"You're scared. You don't want to start a relationship because you might fall for the guy. It might go somewhere, and then your kids will see you as an actual woman, not the maniac robot you tend to be."

Tess opened her mouth to argue, but Angie had known her a long time. Not quite as long as the New Beginnings divorcees, but close.

"I don't know what I'm doing, and you're right. It's scary."

Angie smiled and waved her to the other side of the desk. "Come here."

Tess sat in the chair beside Angie.

"I know you wouldn't think to do this because you're so closed off on the idea of dating Miles, but I think he's just what you need for getting back into the groove."

"Do what?"

Angie pulled out her phone and started typing and scrolling. "After he stopped by with his card, I checked him out. Online, of course, and all as part of my duty as your friend." She handed Tess her phone. "This guy comes from a big money family. Computers and shit, but he's like the goof off."

Tess looked at the phone where Miles stared up at her from the screen. "What is this?"

"Social media. You can look at pretty much everything everyone is up to based on what they post. This guy's Instagram is filled with pictures of him partying. He's not looking to move in and be a dad to your kids. He's out for a good time."

Tess handed Angie her phone back. "And we did."

"Who made the rule that it could only be a one-time deal?"

"Because more than one time leads to

feelings and expectations, and then before you know it, you're in deep."

Angie tapped her thigh. "Not him. Never married, and a different woman in every post. As long as you can control yourself, I think you might've found a safe one."

Tess wheeled away on her chair and went back to work. While she would never actively pray for an emergency, she kind of hoped for one. All the kids slept peacefully and she finished her charts. She'd skipped a break earlier to have time with Miles when he showed without having to admit to him her night was almost done.

When the elevator dinged, she assumed a parent was returning to spend the night. Then a cup of coffee was waved in front of her face. She looked up, and Miles smiled at her.

"You brought coffee?"

"I told you I would. You and Angie said hospital coffee sucks, and I didn't know if you'd be able to leave to get something better." He pointed to a tray holding five more cups. "I brought enough to share, but I didn't know how many nurses would be here."

Angie swooped in. The girl had a nose for coffee. "Hey, Miles."

"Angie," he said with a nod. "I brought coffee."

"For me?"

"For whoever wants some."

Angie grabbed a cup and winked at Tess. The friendly gesture did nothing to settle her nerves. Although Miles didn't look angry, she knew he might be. Their phone conversation hadn't gone well.

"Is this an okay time for your break?" Miles asked.

"Yeah." She stood and slipped her phone into her pocket. "Let's go out here."

She grabbed her cup and led him down the hall past the elevators to a bank of couches. She sat on the edge of one and sipped from the cup. *Damn, this is good coffee.* He settled beside her, close enough to touch.

"So…" she said, not knowing where to start or what he expected.

"Why did you sneak out?"

She scooted forward and set her cup on the table in front of them. "Like I said, I don't get out much. I wasn't totally honest about the reasons. I let you believe it was all work, and while that's part of it, the other part is that I have three kids. I don't have time for a relationship."

"Kids? That's your big secret? But you're single, right?"

"Yeah. I wouldn't lie about that. I've been divorced for years."

"I can work with that." He slid farther back in the couch and spread his arms out on the back.

Huh? Is he hard of hearing? "There's nothing to work with, Miles. I'm sorry I wasn't up-front about only looking for one night, but that's all it can be."

"Why?"

"I work two jobs. I'm here on the weekends when my kids are with their dad, like now. By the time I get home, all I can do is collapse in bed before starting all over. The other weekends, I'm with my kids."

He moved forward again, and she didn't like the look on his face. Like a man on a mission. "What about during the week?"

"While the kids are in camp or school, I do home healthcare work for extra money because it works around their schedules. Then I drive them everywhere they need to be and help with homework and all the really boring stuff someone like you doesn't want to hear about."

He continued to stare, his warm brown eyes inviting. "Everyone has some free time."

She took out her phone and pulled up her calendar. "Look." She pointed to the screen where she had her schedule and all of the kids' activities color coded. "This is my life."

He took the phone and scrolled through the calendar. Tess thought she'd finally convinced him. Her calendar would scare off the hardiest of men.

"Lunch on Monday then?" he asked, returning her phone.

"What?"

"According to your master calendar, you're free for lunch on Monday." He stared at her, waiting for a response.

She had none. Looking at the calendar, she realized he was right. Nothing was scheduled for midday on Monday. Normally, she did housework then. Angie's words echoed in her head. The world wouldn't collapse if the floor wasn't mopped. Miles waited expectantly. "Don't you have to work Monday?"

"I have a flexible schedule. Even a tyrant like my sister would admit I deserve to eat a meal." His seductive smile shot through her. Then he stood. "You have my number. Pick a place, any place, and I'll meet you. On your schedule."

She looked up at him. "Why?" she asked quietly.

"Because we both deserve more than one night." He turned to leave but then paused, reached into his jacket pocket, and pulled out an envelope. "Your friend's necklace," he said and handed it to her. "I'll see you Monday."

Chapter 5

Monday morning, Tess rushed into Sunny's Diner hoping everyone would be there. She needed advice, because after thinking about Miles all weekend, she was still a mess. Nina sat alone at their usual table and Tess sat beside her. "I have a bone to pick with you."

"What?" Nina asked, her usual innocent look in place.

Tess slid the envelope across the table. "You said it was fake. Miles seems to think this is the real thing."

Nina sighed. "You wouldn't have borrowed it if you knew it was real."

"For good reason. Even when I left it, you didn't tell me." Tess's stomach churned with the thought of how much money the necklace was worth.

Nina's eyes flashed, and a broad smile took over her face. "Wait. That means you tracked Miles down and saw him again."

"He actually came looking for me at the hospital."

"I'm glad." She slid her finger under the flap and opened the envelope to pull the necklace out. Opening the envelope wider, she said, "There's something else here."

She passed over a piece of paper, and Tess clamped her jaw. The gift certificate for the spa day. The man was infuriating. "I told him I couldn't take it. He was the winning bid at the auction and he tried giving this to me."

"Already buying you gifts. Sounds interesting."

"Now I'm going to have to meet him for lunch today so I can give this back."

"Lunch? Another date? Yay!"

Trevor sat across from Tess. "Date?"

"Maybe." Tess drank the coffee the waitress set in front of her. While the waitress filled Trevor's cup, their other friends, Evelyn and Owen walked in, and Gabe trailed behind them.

"What's with the weird silence?" Evelyn asked.

Nina spoke up. "Tess is telling us about her date."

"I don't even know if I'm going to go."

"Why the hell not?" Nina asked.

"Where'd you meet him?" Evelyn jumped in.

Nina answered for her. "At the gala last Saturday night."

Trevor set his cup down. "You're going out with him again?"

"He came to the hospital Friday night for

coffee because I left Nina's necklace in the hotel last week. I thought for sure when I told him I had three kids and a crazy schedule, he'd be gone. Instead, he took one look at my calendar and saw I had a free spot today at lunch."

"Assertive guy. Point for him," Evelyn said.

"I don't think I want to go."

"Is he ugly?" Evelyn asked.

Tess shook her head.

"Great in bed, too," Nina added.

"*Shh...*" Tess reprimanded. "I don't need the whole coffee shop to know about my sex life."

"Then what's the problem?" Trevor asked.

"I'm not sure. I don't know if I'm looking for a relationship right now. And Miles? He's *never* been married."

Everyone at the table quieted.

Gabe said, "What does that have to do with anything?"

Tess looked to Evelyn and Nina for support.

"If a guy gets to our age and has never been married, there's a reason," Evelyn said.

"If you're not comfortable with it, don't go," Owen said. "Unless you're looking to get laid again, then go for it."

Tess laid her head on her hand, rubbing her forehead. This was not going the way she'd planned. She'd thought her friends would be more supportive and offer legitimate advice.

"You know what?" Nina said, slapping the table. "You guys are pissing me off."

They all turned and stared at Nina. This fire in her speech appeared to be a new habit.

"What, honey?" Gabe asked.

"All of you. Do you remember what we said when we left the divorce group and started hanging out here? Why we did that?"

No one spoke.

But Tess remembered, and she was sure the others did, too. "We were all ready to start a new beginning."

It was the whole reason they'd called themselves New Beginnings.

"That's why I wanted to be part of this group. I suck at figuring people out, but I thought you could guide me. And you know what? You guys suck. You're all living stagnant lives just like me. Trevor and Gabe live mostly like hermits. Tess, you live to take care of everyone other than yourself." She looked across to Owen and Evelyn and pointed. "And don't even get me started on the two of you, dancing around each other like the rest of us can't see it."

Tess realized that her friend was smart and intuitive. Nina figured people out a whole lot better than she gave herself credit for.

"You're right," Tess said.

Making eye contact with each of her friends around the table, Nina continued, "I'm throwing down the gauntlet. I'm challenging each of you to get out and find someone who makes your life better. We all want to meet someone special, but there's no way for that to happen unless we put ourselves out there.

"Miles might not be the guy you spend the rest of your life with, Tess, and that's okay. You can have a relationship and have a great time without settling into forever. And maybe I don't know anything, and he is the one for you. Either way, there's no way to know unless you try."

She was the second friend this week to speak similar words. First Angie, now Nina. Maybe they were right. She had been holding herself back, and it was damn lonely.

"Okay," she said with a nod, bolstering her confidence. "I'm going to lunch. Assuming Miles is still free. I need to text him where to meet."

"Oh, tell him Agostino's. Awesome Italian food. Relaxed atmosphere," Evelyn said.

"Thanks." Tess made a note in her phone.

Nina crossed her arms and looked at everyone else. "Well?"

"Well, what?" Gabe asked.

"The challenge is for the rest of you, too." She looked at Trevor. "If you still love your ex and you want her back, prove it to her. Nothing happens on its own."

Trevor swallowed hard and stared into his coffee.

Nina moved on to her next target. "Gabe, you need to meet someone and not investigate her at all. You need to get to know her the old-fashioned way and trust what she says to you."

Gabe snorted, and Tess almost cringed. Telling Gabe he couldn't use his computer skills to check someone out was like telling Tess she shouldn't take care of people.

"You look for the worst in everyone."

"Because it saves a lot of time," he said.

"Did you ever investigate me?" Nina

asked. Collectively, everyone at the table sucked in a breath. They all assumed Gabe would have, but they never spoke about it.

"No," he answered, clearly offended. He looked at each of them in turn. "You're my friends. I wouldn't do that."

Nina continued, "Why not?"

"Because I know you."

"But you got to know us. Yeah, it was an overly personal situation, and we've seen one another pretty much at our worst, but if you can avoid digging into *our* lives, you should be able to do the same for a woman you like."

"Point taken. But so many are liars."

"That's a chance you take," Tess said. "It's a scary prospect to put yourself out there, especially since we all did it, and our marriages failed. But Nina is right. I, for one, accept your challenge. Miles will be my starter date."

"Starter date. I like that idea," Nina said.

Owen and Evelyn were quiet at their end of the table.

Nina pointed at them again. "I'm not done. You two need to shit or get off the pot."

"Ever the classy speaker, Nina," Evelyn responded.

Nina checked her watch. "Thanks for the fun, but I have to go. I'm meeting a client in twenty." She tossed a couple of bucks on the table and swished out the door.

"Hey, did anyone else notice how she ripped into all of us but didn't address herself for her supposed challenge?" Evelyn asked.

Tess, Trevor, and Gabe all burst out laughing.

"I don't see what's so funny."

Tess used her napkin to dab at her eyes. "You don't like that she had the intuition and guts to call us out." She finished her coffee and stood. "I have to run, too. Have a great week."

As she walked to her car, she texted Miles

with the name and address of Agostino's. Even if he chose not to show, she'd have a good meal and feel better about herself for making the attempt.

Before she pulled out of her parking spot, her phone rang. "Hello."

"I'm surprised you texted," Miles said.

"I almost didn't."

"What made you change your mind?"

"My friend Nina. She convinced me I should have some fun." His low, rumbling laugh vibrated through her. "If it's fun you're looking for, I can do a whole lot better than lunch at an Italian restaurant."

Tess felt her cheeks warm, and she was grateful he couldn't see her. "I thought you wanted to get to know me."

"I'd like to get to know all of you."

She couldn't lie to herself and pretend the suggestion didn't hold appeal. "If you already have plans for lunch, I understand. Maybe we can try some other time."

"Uh-uh. I didn't say I had other plans. I offered a different spin on the plans, but lunch would be wonderful. I'm looking forward to seeing you at noon."

She shouldn't have been giddy that he'd accepted. Or that he was looking forward to it. It was just a lunch date. But it had been years since she'd even tried to date. "See you then."

"Tess?"

"Yeah?"

"Think about my other proposal." He chuckled and disconnected without waiting for her to respond.

She was definitely thinking about it.

Three hours later, Miles still had a smile on his face, thinking about Tess. His sister,

Sabrina, asked him to come to her office and he whistled as he walked down the hall. He didn't know what his sister wanted, but nothing could ruin his mood. Tess had not only agreed to see him again, but she'd made the plans to do so.

He didn't want to inspect too closely why he liked that idea. He realized how strange it was. He had his pick of women who would offer a no-strings arrangement. In all honesty, though, more often than not, those women thought they offered simplicity, but they all became complicated after a while.

Tess was an unusual mix. She had a life and didn't appear to be looking for a man to fulfill anything other than her biological need for an orgasm. That was something he could happily supply. And since she already had a bunch of kids, she wasn't looking to settle down and start a family.

She might be the perfect woman.

Miles rapped on Sabrina's door before

swinging it open. As soon as he took in the scene, his smile faltered. His family sat around Sabrina's desk and all heads turned his way when he entered. It was more like a firing squad than a meeting.

"What's going on?" he asked.

Sabrina gestured to a chair beside his mom. "I was telling Mom and Brad about my idea for the foundation in Dad's name."

"And?"

Their mother patted the chair. "Have a seat. You look like you're walking to the gallows. We want to talk and iron out some details."

"Details? I haven't said I wanted this job."

Sabrina folded her hands on the desk, and his mother raised a brow at him before speaking. "I think it's a wonderful idea. Why on earth wouldn't you want the position?"

"Because running a charitable foundation is completely different than giving away your money. It's no different than running a corporation." He unbuttoned his jacket and sat. He couldn't fathom why they'd assumed he would jump at the chance to do this. They knew him.

"We all agree it's the next logical step," Sabrina said. "We want to move forward, and we don't have time for you to play games."

"And if I don't take the position?"

Sabrina shook her head. "We'll find someone who will, and you'll be out of a job."

"So you called me in here to tell me to do what you want or I'm fired." His anger crept up and threatened to strangle him.

His mom reached over and laid a hand on his fist. "Let's not blow things out of proportion. This is a good idea. Your father would be so proud to have this in his name. And to have you running it..." Her voice became thick.

Miles inhaled deeply.

Brad cleared his throat. "What do you

expect us to do? Your life has been easy enough."

"What?" He glared at his brother.

"Grow the hell up. Dad created a bogus position for you. We're moving forward to make sure Dad's name lives on. If you can't see that, you're more self-centered than I thought."

Mom tightened her hand on Miles's. "Bradley, watch your mouth. There's no call for speaking to your brother like that."

"Someone needs to. I just said what we're all thinking."

"Yeah? What else are you *all* thinking?"

Brad scowling at him was like being in a stare-down with their father. Brad had filled Dad's shoes better than anyone imagined.

"It's time to make your own mark. Sabrina and Mom seem to think you're the man for this job. Personally, I think you'll fuck it up. But I could respect you if you at least tried."

Miles stood and rebuttoned his jacket.

"Go to hell, Brad. I've never fucked up anything I decided to take on. Mom and Sabrina want me on this because I'm damn good at what I do."

"Easy when you've never taken on a challenge."

Brad's words sank in, and Miles had nothing to say. His brother was right. He'd never had a good enough reason to chase a challenge. What was wrong with wanting an easy life?

The muscle in his jaw pulsed. "You win, Brad. Challenge accepted."

He didn't wait to be dismissed. He spun and left before he committed to anything else stupid. Even as he strode back down the hall to his office, his words weighed on his shoulders. *What the hell did I just agree to?*

Checking the time, he realized he had to leave to meet Tess. He let Eleanor know he wouldn't be back for a while. He had no intention of rushing his lunch. As agitated as he felt at the moment, he might not come back for the day.

After letting his driver know where they were going, he sat in the back of the car and played on social media in an attempt to clear his head. Unfortunately, it didn't work. When they arrived at the restaurant, he saw Tess standing outside. The sight of her did more to relax him in ten seconds than the fifteen-minute ride had.

As she looked down the street, she ran a hand over her hair, which was pulled back in a ponytail. She wore jeans and a T-shirt, and her face was nearly makeup free. She looked so different from Theresa at the gala. This was nurse Tess.

His driver pulled up to the curb, and Miles swung the door open. Miles started to climb out, but Tess met him.

"I'm so sorry. I had no idea, and I'm going to kill Evelyn when I see her."

Miles turned to Dave. "Stay here for a

minute." Then he stepped on the curb and took Tess's hand. "Hi." He bent and kissed her cheek, which seemed to startle her, but she didn't pull away.

"Hi," she said with a soft smile.

"Now. What are you apologizing for? And who is Evelyn?"

"Evelyn is my friend—right now that might be former friend—who suggested this restaurant, which I am completely underdressed for. What she also failed to mention is that they don't take reservations for lunch and there's an hour wait right now."

Miles swallowed his laugh. "How much time do you have?"

She checked her phone. "An hour and a half."

"Plenty of time. Did you drive here?"

"Yes. I'm at a meter down the block. But I can't sit here all afternoon. I have another job to get to before the kids get out of camp."

"Is your spot paid for two hours?"

She nodded.

"Excellent. Get in." He opened the car door for her. She stared at it.

"We'll travel together for lunch. I'll get you back here in plenty of time."

She licked her lips, which had his blood racing, and then pointed at his suit. "I'm not dressed to go to a fancy restaurant."

"You look fine, Tess. Get in the car."

She slid in, and he sat beside her.

Dave looked over his shoulder. "Where to, Mr. Prescott?"

Miles smiled. Dave only called him Mr. Prescott when someone else rode in the car. Miles laid a hand on Tess's leg. "I live close. I can have lunch delivered within thirty minutes and there's no dress code. Would that be okay?"

She stared into his eyes, and he hoped she would agree. He didn't want to be around other people right now, but he didn't want to postpone their date, either.

"As soon as we get there, you can text your friend the address."

Her breath quickened, and she nodded.

"Take me home, Dave," Miles said as he opened the app on his phone to order food. "Preference for lunch?"

"I'm not picky. Whatever you want."

He placed an order with the Italian restaurant near his condo. They knew him, and he tipped well, so his food always arrived fast. After placing the order, he settled back in his seat, but Tess still sat stiffly. He took her hand again. "If you're uncomfortable, we can go somewhere else. I just had a run-in with my siblings at work and I'm not in the mood to deal with people if I can avoid it."

Her shoulders relaxed. "We can do this some other time. It's okay."

"No," he answered quickly. "I don't want

to cancel and I don't want you to feel uncomfortable. I'd like to spend time with you. You set the pace for what happens between us."

She smiled and winked. "That's good because I like to be in charge."

Her saucy attitude pulled a laugh from him that he didn't think possible.

"Want to talk about it?" she asked.

"What?"

"Whatever happened at work. Remember, I'm a nurse, so by nature, I'm an excellent listener."

Miles shook his head. "I'm not even sure, really. My sister wants to start a charitable foundation in my dad's name, and she wants me to run it."

"That sounds exciting."

It should be exciting, and part of him knew it. "She broached the subject with me last week. I've been thinking about it. Today, they ambushed me and told me I either take the position or lose my job."

"Why would they do that?"

"My sister really wants this, and instead of waiting for my answer, she got my mom on board."

"That's a bad thing?"

Miles knew he sounded like a spoiled child, but he wasn't sure how to explain the situation. "None of it is bad. My sister's idea is good. But my brother was in the meeting, and we butt heads. He puts me on the defensive, and I don't like it."

The car pulled to a stop, and Miles glanced out the window. "This is our stop. You ready?"

"I hope the food you ordered is good. I'm famished."

Miles opened the door and held out a hand to help her from the car. The short ride with her, talking about the issues with his family, had helped. She truly was a good listener. He couldn't recall another woman having this effect on him. Relaxed and excited all at once.

Getting to know this intriguing woman was the best decision he'd made in a while.

Chapter 6

Nervous flutters filled Tess's stomach, so she had no idea why she was talking about being hungry. Miles held her hand and led her into a gorgeous modern building as the car pulled away. What the heck was she doing going into a man's house? A man who had a driver and lived in a condo like this?

At the front door, Miles stopped. "You want to text your friend?"

"I will. Thanks."

He unlocked the door but still held her hand. Tess didn't know why she found that charming, but she did. He didn't say anything as they stepped into the elevator. The silence continued until they walked to his condo.

He opened his door, and Tess took in the view. The floor plan was open concept and sunlight filled the space. Everything was meticulous and beautiful, and she realized how little she belonged there. She'd never been in such a luxurious home. Hell, she couldn't remember the last time she'd been in such a clean house.

"Home sweet home," Miles said, tugging her hand. "Still okay?"

Tess nodded.

Miles stepped in front of her and lowered his face until they were eye to eye. "If something's bothering you, we can go out for lunch."

"No. You already ordered food. Nothing's wrong. I was taking in how beautiful your condo is." It wasn't a total lie. The space was gorgeous. It just made her feel inadequate.

"Let me give you the grand tour. Living room," he said as he swept his arm out. "On the other side of that counter is the kitchen, a room I rarely use."

She laughed at his silliness. The floor plan allowed her to fully see both the living room and kitchen from the front door.

"My bedroom's upstairs." He winked at her.

"Bathroom?"

He smiled and pointed. "Around the corner from the kitchen. Unless you'd like to go upstairs."

Tess rolled her eyes and gave him a playful look. Miles was a huge flirt, and she loved it. She followed his directions to the bathroom and waited for the nervousness to subside while washing her hands. She didn't even know why butterflies were taking over her stomach. This might be her first date with Miles, but a date should be easier to navigate than having sex for the first time, and that had been remarkable.

She dried her hands on a plush, unstained towel and fixed her ponytail. She should've put more effort into this date. Miles was used to hanging around glamorous people. She pressed her lips together. *This is who I am.* Miles would either like her or not.

Satisfied with her pep talk, she retraced her steps to the living room where Miles was opening enough containers of food to feed a village.

"I was about to send a search party," he said.

"Everyone knows the first time a woman is in your bathroom, she's gonna snoop," she joked.

He nodded as though she were serious. "Then you should've taken the bathroom upstairs."

She had a reason for not using that

bathroom, and she had a feeling he knew exactly why. But she said, "That would be a little too obvious. Some of us like to be subtle. Besides, maybe I'm saving that for when I want to search your underwear drawer."

The glint in his eyes and the grin on his face as he came nearer made his intentions clear. Tess momentarily thought of backing away, but her body overrode her brain and instead she stepped forward.

Miles stopped short of actual contact, but she felt his touch all over. Something about the way he looked at her, like he was hanging on her every word and couldn't get enough, gave her a rush. So much of her time and focus was always on others, usually children, that she was out of practice being the focus of attention.

His gaze dipped to her lips and then farther down. Her body tingled, begging for his touch.

"Hungry?" he asked.

She licked her lips and nodded. He began to turn toward the food, but Tess grabbed his arm and pulled him back. Their bodies collided, and her heart thundered. She was damn hungry for this. She wanted to taste him.

Although she'd only had him the one night, his proximity prompted a craving. She wanted to act on it, so she did. Leaning in, she pressed her lips to his gently, a slight shift for access. Miles needed no further direction. His tongue entered her mouth and toyed with hers. He encircled her with his arms and held her flush against him.

They stood together for long moments, exploring each other's mouths, hands pulling, grasping, caressing. Having sex with Miles had not been her intention when she'd accepted his invitation, but now that was all she could think about. His erection grew against her, and her underwear was damp.

Miles pulled away first, breathing heavily. "Damn. I didn't expect that."

Tess wiped at her lips, her fingers a little shaky. "Neither did I. I don't know what I was thinking."

He brushed a loose lock of hair away from her face. "I get the impression you weren't thinking, which is what made it so freaking hot. Every time we've talked since that night, you've been trying to rationalize why we can't do this. But just now, your body made one hell of an argument for the pro column."

"You're right, Miles, but I'm at a loss. I've dated very little since my divorce and when I did, it was usually disastrous. I don't know how to do this."

With a hand on her hip, he pulled her close enough to grind against her, the hard ridge of his dick making her want to strip. "Trust me, you know how to do this."

She rolled her eyes again. "I wasn't talking about sex. After the gala, there's obviously no question we're compatible, but I don't know how to fit a relationship into my life. I refuse to bring random men into the lives of my kids. I won't upset their stability."

"Not asking you to." He lowered his head and nibbled on her neck, causing her brain to fog. "Let's see where things go."

Could she do this? Tess tried to focus, but Miles's tongue was doing amazing things to her erogenous zones, and she was melting into a puddle.

Miles pulled away again, releasing her hip, and Tess swayed toward him, seeking more of his touch.

"Here's the deal, Tess. I want you. I want to strip you down and take you right here. But if you don't want to, I respect that. Lunch is on the table waiting for us."

He put the decision squarely on her because she was the one with the reservations. She looked into his warm brown lust-filled eyes. She wanted this, too, but was that enough? Nina's words from earlier came back. So what if Miles wasn't her forever guy? She didn't need a forever guy, and Miles would do quite nicely for right now.

"I think if we hurry, we can have both."

His grin turned a little wicked. "Please tell me the nakedness comes before lunch."

"Well, we should work up an appetite, right?"

"I like the way you think." He kissed her again, hard and deep, while tugging at her shirt. His hands skated under the cotton, and he leaned his forehead against hers. "So we're doing this?"

Tess smiled. "We're doing this." She paused and stepped back. "Upstairs."

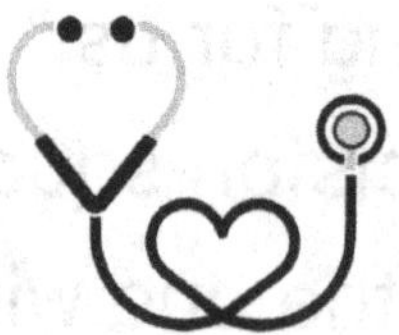

Miles led Tess up to his bedroom. He pulled the curtains open, allowing sunlight to flood the room. She toed off her gym shoes and crossed her arms in front of her to peel away her T-shirt. His mouth watered at the sight.

This was what he needed to put his family out of his head. Their ambush and expectations didn't touch him here. Following her lead, he kicked off his shoes. He draped his jacket over the chair and loosened his tie. By the time he got his shirt unbuttoned, Tess was down to her underwear.

She turned her hand over in the air. "Get a move on. You're taking too long."

"Sorry. Next time I'll be more efficient. I'll pick you up in my boxers."

She smiled. "I'd like to see that." She stepped closer, tugged at his waistband to undo his belt, and made quick work of the button. His shirt joined the jacket as Tess lowered her body to push his pants to the floor.

As he stepped out of the pants, she stood, trailing her fingers along his thighs and then his abdomen. His muscles flinched and flexed under her touch. Grabbing her arms, he pulled her to his mouth. "Come here."

With his lips on hers, he guided her to the bed. He pushed her down gently to the mattress, and she scooted back, making room for him. Much like she had done to him, he allowed his hands to wander up her legs. At her panties, he tugged at the waistband, so she lifted her hips for him to remove them.

He thought he was going to continue up her body, but the sight of her bared to him was far too tempting. He smelled her arousal, making his own desire pulsate through his entire body. Stretching out, he slid his hands under her ass and gave her cheeks a squeeze. Then he brought her pussy to his mouth. Using his tongue and lips, he teased her and stroked her until she moaned like he knew she would.

It was low, as if she'd tried to trap the sound in her throat. He pressed on, wanting her to let go. Her heels sought purchase on the edge of the bed, and she raised her hips to him, chasing his moving tongue. He looked up over her soft body to see her face.

Eyes closed, mouth slightly open, head thrown back, Tess was fully in the moment, even if she refused to let the world know. He lapped at her and pressed against her clit until she ground herself against him and grabbed his head to hold him in place as she came.

He caressed her thighs and her ass as she came back to him. When her feet slid from the edge of the mattress, he reached for a condom.

"Oh, God that was good."

"It'll get better."

With an arm thrown over her eyes, she said, "Don't know if that's possible."

Settling himself over her, he brushed her

arm aside to look into her eyes. "Are you challenging me?" Now that was a challenge he would gladly rise to.

"Not really."

"I think you were." He slid into her, and her breath caught. When he was fully seated inside her body, cradled in her wet warmth, he kissed the side of her neck in all the places that had caused her breathlessness downstairs. "This is better," he whispered.

The moment provided him with the escape he needed. One where he could be himself, lost in pleasure. He peeled back the cups of Tess's bra and sucked hard on her nipple, drawing another quiet moan. Her nails scraped against his back.

"We're all alone, you know. Fully insulated walls."

"Huh?" she asked, her gasp urging him to move faster.

"You're so quiet. Let go. Be loud. Scream if you want."

She laughed quietly. "I'm not a loud person in general. And for a lot of years, I've needed to be quiet."

The soft reminder of her kids and her ex-husband could've ruined the moment, but Miles wasn't going to go there. "So now's your chance." He thrust deeper, lifting her hips up. "Let it out. I want to hear you scream."

"Sorry to disappoint you, but I'm not a screamer."

He paused his thrusts and smoothed her hair from her face. "You are no disappointment."

Curling her legs around him, she pumped her hips and grinned. "Good to know."

For whatever reason, Miles had the urge to make her pleasure his number one priority. Whether she screamed or not didn't matter. He wanted her to come so hard she couldn't say no to seeing him again. He played with her body until she was squirming and writhing and moaning his name along with God's.

When her body gripped him, he couldn't hold out anymore. Her muscles pulsed and pulled him, and he was lost. For long moments after, he barely held his weight above her. The contact of their bodies had them connected in every way possible. And he had no desire to move. Then Tess laughed. It was deep and low and a little dirty. When he pushed up to look into her eyes, her entire face was lit with her smile.

"I stand corrected. That was fucking amazing."

Miles no longer cared about what had happened at the office or what his family expected. Seeing that look on Tess's face, knowing he'd put it there, was enough for him. "Glad to be of service."

Her face sobered. "I didn't mean it like that. I mean, you had a good time, too, didn't you?"

"Are you kidding? I won't be thinking about anything else until I can see you again. Servicing your incredible body, making you laugh like that? It's pretty fucking hot. I wish you could stay so we could do it all over again."

He lowered and kissed her, licking the seam of her lips. She sighed into his mouth, and he captured her breath.

"I really do have to go," she whispered.

He closed his eyes, dreading having to remove himself from her warmth. Her pussy, her mouth, her smiling eyes. He knew the minute he pulled away, he'd lose them all. "When can I see you again?"

Her eyes looked sad. "I don't know, Miles. I told you—"

"You told me you didn't have any time, but we made time today."

She smiled again. "I'm really glad we did."

"Then tell me when we can meet again."

"For this?"

"For whatever you want."

She licked her lips again, so he pulled out of her and rolled off before he was tempted to keep her in his bed.

"I'll check my calendar when we get downstairs."

He'd take it. If he had his way, he'd have his own color-coded regular appointment on her schedule. He rose and disposed of the condom. Pointing to the bathroom, he said, "Snoop away. I'll go set up lunch."

He put his underwear back on and left the room so she could clean up and redress without him ogling her. In the living room, he opened the containers of pasta and grabbed plates from the kitchen. Eyeing the clock, he wondered if Tess had time to eat.

Moments later, she descended the stairs. It wasn't often he brought a woman to his home, and he'd certainly never watched as one came down from his bedroom. But watching Tess did something to him.

He wasn't sure what.

Tess had no idea what she was doing. She didn't do this. Go to a man's house in the middle of the day to have sex. A man she barely knew. *This isn't who I am. Is it?* When she reached the bottom of the stairs, she turned to find Miles standing in the middle of the living room, carton of food in hand, staring at her.

She glanced around the room. "Is something wrong?"

He blinked and shook his head. "No. It is getting a little late. Do you still have time to eat?"

She went to her purse and pulled out her phone to check the time and calculate how long it would take to get back to her car and then to Mr. Dunphey's house. "If I inhale the food like a teenage boy, maybe."

Suddenly, Miles stood at her side, holding a forkful of pasta up to her mouth. She let him feed her.

"I promise next time, we'll eat first."

Her heart beat faster at the mention of there being a next time. With a mouthful of food, she said, "How will it be better for me to rush out of your bed instead of rushing without eating?"

"I feel bad we didn't have much of a lunch date." He held up another forkful.

"I can feed myself."

"You have to check your calendar for free time."

She laughed at "free time" but accepted the food and opened her calendar app. All the colors spread out, filling her days. Miles moved so he stood behind her, reading over her shoulder.

His warmth seeped through her T-shirt,

and it took all of her control to not lean back into him.

"Don't you trust me?" she asked.

He held up more pasta. "No offense, but last time we talked, you said you had no time."

"Yet here I am."

"Only because I looked at your calendar."

She scrolled down.

"It looks to me like you have some free time almost every day for lunch."

It was only an hour or two. Was it bad that she wanted more of this? "I guess. I never think of that as free time because most of the time I stay at work or do stuff around the house."

"Everybody's got to eat."

He pushed more pasta into her mouth. She wasn't even tasting it, but she was enjoying his arms around her as he took care of her. An odd feeling. Someone taking care of her. Making sure she felt good. Ensuring she ate. "What does your schedule look like?"

"I make my own schedule."

"That's not entirely true. You get dressed and go into the office. Didn't you say you're about to start a foundation? That's huge. I don't even know what's involved, but it's gotta take a lot."

"Don't remind me," he mumbled as he nipped her earlobe.

A shiver skated down her back. She blinked and tried to focus on the calendar. Figuring out when to get chores done and still leave time to meet Miles was easier said than done.

"Tuesday," he said against the side of her neck.

Lord, it was hard to concentrate when he did things like that. "Thursday would be better. My Tuesday client tends to go over. I always write her in with the hope I'll be out on time, but it hasn't happened yet."

"What about Wednesday?"

"I work all day at the hospital."

Miles set the fork on the plate and wrapped his free arm around her waist, holding her against him. "Thursday it is. Where would you like to go?"

"Hmmm?" Her mind had wandered off again with the feel of him pressed against her back. Memories of their night at the hotel, with her hands pressed against the window, rushed through her head.

Miles stepped away and moved to stand in front of her. "Where do you want to meet?"

She shrugged. "I'm going to be on the northwest side of the city. But I'll have almost three hours free, so I can meet wherever you want. I'm assuming your office is downtown?"

"It is."

"Then let's pick someplace in between."

"And waste half the possible time with you on traveling? Uh-uh. I'll leave work early and come to you. Three hours might be just enough time."

The lust in his eyes conjured all kinds of dirty thoughts in Tess. What this man could do in three hours would be enough to fuel her fantasies for many weeks to come. "What's near here?" she asked without considering how forward it sounded. She was too old to play games. If they were going to have a sexual relationship, why not just say what it was?

"I like the way you think. There's a diner two blocks down on Lincoln. Text me when you leave your job."

"Okay." She gathered her purse and dropped her phone in the side pocket. "See you Thursday."

"Wait," he called. "Take this food with you."

"Why? You can stay and eat."

"There's plenty here. You can probably reheat it and not have to cook dinner." He was already boxing up the containers and sliding everything back into the brown paper bag.

"Thank you. That's very thoughtful." Tess meant it. Most guys would've thought nothing of just sending her on her way.

He handed her the bag, his fingers brushing hers as he let go. "Anytime. Have a good afternoon."

She laughed. "It'll be hard to beat lunchtime."

He wrapped a hand around the back of her neck and pulled her close for a kiss. "My driver is at the curb. He'll take you to your car."

She blinked. "You're not coming?" He pointed to the fact that he was still standing in his boxers. "He'll come back for me."

"Thank you. For everything."

"See you Thursday."

Tess slipped out the front door before she totally lost her mind and canceled her afternoon appointment to spend the rest of the day in bed with him.

Outside, the sun shone brightly, making her squint. The driver exited the car and walked around to open the back door for her.

She smiled. "Thank you. But that's unnecessary. I can get the door."

He nodded and closed the door behind her once she was seated. Then he got behind the wheel and asked, "Where to?"

"Agostino's, where you picked me up." *Damn, this is a little too* Pretty Woman *for me.* He'd picked her up on the street and now he was returning her to where he'd found her. She shook her head. Miles wasn't like that. He was just being efficient by having them drive together earlier. Plus, it wasn't like he'd taken her to some seedy motel.

He took her to his condo. He thought nothing of having her in his home. The drive back to the restaurant was quick and as they neared, Tess said, "You can drop me by the front door."

The driver looked at her in the rearview mirror. "Mr. Prescott said I'm supposed to take you right to your car."

Tess rolled her eyes. Of course he had. "Fine. Go to the end of the block and turn right. That's where I'm parked. I'm the minivan." She glanced at her phone. She'd have just enough time to get to Mr. Dunphey's house, assuming traffic wasn't horrible.

The car stopped beside hers and as the driver moved to get out, she waved him off. "I'm good. Thank you for the ride."

"No problem."

She stepped from the car, bag of food in hand, and clicked the button for her car. As she neared the driver's side door, she saw an orange ticket on her windshield.

Damn it. Are you kidding? The meter had expired less than five minutes ago. She grabbed the offensive paper and tossed it on the dashboard. Reaching across the car, she set the food on the floor of the passenger side. At least she wouldn't have to cook tonight. And she'd had a great time with Miles. So what if it cost her sixty-five bucks?

As she put the key in the ignition, she realized Miles's driver hadn't left yet. He was blocking her in. She started the engine, figuring he must be waiting to make sure her piece of crap minivan would start. Then her phone rang. Miles.

"Hello?"

"Hey. Give Dave the ticket."

"What?" A sharp rap at her window made her jump. Miles's driver. She rolled the window down.

"Give Dave the ticket."

"How did you...? Wait." She looked up at Dave through the window. "Did you just spy on me and call Miles?" she asked him.

In her ear, Miles answered, "Yes, he did.

As he should have. I asked you to come to my place, and I promised to have you back in time to get your car. I'll pay the ticket."

"Getting in your car was my choice. I can pay my own ticket." She leaned a little out the window and said, "You can leave now, Dave. We're good."

Dave didn't move.

"Tell Dave to leave," she said into the phone.

"Give him the ticket."

"You're making me late to my next job. I don't have time to argue with you."

His heavy sigh came over the phone, reminding her of what he sounded like when he was worked up. "Hand Dave your phone."

She handed Dave the phone, and a moment later, he returned it to her and retreated to his car.

"Thank you," she said to Miles.

"This isn't over. I just don't want you to be late."

She disconnected and pulled out of the spot. A range of emotions bombarded her. Her body was as relaxed as it had ever been. A couple of powerful orgasms had that effect. But she was conflicted. He'd stood in his living room, literally feeding her, which was sweet. But then to have his driver spy on her and try to take her ticket... She wasn't sure how to feel. Part of her liked that he wanted to take responsibility for that, but another part of her thought he was being a little overbearing. She didn't need him to take care of her.

She tabled all those confused thoughts and focused on going to work.

Chapter 7

The next few days were a blur of activity, which was par for the course in Tess's life. She ran around dropping kids off at day camp, sped from job to job, and constantly wondered in what way she was failing today. By the time Thursday came, all she wanted was an escape. She couldn't wait to see Miles. After her first appointment in the morning—Mrs. Casey, who had just had knee replacement surgery—she texted Miles.

Instead of meeting at the diner, can we go straight to your place?

His response was short.

Sure.

No questions, no comment. At first, she thought he might be annoyed by her request. He was the one who had said more than once that he wanted to get to know her, but when she suggested his place, he had no problem with forgoing the "date" portion of their time together.

12:30?

She stared at his text. He wasn't bothered at all by the change of plans? She responded with one word of her own.

Yep.

As she checked on her next client, Mr.

Kincaid—a bedridden man in hospice—she considered this thing with Miles.

She worked through her routine on autopilot. Hospice was hard for her. Dread and fear and utter grief permeated every house. People spoke in hushed tones as if they were already at a funeral. For the most part, no one talked to her. They let her go about her business, which offered her a chance to think about her own life.

She'd thought she'd be okay having a relationship with Miles without giving it a label. She didn't know if she was ready for a relationship. That was part of why she hadn't done much dating. She didn't need another person to take care of.

Right now, this thing with Miles, whatever it was, was mutually beneficial. Maybe she could keep it like this. Meet once a week or so to have sex and share a meal if they had time.

Finishing up with Mr. Kincaid, she made

notes and checked in with the service that sent her. Then she said her goodbyes to Mrs. Kincaid. Once outside, Tess took a deep breath, filling her lungs with fresh air. She needed a cleansing breath to make sure the sadness from the house didn't cling to her as she went about the rest of her day.

She drove to Miles's condo and circled around looking for a spot to park. When she'd made this suggestion, she hadn't considered the dearth of parking here. On her third time past his house, her phone rang. She pressed the button to put Miles on speaker.

"Hello."

"Almost here?"

"I'm looking for parking."

"Drive around back. I have an extra spot. Number twelve. I'll open the gate for you."

"Okay." Tess couldn't imagine the life Miles led. Personal drivers, a gated parking garage, trendy condo.

She drove down the alley and, sure

enough, as she neared, the wrought iron gate slid open. She quickly found the spot and parked. Now to find her way to the front entrance. She looked around and a door in the corner of the garage opened.

"Tess." Miles stood at the door, waving her over.

"I'm glad you came down for me. I don't think I'd know how to get out of here."

"It's not that complicated." As soon as she was close enough, he slid an arm around her waist and pulled her through the door. "Hi." He pressed a kiss to her cheek and led the way to the elevator. "So why the change of plans?"

"It's been a crazy week. I wanted a break." She huffed out something that sounded kind of like a laugh.

"What?" The elevator dinged, and he moved his arm to rest it around her shoulders as they walked to his door.

"It sounds ridiculous. This week wasn't

any different than any other. I don't know why it's getting to me."

"Come in and tell me about it." He shoved his door open.

Tess stepped into the living room and turned so her body was in front of him. "I don't want to talk."

"That's okay, too." He skimmed his hands up her arms. "Tell me what you do want."

"Take me to bed. Give me the escape I need." Tess liked asking for what she wanted. She'd spent too much of her life not doing that. All of her thoughts fled as Miles captured her mouth, assaulting her with kisses.

He took her upstairs without a word. In his bedroom, she reached for her shirt to pull it over her head.

His hand on hers made her stop. "You want an escape, so let me."

Tess dropped her hands to her side to see what Miles would do. He trailed his fingers from her hand up her arm and to her collarbone. The soft lingering touch caused goosebumps to rise all over her skin. He stroked her abdomen where her shirt met her pants without pulling her shirt up. A gentle glide under the edge of the cotton.

Then he slid his hands under and pulled the shirt over her head. He lowered his lips to her neck while his hand continued to stroke her bare skin. It seemed like an eternity before he flicked the clasp on her bra and popped the button on her jeans, but then suddenly, she was lying naked on his bed.

They didn't speak. The room was filled with heavy breathing and the sounds of their kisses, but no words. Miles took his time with her body, playing and exploring like she was his favorite new toy. In the back of her mind, she felt a little guilty, because he was doing all the giving, making sure she was pleasured and enjoyed herself.

She did none of the work. She didn't even

have to request what she liked. It was as if he just knew.

And while she was lying in Miles's bed, nothing else mattered. She had no worries, no weight pulling her down.

He allowed her to be Tess, the woman.

It was a frightening thought as she lay spent and panting with his arm curled around her hip. She wasn't sure she remembered how to be just Tess.

Miles knew he should get up and check the time so Tess wouldn't be late to wherever she needed to go, maybe offer her lunch. He almost laughed at that. They kept making plans to have a meal together, but it never seemed to happen. Not that he could complain about how his afternoon had turned out, but he hadn't wanted his time with Tess to be just about sex.

But today, something about the way she'd said she needed an escape meant he couldn't say no. He couldn't remind her he wanted to get to know her better. Instead, he'd given her what she'd asked for.

She lay in his arms with no sign of moving. He trailed his fingers up her back. "Why do you have so many jobs?"

"Gotta work," she mumbled.

"Why not just work at the hospital?"

She rolled her head to look up at him from her resting spot on his chest. "I work long shifts at the hospital every other weekend, and one day shift on Wednesdays. That's my main paycheck. I supplement with home healthcare because the hospital isn't enough."

"Why not work more at the hospital?"

"I work shifts most people don't want—overnights on the weekend. The pay is premium. But I only do that every other weekend, when the kids are with their father. If I try to go full-time, I'd get variable shifts, which doesn't work well for a single parent."

"Can't you just get a regular shift?"

"Doesn't work that way. The schedule rotates to be fair."

"Except for you. You always get the crap."

"I ask for the crap. Like I said, good money."

"Tell me about your kids."

She took a deep breath and shook her head. "I'd rather not. They aren't part of this," she said, laying her hand on his chest.

Her reaction stung. It wasn't as if he'd asked to move in with her family. He wanted to get to know her. "Why do you try so hard to work around your kids' schedule? Working parents use babysitters all the time. I had a nanny my whole childhood, and I turned out okay."

He'd meant to make her smile, but all he got was another sigh. She shifted again, lowering her head back to his chest, no longer looking at him. He'd overstepped another invisible boundary.

"My mom was a single parent. I never knew my dad. He took off when she was pregnant. Growing up, I had a lot of friends with at-home moms, and I thought it was great. Don't get me wrong, my friends pointed out all of the downsides, like not being able to do what you want. But especially when I was really young, the idea of having someone at home to help with homework or make me a snack, ask about my day—I didn't have that. I wanted it for my children."

Tess began tracing shapes on his chest as she spoke. Even though it tickled, he didn't move because he wanted her to continue.

"That was one thing William and I agreed on. He wanted me to stay at home and take care of the kids. And I did for years. But when Andrew was a toddler, I wanted to go back to work part-time. I missed being a nurse. I also mistakenly thought my paycheck would relieve some of the burden on William. We were already drifting apart. Going back to work only made it worse."

He didn't understand how her ex could have a problem with her working. She was obviously passionate about it. She loved being a nurse. It was the first thing he'd noticed about her at the gala.

"So he didn't want you to work at all?"

Tess's hand stopped moving. "You don't want to hear about my ex. It's definitely not a conversation for now. Not here. I might be woefully out of practice when it comes to dating, but even I know I shouldn't be talking about another man while lying naked with you."

He reached and tilted her face toward him again. "I don't care if you want to talk about your ex. He's obviously a loser, so I can only imagine how amazing I look in comparison."

This time he accomplished his goal of making her smile.

"Do you have time for lunch today?" he asked and stroked her cheek.

She pushed up off his chest. "I'm not sure. What time is it?" She glanced around the room.

He grunted and got off the bed to grab his phone. "Almost two."

"I have to leave by three."

"Awesome. Get dressed." He reached to the floor, picked up her discarded clothes, and tossed them at her.

"You don't have to, you know," she said as she stepped into her underwear.

"Don't have to what?"

"Have lunch with me. Take more time out of your day. Make this..."

He buttoned his pants and studied her. "Make this what?" She suddenly looked uncomfortable. "A date?" he supplied.

She nodded but didn't look at him. She stared at her T-shirt, as if pulling it on had become a confusing task.

He crossed the room to where she stood and waited for her eyes to meet his. "What is that supposed to mean?"

She lifted a shoulder. "It's just that...I don't know. I thought you were looking for sex."

"I am. So are you. That doesn't mean that has to be all there is. We can hang out and have fun, too."

"For how long, Miles?"

"Huh?"

"If we try to make this a normal relationship, at some point, it's going to stop working for you. You're going to want more from me, and I don't know how much more I have to give."

There it was again, the look on her face that showed all the worry and burden she carried with her. Like she believed she had to do it alone. Not that he was volunteering to help carry the load, but if he could give her a respite now and then, it would be good for both of them.

"I'm fine with whatever you can give, Tess. If coming here to have sex is what you want, why can't we be friends, too? I like talking and spending time with you. No pressure."

She studied his face as if searching for some answer. Then she offered a short nod. "Okay."

He didn't know why, but Miles felt like he'd just won a battle. He dressed and debated what he wanted to do with Tess for lunch. As much as he liked the idea of keeping her all to himself and ordering food in, he didn't want to treat her as if she had nothing else to offer but sex. He really did want to get to know her.

"Come on. I'll drive."

She raised an eyebrow. "I feel weird having a car with a driver. Let's take my car."

He grabbed his keys off the dresser. "I mean *I'll* drive." He jingled the keys in front of her. "I promise I'll have you back here in time to get to your next job."

"I think you have control issues."

He laughed. "No more than you do, Miss Bossy Pants."

"I'm only bossy because I have a lot to do. I don't have time for people to figure out what to do and how to do it. It's easier if I tell them. It's not so much about being in control as it is about being efficient."

"Whatever you need to tell yourself," he said. He led her down to the garage. He drove most places, except to and from work. A corporate car was one of the perks his position afforded him. He used that commute time to make more calls. But on his own time, he liked to drive. Tess was right, though; he liked to be in control.

Tess didn't know who she was any more. She and Miles had a lovely lunch at an outdoor café. It felt strange to have a relaxing lunch in the sun without having to order for anyone else, or break up an argument, or rush through her meal because she needed to get someone to practice or class. Miles proved to be an excellent lunch date.

He continued to ask questions about her life and listened to her responses. He also respected her choice to leave some topics off-limits. Like the kids. She thought she'd run out of things to talk about with him, but she didn't. In her everyday life, the kids took up so much space, even when she wasn't with them, she'd forgotten what it was like to talk about anything and everything else.

She and Miles shared childhood stories. As she suspected, Miles had been a troublemaker, albeit a good-natured one. He charmed everyone, including her.

She'd also forgotten what it was like to have a man focus on her, as if she were the prize. And it wasn't even about sex, because he'd already gotten that.

As he pulled back into his parking spot in the garage, he held her hand. "I had a great time today."

"So did I," she answered.

"Can I call you later?"

She froze as she gathered her purse to head to her car. "Why?"

"To talk."

She stared at him.

He reached across the car, wrapped his long fingers around the back of her neck, and pulled her in for a kiss. He swiped his tongue against hers, making her dizzy.

"As much as I enjoyed having sex with you today, I also had a great time talking over lunch. Since I know you can't come over to fuck my brains out tonight, I'd like to talk to you."

"Okay," she found herself agreeing.

His fingers massaged her neck for a moment. "Until tonight then."

"Bye." She slipped away from him and out of the car.

As she drove, Tess thought about Miles's request to call her. So they would talk. Like a real couple.

Huh. How had he maneuvered her into that? Talking after work, sharing meals, having sex—all hallmarks of a relationship. And they'd managed to do them all in one day. She drove to her client's house with the realization she'd been right about Miles in more than one way. He was trouble, and he did like to be in control.

At the moment, though, she couldn't quite remember the downside to either of those.

Later that evening, as she sat on the uncomfortable metal of the bleachers at the park, her phone rang and Miles's name popped on the screen. She pushed it to voicemail but immediately felt guilty, so she texted him.

Can't talk. At baseball practice.

You don't strike me as a ballplayer. What position?

Funny. My son is playing.

Another piece to the puzzle.

Huh?

She looked up and saw Andrew still sitting on the bench, waiting for his turn to practice batting. Billy sat beside her, oblivious to everything with his nose in a book about Albert Einstein, so she returned her attention to her phone.

> I now know that of your three kids, at least one is a boy and he likes baseball.

Tess rolled her eyes.

> It's not like I'm keeping government secrets.

> You said kids were off-limits.

She had said that, hadn't she? She

thought about it a moment. It had felt natural to tell him where she was and what she was doing. What was she supposed to do, lie? Then she remembered being in bed with Miles and she had her answer.

That was when we were naked.

Got it. Naked=No kid talk

Tess snorted loud enough for Billy to actually look up. She waved at him to continue ignoring her and go back to his book, and he did.

Are you having fun?

She wanted to laugh at that, too, but she didn't want to draw attention to herself.

No way. Watching kids this
young play baseball is
torture. Mostly they stand
around and talk or pull up
grass and dandelions.
Painful.

Ouch. Why go then?

He's my kid. He wants
baseball, we do baseball.

They continued chatting via text. As it
turned out, Miles had played baseball in high
school and college. He tried to convince her
of the virtues of the game, but she wasn't
buying it. Before she knew it, practice was
over. She sent one more text telling Miles she
had to go. He replied with a winkie-face
emoji. The simple conversation made the
time she usually spent doing mundane
things, like creating her grocery list, fly by.

She tapped Billy's shoulder. "Practice is over. Ready?"

"Who were you talking to?"

"What do you mean?"

Closing his book, he shot a look at her over his shoulder. "You usually sit here, staring between Andrew and the time. You were laughing."

"A friend, nosey pants. I'm allowed to have those, you know."

"I know."

Andrew came running up to them. "Did you see? I caught a fly ball."

"Yeah, buddy. We saw." She had seen and even cheered for him. Billy mostly pretended, and Tess let him. "Come on. Let's go get your sister."

They piled into the car and drove to the pool to pick up Zoe, who was getting out of swim team practice. Such was her night, filled with driving to and from, handling requests for snacks because everyone was *starving* even though she'd fed them all dinner before they started on this trek. Just like every other night of her life.

Except it wasn't.

Tonight, things had gone smoother. She'd been relaxed, no doubt thanks to the orgasms she'd received earlier in the day. But more than that, having that little break with Miles made her happy.

As they entered the house, Andrew and Zoe started arguing over who got the bathroom first. Tess shook her head. She knew Andrew only did it to start the argument with his sister. Why Zoe let him get to her Tess didn't understand. During the school year, the rule was youngest to oldest simply because Zoe could stay up a little later. During the summer, she let some of the rules slide.

"Enough. Drop the dirty stuff in the laundry room and flip a freaking coin if you can't figure it out without a fight."

They grumbled, and Billy plowed past them with his book to retreat to his room. Tess didn't know what to do with him. He spent his days at a science camp. He had zero interest in sports, much to his father's dismay. William had wanted his firstborn son to be a star player of some sort.

Billy preferred to learn and think and create, which Tess loved, but sometimes she worried he spent too much time in his own head.

"Fine," Zoe said. "Take a shower first, but if you use all the hot water, I'm going to dump ice water on you first thing in the morning."

"You can't do that."

"Watch me."

"Mom!"

Tess opened the dishwasher to empty and reload it with the night's dishes. "She has a valid point, Andrew. There's no reason for you to stay in there so long there's no hot water for your sister. You have a little body. You should be out in record time.”

He took off for the bathroom.

Zoe stood in the middle of the kitchen and stared at her.

“What?”

“You wouldn’t care if I dumped water on him?”

“Of course I’d care. It would make a huge mess. But sometimes you have to understand the power of a well-placed threat. It was enough for him to think I’d let you get away with it.”

“You’re a little bit evil,” Zoe said with what Tess chose to believe was a hint of admiration. Then she wandered off, leaving the trailing scent of chlorine in the room.

Tess put away the few clean dishes that were still in the machine from yesterday and then reloaded it. By the time she had the dishwasher loaded and the counters wiped down, Andrew was back in the kitchen looking for a snack. She handed him a banana.

He took it and ran to the living room.

"Half an hour of TV then bed."

"I know."

It was the *I know* of someone who had no intention of doing what he knew he was supposed to. As she grabbed dirty clothes from around the house—seriously, why did the kids throw dirty clothes *everywhere*?—her phone vibrated in her pocket. She assumed it was her mom checking to see if Tess needed her to babysit this week, but when she pulled the phone out, she saw Miles's name on the screen. With an armful of clothes, she pressed the screen.

"Hello," she said as she hurried to the laundry room.

"Hey, gorgeous."

Something about the flirty greeting made her insides turn to mush.

"Is now a good time? You said I could call to talk."

"We already did."

"We texted. I wanted to hear your voice."

Her mushiness turned to goo. This guy was too charming. He shouldn't have this effect on her. She knew better.

Miles didn't know why he'd called. Well, he did, but he didn't want to examine it too closely. He'd had a great time with Tess this afternoon, both in bed and out. He wanted more. Their texting earlier was proof she wanted more, too.

"What are you doing?" he asked.

"Laundry."

"Boy, you really know how to relax."

She laughed, but it sounded harsh. "This is my life."

"Can you talk for a few minutes?" He heard some shuffling and banging on her end and then the sound of a machine starting up.

"Now I can."

"Why couldn't you talk at the baseball field?" She was so quiet he thought he'd lost the call.

"My son was sitting next to me." Another brief pause. "My older son. I didn't want to have to explain who I was talking to or worse, have him overhear something he shouldn't."

He tried not to let it bother him that she felt the need to keep him a secret. "Theresa, are you saying you can't control your mouth when you talk to me?"

"I'm not the problem," she answered, chuckling. "You say things that are inappropriate for little ears."

"Are you alone now?"

"For a few minutes. I'm in the laundry

room. I can usually hide out here for a little bit. They don't come in because they're afraid I'll put them to work."

He sat back on his couch and closed his eyes. He imagined her hiding behind a door, peering through a crack to make sure she was alone. "Then I can be as dirty as I want."

She sucked in a sharp breath.

"You want me to be dirty, Theresa?"

"Not now. I have to face my kids before they go to bed."

"But I have you now, for at least a few minutes. Close your eyes."

"What?"

"I'm going to give you something to think about, something to relax you." He waited a beat. "Are your eyes closed?" Nothing.

"Theresa?"

"Fine. They're closed, but if my kids start yelling because they're burning down the house, it's on you."

Man, he knew she didn't like relinquishing

any control, but he hadn't pegged her for a drama queen. "I'll buy you a new house if they burn it down. Eyes closed?"

"I said yes."

"Close them for real this time."

She snickered. "Okay."

He liked that they could laugh and tease even in the heat of a moment. "Imagine sitting on my couch. Naked. The leather cool against your skin."

"I would never sit naked in the living room."

"You will in my house." He ran his hand across the leather cushion beside him, imagining her lying there. "I'd pour you a glass of expensive champagne because I know you like it, though you'd never buy it for yourself."

"Mmm...I can almost taste it."

He knew she was playing along to appease him, but the fact she was at least trying was enough. For now.

"I'd pick up your legs and stretch them out onto my lap. I'd massage your feet, kneading into the arch until you moan."

She sighed, and he knew he had her. "My thumbs press deep into your muscles until you're limp."

"You know, I thought you were going to seduce me with dirty talk, but this might be better."

"I prefer my seduction to take place in person, but if you want dirty talk, I can accommodate that, too. I'd take the bottle of champagne and pour it over your perfect breasts and then lick them clean."

"You're gonna ruin that expensive couch of yours," she said, but her voice was low and husky.

"Then I'll buy a new one. It would be worth it to watch you soar with pleasure when I suck a nipple in my mouth until your back arches, searching for more."

Her breath quickened, and in his mind, he saw her chest heaving with excitement.

"The bubbles tickle your skin as they trail down your stomach. I'd work my way with my lips and tongue until I could lap at your pussy. It's already wet for me. Isn't it, Theresa?" He waited a second, but she didn't respond. No quick, snarky comment. She was in the moment with him. "I'd kiss your pussy like I own it. Flick the tip of my tongue against your clit, just enough to make your hips jump. A hint of what's to come. I'm gonna take my time with you because I love the taste of you on my lips, in my mouth. A slow build until you're scratching at my shoulders, pulling at my hair, anything to hold me in place to get what you want."

"You're killing me here," she whispered.

"You want it bad, don't you?" She didn't respond.

"Theresa?"

"Yes. I nodded, but you can't see me."

What he wouldn't give to see her right now, full of desire, dying to get off. On him. "You're not touching yourself, are you?"

"No. But I want to."

"Don't. Let me take care of you."

A heavy sigh crawled into his ear. "You know that's not possible."

He wanted to make it possible.

"Come over for lunch tomorrow."

"I can't. I'm working."

"Before? After?"

"You're making it really hard to resist."

"So don't. Everyone needs a break. I'm suggesting you take a break with me."

She became silent again, and he knew she was warring with whatever she had on her schedule that would compete with him.

"I guess I can go grocery shopping tomorrow night."

"What does that mean?"

"I can come by before work. Nine o'clock?"

"Excellent."

"What about your job?"

"Don't worry about my job. See you tomorrow morning. I'll be thinking about you tonight." He shifted his hard dick in his pants. He didn't think he'd make it 'til morning.

"You certainly gave me plenty to think about."

"Only thinking, Theresa. No touching. That's for me."

"We'll see."

His cocky girl was back, and he liked it. "Have a good night. But not too good."

"You, too."

Chapter 8

Days later, Tess was sitting at the table at Sunny's Diner waiting for her friends. Nina came through the door, and before she'd gotten to the table, Evelyn strode in as well. Tess was glad the women showed first. As much as she loved Trevor, Owen, and Gabe, sometimes she needed girl talk. Nina slid onto a chair across from her.

"Oh my God. You're like…glowing. You dirty girl. You've been having sex."

Tess leaned forward. "Shh. I told you I

don't want the whole diner to know about my sex life."

"Sex life?" Evelyn asked. "You have one of those?"

"Jeez. And here I thought I wanted to talk to the two of you before the guys got here." Then Tess remembered the Agostino's fiasco and turned to Evelyn. With a pointed finger, she said, "You're a bitch."

"What did I do?"

"Oh, *Go to Agostino's. Casual Italian food.* Liar. No mention of a dress code or the hour-long wait. For lunch."

Evelyn lifted a shoulder with a smirk. "I figured the wait would give you a chance to get to know each other."

"They've *been* getting to know each other. Biblically," Nina said.

Tess snorted. "There's nothing biblical about what we've been doing."

"Spill," Evelyn said as she held up her cup for the waitress and her never-ending pot.

Tess explained how the last week had gone, including her reservations about what she had going with Miles.

Evelyn looked confused. "You're obviously enjoying what this guy is doing, so what's the problem?"

"I don't know. He's pretty amazing. He doesn't ever pressure me to make plans for a real date. He completely accommodates my schedule so I don't have to worry about the kids."

"You have a boy toy," Nina said with reverence.

"He is not a boy toy." Tess cringed at the phrase.

"What would you call it? You only meet him to have sex. On your terms. On your schedule."

Tess set her cup down. "That's just it. That's what I expected, but he calls me and texts me and we talk. Before sex, after sex, at lunch. Or breakfast." She looked at two of her closest friends and hoped they could figure out what was bugging her. "It's like…I don't know. We have this whole clandestine relationship that's too good to be true."

Evelyn leaned back in her chair and toyed with the spoon in her coffee, not making eye contact with Tess. "Maybe he is," she finally said.

"What do you mean?" Evelyn took a deep breath. "Are you sure there's not someone else?"

Tess started to laugh, but then she saw that Evelyn was serious. "He has the reputation of a playboy, so I know there's no one serious." Suddenly, a sinking feeling hit her. Was she one of a string of women? Was he fitting easily into her life not because he was accommodating her, but because the rest of his free time was otherwise occupied?

"Stop it," Nina said. Looking at Evelyn, she said, "Why would you make Tess doubt Miles? Can't you see how happy she is?"

Evelyn didn't back down. "A guy looking for a real relationship isn't going to jump through hoops. He isn't going to be satisfied with lunch dates only."

"Whoa." Tess put up a hand, but Nina jumped in as if Tess hadn't said anything.

"A good man will. In fact, we know some. Trevor and Owen and G—okay, maybe not Gabe. But Trevor and Owen would."

A hand fell on Tess's shoulder. "Trevor and Owen would what?" Trevor asked.

Tess's cheeks flamed. Luckily, she wasn't required to speak.

Nina looked up at him with a smile. "You'd make accommodations to fit in a woman's life if you really liked her."

Trevor sat down and turned over his coffee cup. "What do you mean?"

Owen came in and slid into the seat across from Trevor, waving the waitress over for coffee.

Nina turned to the both of them. "Tess has been spending time with Miles."

"Miles?" Owen asked.

"Guy from the hospital gala," Trevor provided.

"She's been seeing him in the middle of the day when she's free. He arranges his schedule to suit hers. Evelyn_" Nina rolled her eyes over to their friend—"seems to think the only reason a guy would do that is because he has someone else in his life."

"What do Owen and I have to do with that?"

Owen perked up at the mention of his name.

Nina lifted her shoulders. "You two are my example of guys who would go out of their way to spend time with a woman because you liked her. Even if it meant unconventional date times."

Trevor nodded.

"See?" Nina said. "Don't let Evelyn make you doubt."

"You're talking as if a long-term relationship is a foregone conclusion here. It's not. Miles is a great time. But he's not looking for a commitment. I thought I was ready for a relationship. Now I'm not so sure. We're enjoying each other's company. No pressure. He's happy with whatever I can give." She turned her coffee cup in circles, thinking about the texts and phone calls she'd had with him over the last few days. "Sometimes, though, it feels like it's more. I don't know what to do with that."

"What do you want this to be?" Trevor asked. "Friends with benefits?"

Gabe finally joined them in time to say, "Who's got a fuck buddy?"

Tess cringed again. That wasn't any better than boy toy.

"No one would blame you if that's all it was," Trevor continued. "We've all been there. A warm body on a cold, lonely night helps. If you want more and this guy doesn't, then that's a problem. You'll end up hurt. I think that's what Evelyn wants you to consider."

"I know. I'm being cautious. Kind of." She sighed, lifted her cup, and smirked over the rim. "But I'm having such a good time."

Owen's cup clinked against the table. "As long as you go in with your eyes open, there's nothing to worry about."

She'd thought her eyes were open, but Evelyn had made her think otherwise. It wasn't as if she and Miles had had a heart-to-heart about expectations. Maybe they should. But that might feel too much like the talk. She wasn't even sure what other boundaries she'd need to put in place. She was already protecting the kids. Did she need to think of more?

"Who's next?" Nina asked.

They all gave her a blank look.

"I issued a challenge to all of you last week. Do you think I've forgotten?"

Glad to no longer be the center of attention, Tess sat back and enjoyed her coffee. Nina stared at Trevor. "Have you talked to Lisa?"

Trevor groaned, and Nina reached across the table and covered his hand with hers. "If you're still in love with her, tell her."

"I don't know what I am with her. We'll always be connected because of the kids. I don't know if I'm holding on to the image of what I thought we'd be, a holdover from before I blew up my life, or if it's something I want now, a fresh start."

"You need to figure it out. Otherwise your life will continue to stagnate."

"And what about you?" Evelyn asked Nina. "You yelled at us last week about how we're not doing anything to move on. What are you doing?"

Color rose in Nina's cheeks. "I'm ready to

date. In fact, I'm going to a speed-dating thing this weekend. Without being prompted by any of you, I might add."

"Damn. Speed dating? People still do that?" Trevor asked.

"I guess things really do come back around," Tess said. She'd never speed-dated, but she had friends who'd given it a shot years ago. More often than not, the stories had been horrible.

"Good luck," Tess offered Nina. "We expect a full report next week."

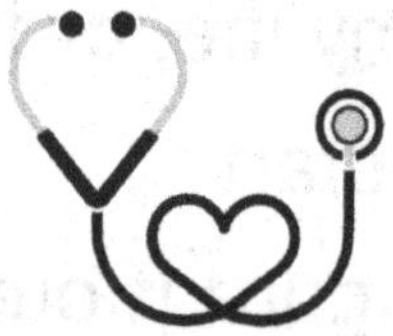

Monday evening, Miles stretched out on his couch as he loosened his tie. His afternoon had been filled with meetings with his sister and various people she thought should play a role in the new foundation. After a lonely weekend, he missed Tess. Although they'd texted and spoken late at night after her kids had gone to bed, he wanted to see her.

She'd warned him this would happen, and he hadn't listened. He couldn't remember the last time a woman had burrowed so deep under his skin. She was right. He wanted more.

But he knew if he pushed, she'd walk right out of his life. So he'd suck it up until she was ready to give more. He looked at the time. Six thirty. She'd be at baseball practice. Instead of calling, he texted.

How's practice?

Boring as usual.

Better than back-to-school shopping though.

He remembered how she'd spent her weekend.

Not by much.

What position does he
play?

Miles was bothered that he didn't even
know her kids' names.

Right field.

Before Miles had a chance to comment,
she added,

He's not very good.

Miles didn't correct her. He remembered
Little League. Right field was a safe place to
put a kid who wasn't confident and didn't play
well.

But he's having fun, right?

He loves it.

That's all that matters.

She was silent for so long, he wondered what was going on. They routinely texted for most of the practice.

Tess? Everything okay?

Give me a few.

While he waited, he went to the kitchen, popped the cap off a bottle of beer, and surveyed his refrigerator for food. He did this two or three times a week and didn't understand why. It wasn't like some fairy came around and filled the fridge. He needed to get into a routine of actually shopping.

He took his beer back to the couch. When he turned the TV on, he found the Cubs game. He snapped a picture of the TV screen and sent it to Tess.

Every team needs a right fielder.

It took another five minutes for her to respond.

> Sorry. I got tied up with something here.

> What?

> For a change my ex showed up to watch Andrew's practice.

The beer sloshed in Miles's empty stomach. He knew he shouldn't be jealous of Tess's ex. They had history. Hell, they had kids. He knew she couldn't cut the man out of her life completely. But he was jealous. He wanted to be there, too, to be a part of her life.

> Problem?

No more than usual. Thanks
for the picture. It's a good
reminder.

It only took another week
for me to get more
information. I now know
that you have 2 boys and
the youngest's name is
Andrew. Sooner or later,
you'll let all your secrets
slip.

She responded with an emoji with its
tongue stuck out. He could almost hear her
laugh.

I don't have secrets. My full
name is Theresa, but
friends call me Tess. Except
for this guy I'm seeing.
When he gets all hot and
bothered, he calls me
Theresa, and it's sexy.

He read the text and her words did make
him hot and bothered.

I have 3 kids: Zoe 14, Billy
10, Andrew 8. I've been
divorced for five years from
their father who is a doctor.
I've only been on a handful
of dates in those years.

Sounds lonely.

It has been. Your turn.

My turn for what?

Spill your secrets.

I'm an open book.

Liar.

He drained his beer and set the bottle on the table. Sinking into the couch, he tried to formulate what he needed to say.

I'm the baby of the family— 2 older siblings. My whole family treats me like I'm incompetent because I like to enjoy life. My father created a job for me at the company because he thought I would end up a loser otherwise.

Harsh.

> I come from a family of
> ambitious people. They're
> not bad though. I haven't
> had a serious relationship
> since college. No real
> reason. Just haven't found
> the right someone.

Miles felt okay spilling his guts. Telling Tess things via text was much easier than talking face-to-face in a serious conversation.

> Come on. You have to have
> some deep dark secret.

> You didn't tell any deep
> dark secret.

Okay—how about this?
When I go to St. Mark's
gala every year, I plan to
find a one-night hookup
after the ball. It's the only
time I get to let loose and
have a night of great sex. I
never saw you coming.

Damn. She knew how to throw a curveball
at him. So he tossed one right back.

I didn't see you coming,
either. And you were right. I
want more, Theresa. Much
more. But I'll wait until
you're ready.

On that note, I have to go.
Practice is over. Have to get
kids home.

Talk later?

Sure.

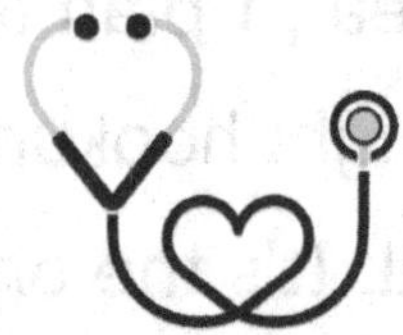

Two days later, Tess woke up and realized she'd fallen asleep and missed her usual call with Miles. After sending a quick apology text, she began her mad dash to get everyone ready. Her mom arrived to help get the kids off to camp.

"William said he'll get the kids and feed them dinner, so I shouldn't need you this afternoon."

"Hmm-mm," her mom said with a skeptical look.

"He's been doing better, Mom. Thanks for always being here. I wouldn't be able to take this shift without your help."

"Anything for you. And my grandkids. William can go to hell."

"It's a good thing I'm not asking you to do him any favors then. Schedule is on the fridge. Remind Zoe to take it so she can give it to William."

"The man shouldn't have to depend on his fourteen-year-old daughter to figure things out." Her mom moved to the kitchen and began cleaning, as she did every week when she babysat for Tess.

"I'm doing the best I can. Please don't say things like that to the kids. No matter what you think of him, he's still their dad." She kissed her mom's cheek. "And you don't have to clean my house."

"For your information, I get all my insults about William in while talking to you. And I clean to help you. I remember how hard it was to do it all, and I only had you." She continued wiping the counter.

"Thanks again."

Tess went to work, hoping for a quiet shift.

As she stowed her purse in her locker, Angie turned the corner.

"Hey, girl. Long time, no see. What's going on?"

"Same stuff, different day."

In between taking care of patients, talking to worried parents, and updating charts, Tess managed to fill Angie in on her love life—sex life—whatever. "So is it getting serious with Miles?" Angie asked when they took a brief break for coffee.

Tess shook her head. "Not serious. We're having fun together, getting to know each other. I'm not rushing to bring him into my life. We're seeing where things go."

"Spoken like a woman who's lying to herself."

"What?"

"I've been listening to you talk about him all morning. While you led with the amazing sex, everything else you've told me is about you and him talking. You really like him."

"I also said we're getting to know each other. Talking is a good way for that to happen. It doesn't mean I'm falling in love with the guy."

"Not yet," Angie said with a smirk over the rim of her coffee.

Tess didn't respond. Any further protest would sound over the top. She didn't love Miles. She could, though, and that was what Angie was getting at. Tess had convinced herself she wasn't looking for love or anything permanent right now. She wasn't sure if it was because she didn't want it, or because Miles seemed like he didn't. She excelled at protecting herself.

That cup of coffee was the last break Tess had all day. They had four new patients admitted, and right before her shift ended, one of her patients went into cardiac arrest.

Emily had been with her for months. She'd had three surgeries, and up until that evening, the toddler had been doing better.

Tess had been sure Emily would be running her parents ragged soon.

Instead, by the time Tess got ready to leave for the night, all she could think about was the look on Emily's parents' faces when they were told Emily couldn't be saved. They'd done everything they could. Emily's mom had crumpled to the floor and her dad had followed her down and wrapped his wife in his arms.

Their grief was a tangible, heavy thing, and Tess needed air. She punched out, grabbed her purse, and walked out of the hospital. She didn't stop to talk to anyone. Once outside on the street, she breathed deeply and pulled out her phone. Five texts and two missed calls from William.

Fuck. He didn't leave a message, so she scrolled through the texts. They were all asking where she was. She was an hour later than she should've been, but of all the people in her life, William should understand how it worked. How many dinners, recitals, and games had he missed over the years because of work?

She debated texting but decided to call.

"It's about time," William answered. "Is everything okay?"

"I'm sorry. I had a patient code. I'm on my way to the train now."

"What am I supposed to do?"

She sighed. "Did you feed the kids?"

"Yes." He sounded irritated that she would even ask. "And I took Andrew to baseball practice. And Zoe to swim team. We're all home now."

Home. It was no longer his home, and Tess spitefully wanted to point that out but didn't. "Thank you. Tell them to get ready for bed. I'll be home soon."

"Am I just supposed to sit here and wait?"

"What would you like me to do, William? I can't control what happens at work any more than you can. If it's that big a deal for you to stay there with *our* kids, call my mother. I'm sure she'll rearrange her life to be there."

"Like that'll happen. Just hurry." Then he disconnected.

Tess climbed the steps to the El platform and swiped her card. The weight of everything pulled at her. Her throat tightened, and tears clawed at the backs of her eyes. When the train roared up and the doors swished open, she stepped on and took a window seat. She laid her head against the cool glass and closed her eyes.

She'd had patients die before. It was part of the job. Normally, she handled it better than this. It was one of the reasons William had said she shouldn't work. She needed to be compassionate without being emotional. Tess accepted she wasn't wired that way.

But today, after watching little Emily die and her parents fall apart, her exhaustion and William being an ass was all too much. She wanted to curl into herself and cry. Doing so on the train didn't seem like a good idea, so she thought about things that brought her happiness.

The look of surprise on Andrew's face when his bat actually connected with the ball. Zoe's high five when she dropped time in breaststroke. Billy sitting completely absorbed in a book. Miles's teasing voice over the phone.

She sat straight and opened her eyes. Where the hell had that come from? Her happy thoughts were always of her kids.

The train neared her stop and she got up. The weight of her sadness made her move slowly, and the jerking motion of the car had her planting her feet. The doors swooshed open and she texted William that she'd be home soon.

When she got to her house, he was waiting outside. Damn. Maybe he was just in a hurry and was rushing to his car. Maybe he wouldn't feel the need to pile on more crap.

"You need to come up with a better plan than this, Tess."

"What am I supposed to do, William? It's one shift a week that I need help with. Everything else in my life works around the kids. I don't ask you for anything but this. One night a week to have a meal with your kids and take them to their activities." She was too tired to fight. She had plenty of ammunition she could pull out, but she lacked the energy.

"I know. But you could've at least called or texted to let me know. Margaret's been holding dinner for me."

Tess closed her eyes. "I would've texted, but it all happened so fast. There was no way for me to predict how long anything would take."

"I know. I'm just frustrated. I don't mind having dinner with them or taking them to sports. But when you're late like this, I don't know what to do. They treat me like a total stranger in this house. They have routines and go about them like I don't exist."

More sadness assaulted Tess. "So talk to them, William. You're their dad. They want you here, but they don't know how to teach you their routines. I can't do that for you."

Before he could say anything else, she turned to the front door. Her emotions couldn't take another hit. William wasn't a bad man or a horrible father. He was just utterly clueless. And she was tired of him blaming her because of it.

She pushed through the front door, and her phone vibrated with a text. Miles.

Good time to talk?

Sorry. I won't be good company tonight. Going to tuck the kids in.

Call if you want to talk.

She left it at that and went upstairs to hug her kids. Billy and Andrew were already in bed, Billy with a book and Andrew talking to his big brother, giving a play-by-play of baseball practice. Billy let him ramble as if he hadn't been there, too.

"Good practice?" Tess asked as she came into the room.

"It was awesome. You should've seen me, Mom. I caught a fly ball. And I threw it to first base, and it made it all the way there."

"Sounds like I missed a good time."

"Yeah," Billy said from the other side of the room. "Would've been nice to have a parent actually see it."

Tess bit back her response.

Andrew sat up and glared at his brother. "Dad was there. He saw. I'll try to do it again so you can see, Mom."

"I'm sorry I missed it."

"That's okay." Andrew threw his arms around her neck and squeezed.

"Good night. No more chatting. You need to get into your routine for school." She tucked the blanket around him and went to Billy's bed to kiss him on the head. "Only a half hour of reading. Then lights out." Lowering to his ear, she whispered, "Try not to make nasty comments about your dad."

Billy narrowed his eyes, looking so much like his father when he did so. "He only comes to practice once a week. He could pay attention. At least a little."

"He tries."

"No, he doesn't."

Instead of arguing, Tess kissed his head again. "Good night."

"'Night, Mom."

She went across the hall to Zoe's room and knocked on the door. Zoe sat at her desk, tapping away on the computer. "Hey," Tess called. "What're you doing?"

"Just chatting."

"Okay. Be in bed by ten."

Zoe looked up from the screen. "You okay?"

"Yeah, why?"

"You didn't ask forty questions about what we ate for dinner or if Dad got us everywhere on time or if the boys behaved."

Tess smiled. "Rough night at work. Glad to be home."

Zoe stared at her a minute. "Someone died."

It wasn't a question. Tess swallowed and nodded. "Ten o'clock," she repeated, forcing the words past the lump that had returned to her throat.

She closed Zoe's door and went through the house on her nightly ritual of gathering dirty clothes and emptying sports bags. Her phone buzzed again.

Ready to talk?

Hell no. Pushing towels into the washer, she debated answering. She didn't have the energy for light-hearted conversation with Miles tonight.

After starting the machine, she leaned against it and stared at her phone. Then she remembered sitting on the train and thinking happy thoughts. Talking to Miles made her happy.

She needed some happy tonight.

Chapter 9

Miles sat on his couch like he did every night, waiting to talk to Tess, but she wasn't answering. At this point, he knew her nightly routine. He could ballpark how long it would take for her to tuck the kids in based on their previous conversations. She should be done.

He scrolled through TV channels and waited. Finally, his phone rang. "Hello."

"Hey."

"I'm glad you called. How was your day?"

"Crappy." She choked the word out.

Miles sat up straight and muted the TV. "What's wrong?"

"Nothing. Bad night at work."

"What happened?"

"A patient died."

Miles sat stunned. He didn't know what words of comfort to offer. She'd lost a kid. "I'm sorry. Tell me about it."

"I can't." She sniffed, and he realized that she'd started to cry.

Before he thought about it, he grabbed his keys. "I'm coming over."

"No," she whispered. "I'm fine."

"No, you're not." Then he realized he didn't know where she lived. "What's your address?"

"You can't come here. My kids."

What was the big deal? He wasn't suggesting getting naked in her living room. "I won't come in. We'll sit outside. It's a nice night."

Nothing but silence.

"Tess, you shouldn't be alone. You're upset. Let me be there for you." He thought he'd have to do some more convincing, but she rattled off her address. "I'll be there soon."

He drove to her house as fast as he could. The entire drive, he questioned what he was doing. No matter how many times he went over it in his head, he couldn't come up with an answer. All he knew for sure was that he hated the thought of Tess sitting alone and crying.

Hell, he couldn't even imagine her crying. She always had her shit together, like nothing affected her.

He parked on the street in front of her house and texted to let her know he was there. She responded that she'd be out in a minute.

He left his car and waited on the front porch. It was a nice brick bungalow on a quiet residential street. Looking down the block, he could picture families barbecuing and kids playing in the grass. It was the kind of neighborhood you saw in movies. He'd never considered what it would be like to live in such a place, but now he let his mind wander.

The front door opened, and Tess came onto the porch. She stopped and looked at him as if at a loss for words.

Instead of trying to figure out what to say, he stepped forward and wrapped her in a hug.

"You didn't have to come here," she mumbled against his chest.

"Yeah, I did." The truth of the statement surprised him.

Tess stood still and let him hold her for a minute before stepping away. "I told Zoe I was going for a walk."

He wasn't sure if she was hinting that he should go, or what.

She took his hand. "I try really hard not to lie to my kids, so let's walk."

"Okay." They held hands as they descended the steps and headed down the block. "Want to tell me about it?"

Tess shook her head, her ponytail flopping around with the movement. They walked in silence for about half a block. Then she said, "A patient died tonight. A little girl who had heart surgery. Multiple operations. We thought she was improving. I normally handle a death better than this."

"I think you're handling it pretty well. You watched a little girl that you cared for die. I wouldn't even know where to begin."

"It's part of the job that always hits me. I've never been good at turning off my emotions. But tonight, I can't get the image of her parents out of my head. They just crumbled. Their whole world. Gone. The way they held each other, like that was the only thing keeping them here." She sucked in a breath on a hiccup and swallowed hard. Miles stopped and held her again. This time she stayed in his arms until she calmed and the shuddering stopped. He rubbed a hand down her back, hoping to soothe her.

"Really. I'm not normally this emotional. It was Emily's death and then her parents' despair. Then to top it off, William."

"William?" Miles asked.

She nodded against his chest. "My ex. I left the hospital and had a bunch of texts from him asking why I was late. I was already in a bad place, so I didn't deal well with him."

"Why did you have to?"

She moved away, wiping her face. "When I work my Wednesday shift, my mom comes over in the morning to get the kids off to camp or school. William picks them up, feeds them dinner, and takes them to extracurriculars. I'm usually home by the time practice is done. Tonight I wasn't."

Miles got pissed off on her behalf. He

wanted to let William know what an asshole he was being. "You had a good reason."

"I know. William does, too." She sighed again and crossed her arms, staring at her feet.

Miles didn't like the distance. "What is it?"

"I feel like a bitch for saying this, so if it comes out wrong, just… I don't know." She looked up at him. "William is always going to be in my life. Sometimes it's hard dealing with him, and I'm sure he'd say the same about me. But we're doing what we can. I don't need you to rush to my rescue."

"I'm not trying to—"

Tess gave him a watery smile. "You are. Your whole body tensed when I talked about William."

"He should be nicer to you."

"Yeah, he should. And I should be nicer to him." She glanced up at the night sky. "Maybe he should be a topic we don't discuss."

He stepped closer and unfolded her arms so he could take her hand again. "In a perfect world, that might be a possibility, but like you said, he's always going to be part of your life. How about I promise to try to listen without getting pissed off?"

"Is that possible?"

"I said I could try. I don't want you holding part of yourself back because you think I'm going to get mad."

"What about you?"

"What about me? I don't have an ex who's an ongoing part of my life."

They continued their walk, still holding hands. "Oh, no, I don't think I want to hear about any of your exes. I was referring to not keeping things tucked away."

He couldn't help but laugh. "Are you trying to tell me you're the jealous type?"

"In general, no, but I don't think my ego is strong enough to hear about all the young, beautiful women in your life."

Her comment, while seemingly flippant, made him pause again. When he stopped, she looked up at him. "There is no line of women in my life."

Tess tilted her head and licked her lips before speaking. He wished he could ignore the movement or say it had no effect on him, but he would be lying.

"You have a history, as do I. My point is that our situations are different, and I'm not sure how to handle it. You tell me you don't care if I talk about my ex, yet I know I don't want to hear about yours. It's petty and unfair."

They walked in silence. Miles thought about everything she'd said. Seriously thought about it. With the women he'd been with in the past, he didn't discuss relationships. His last serious relationship had been in college, and back then, no one discussed exes because it always led to jealousy.

Miles wasn't jealous of her ex. The man had been stupid enough to let her go, so there was nothing to be jealous of. Past sexploits were fodder for conversations with friends, not the woman he was involved with. They turned the corner, and Miles saw Tess's house down the block.

Now a little ping of jealousy pricked him. He wouldn't be allowed in. Until that moment, he hadn't even realized he wanted to. He wanted to be part of her whole life, not just the pieces she carved out. He pulled her to a stop again, close enough to see her house, but far enough that they still had privacy.

"I'm not jealous of your ex. I got a little pissed off when you told me he'd done something to upset you, but you can talk about him without worrying that I'll start trouble for you. And I don't want to tell you about any previous lovers. They don't matter. All that matters right now is you and me." He wrapped his arm around her waist and pulled her to him.

He lowered his mouth to hers and kissed her until it seemed as if the sadness weighing her down dissipated, until she melted against him and was completely in the moment. The kiss was slow and gentle, and although he wanted to continue tasting her all night, he released her.

"Better?" he asked, stroking his fingers over her knuckles. Her eyes fluttered open, and a slow smile crept onto her face. "I feel a whole lot better about a number of things."

"Then I'm glad I came over."

"Me, too."

Standing in the moonlight with a soft summer breeze blowing over them, an unusual level of contentment washed over him. "Now that we've got all the heavy subjects settled, let's move on to the fun stuff. What're the chances of me sneaking into your bedroom tonight?" Tess laughed, and the sound echoed down the street. Her shoulders shook, and more tears streaked down her cheeks. Her eyes were bright, and the sadness from earlier was buried. "I'm not a teenager anymore. What's worse, I have one, so I won't be setting that kind of precedent."

He snapped his fingers. "So I'm a few years too late for sneaking in."

"More than a few."

"What about sneaking out?"

"What?" He slid an arm around her shoulders as they walked toward her house. He pointed at the building.

"As you can see, it's still standing, and you've been gone for a half hour. How about a proper date? Let me take you out."

She sighed but leaned into him.

"I warned you I would want more. Can you get a babysitter for one night this weekend?"

"It's my work weekend."

"Then tell me what night we can go out."

"I'll call my mom and see when she's available."

His mood skyrocketed. He'd been prepared for her to turn him down. Arguments to convince her had been on the tip of his tongue.

She stopped two doors away from the house. "I'd rather you didn't walk me to the door. I don't want the kids to accidentally see you. I want to talk to them first. Prep them for the idea of me dating."

He pushed down the disappointment. Things would change. Soon.

"Okay." Instead of leaning in to kiss her again, he slid his arm off her shoulder and gave her hand a quick squeeze. "Call me tomorrow."

She nodded and walked toward her house, and he stood by his car to wait for her to open the door.

On the drive home, he considered how

often he'd done the wrong thing when it came to women and relationships. He was far from perfect, but all of those mistakes had led him to tonight and knowing that Tess needed him.

That thought made him unusually happy.

When Tess walked into the house, her mind was stuck on Miles and his gentle touches and comforting caresses. While she hadn't completely broken down crying on his shoulder, she was confident he would've let her.

And the kiss...wow. Every time they came together was a slightly different experience with Miles. There was comfort and pleasure every time, but he continued to add layers. She headed toward the laundry room where a load of clothes would be ready to be switched over to the dryer.

Zoe stood in the kitchen, leaning against the counter, eating a bowl of cereal. Tess shot her a look. With her spoon, Zoe pointed at the clock on the stove. "You said be in bed by ten. I have time."

"Five minutes?"

"Plenty of time." She opened her eyes wide. "Did you have a nice walk?"

"Yes, I did. I feel much better." At least she wasn't lying to her daughter.

The daughter who now snickered at her. "Really, Mom?"

"What?"

"Do you think I don't know you're talking to some guy when you disappear into the laundry room like every night? A couple of nights might be believable, but every night? The machine drowns out your conversation, but I can hear you laughing."

She froze and stared at Zoe. When had

her baby grown up and become so observant?

Zoe set her bowl on the counter. "It's no big deal. You have the right to go out and have fun."

"I don't need your permission."

Zoe smiled. "No, you don't. But you never date. You and Dad broke up a long time ago. He didn't sit around. He dated and now he's married to Margaret."

The emphasis Zoe placed on her stepmother's name was normal. No matter how many times she asked Zoe to be more polite, Zoe wouldn't give Margaret much of a chance.

"Your father..." She didn't know how to continue.

"He didn't have us. I get it, Mom. Half my friends' parents are divorced. They all share stories about who their parents are dating."

"I know you're trying to be nice, but I don't want dating advice from my fourteen-year-old. I also don't want to bring a man into your life until I'm sure of him."

"I didn't say I wanted to meet him. I'm just sayin' you should go on a date instead of sneaking around."

Tess almost laughed about being lectured by her daughter for sneaking around. "You're not bothered by me dating?"

"Why would I? Billy and Andrew won't care, either."

She hadn't been looking for the go-ahead from her kids. At least that's what she told herself. But having Zoe's nonchalant nudge eased the discomfort she'd been feeling about her relationship with Miles. "I'm glad you feel that way, because we're going on a date as soon as Grandma is free to babysit."

Zoe groaned as she picked up her cereal again. "I don't need a babysitter."

"But your brothers do."

"You can leave us alone. God, it's only a couple hours."

Now Tess did laugh. Loud enough that Zoe stuck her tongue out at her. "I'll leave you in charge as soon as you show me you can talk to your brothers without letting every little thing they do irritate you."

Zoe threw her shoulders back and lifted her chin. "Fine. I will." Then she slurped the milk from her bowl, set it in the sink, and kissed Tess's cheek. "Good night."

"Good night. I love you."

"Love you, too, Mom." She got to the door of the kitchen and paused. "I'm glad you found someone who makes you feel better."

Then she disappeared.

It was a little thing, but Tess smiled. Miles did make her feel better. She didn't often lean on other people. And he hadn't hesitated. He'd come over even though she hadn't asked him to. Even though she wouldn't invite him into her house.

She went to the laundry room and pulled the wet stuff from the washer and tossed it into the dryer. Her body went through the motions of her mundane tasks, but her mind was focused on Miles.

Although she'd pointed out she was far from a teenager, he had a way of making her feel like one again.

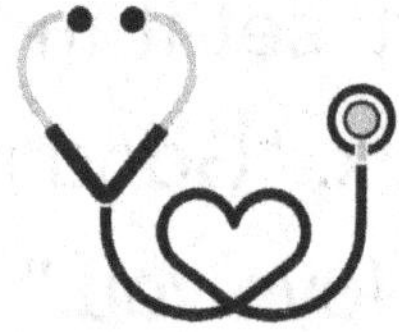

For the past week, Miles had felt mounting pressure from Sabrina to make things happen for the James Prescott Foundation. He'd already retained a team of lawyers to help push through the paperwork. He was in the process of creating a mission statement. In the meantime, he didn't want to abandon all the charities and people who also counted on the Prescotts every year.

Between the constant flood of meetings and Tess's weird schedule, he hadn't been able to see her since he'd gone to her house. And he was missing her. She'd finally agreed to a date, and here it was, Monday night, and he couldn't leave the office fast enough. He wanted every moment with Tess that he could steal.

"I can't stay out late, you know. It's a school night," she'd said when they'd spoken on her break at work. "That was the warning Zoe gave me."

He'd dutifully promised to have her home at a decent hour. With every conversation they had, she was opening up more. She'd begun to share stories of the kids, and Miles had learned not to bring attention to it, or she would get quiet again. He listened and drank in every detail so he could know her better.

As he left his office, he noticed Eleanor's desk was clear. She had small kids at home, and he never kept her late without warning. He turned off the lights and headed down the hall, trying to think about how he could give

Tess both a fabulous date and have her all to himself tonight.

His phone rang with the ringtone he'd assigned to Tess. "Hello, beautiful."

She sighed a little. He loved catching her off guard. "How should I dress for our date?"

"You can wear whatever you want."

"No, I can't. Remember when we were supposed to eat at Agostino's for lunch? That's how I normally dress."

He leaned against the wall near the elevators and pictured her standing in front of her closet deciding what to wear. "Let me amend, then. Wear something nice, Theresa. We won't be eating takeout tonight."

"Are you going to tell me where we are going?"

"Nope. It's a surprise."

"I know you're probably used to women who squeal over surprises, but I'm not one. I like to know what's coming."

"You'll have to be satisfied knowing that I can promise you'll enjoy yourself."

"Not if surprises are involved."

"Trust me."

"I'm trying," she said softly.

Sabrina turned the corner toward his office at the end of the hall. Damn. He'd almost escaped.

"Am I allowed to come to the door to pick you up?"

"Umm…"

"If I need to text you from the car, I will, but I prefer to be a gentleman and ring the doorbell."

"Text when you're close. That way I can be ready to scoot out the door without worrying about having all eyes on you."

"I can withstand an inspection." How scary could a few kids be?

"I'm not ready for that yet."

While he tried to understand, her stance on him meeting her kids felt like she still wasn't sure of him, and it bugged the hell out of him. "I'll see you in about an hour."

"See you then."

He disconnected and slipped his phone back in his pocket as Sabrina neared.

"Cutting out early, little brother?"

"Six o'clock is far from early."

She arched an eyebrow.

"You're a workaholic. I choose not to be."

She tilted her chin at him. "Who are you dating?"

"Who said I was dating?" She rolled her eyes. "Don't you know by now that I monitor everything to do with this family? Your social media accounts have been quiet lately. No posts or pictures of you drinking with a lady on your arm."

"So by not taking pictures with a woman, you've deduced that I'm dating?"

"Absolutely. The people you pose with are unimportant to you. If you're not using her as a prop, it means you care about her. Who is she?"

"I think you should go home. You sound delirious."

She laughed. "That didn't work on me when you were a little boy and cute. It's really not going to work now. Spill."

"There's nothing to spill. I am seeing someone. It's nothing you need to concern yourself with."

"Who is she?"

"No one you would know. She doesn't travel in the same social circles."

"Where did you meet her?"

"At St. Mark's gala."

She snapped her fingers. "The nurse. I suspected when you were acting all squirrelly the week after, and Mom mentioned you met a nice nurse."

Miles stiffened at her comments. Sometimes having a nosey big sister sucked. "I'm never squirrelly."

"Keep telling yourself that." She eyed him up and down and then nodded. "Do we get to meet her?"

Miles tucked his hands in his pockets and shook his head. "We're not there yet."

Sabrina smirked. "Yet."

Shit. He'd forgotten it was Sabrina who'd taught him to listen to the small details when someone spoke.

He pressed the button for the elevator, the need to run intensifying. He pointed toward his office from where she'd come. "Did you need something?"

"I left a file on your desk. It'll keep until tomorrow. Have a good time on your date. I hope you're planning something better than getting drunk at a nightclub."

"Te—not the kind of date this woman would enjoy." He'd almost given her Tess's name.

Of course, Sabrina caught the near slip. "I look forward to meeting the woman who has you being discreet." The elevator dinged, signifying his escape. "See you tomorrow."

With a wave, he stepped away and tried to ignore the look on his sister's face.

Tess stood in front of her closet and regretted turning down Nina's and Evelyn's offers to let her borrow something to wear for her date tonight. What the hell had she been thinking?

That Miles would pick her up, they'd grab some takeout, and go back to his place. That had been the extent of the majority of their "dates," which was fine with Tess. She huffed out a breath. When Miles said he wanted more, she hadn't considered he meant more than just extra time with her. He wanted to actually date.

She didn't know why she found that surprising. Pulling her little black dress from its hanger, she hustled to get ready. Her mom was already downstairs making sure the kids had had a plan for the night. Miles would be here soon and Tess was still wrestling with the idea of whether he should invite him in to meet everyone.

She stepped into the dress and shimmied to get it zippered. After a quick glance in the mirror for a makeup check, she spritzed perfume and went downstairs. Her stomach was rebelling against her. She shouldn't be so nervous. It was a date. Single moms dated all the time, right?

The kids were all sprawled on the living room furniture with the TV on. In addition, Zoe was staring at her phone and Billy had a book. But at least they were together.

Her mom came up behind her. "You look nice."

"Thanks." She looked at the huge bowl of

popcorn her mom had made. "No more junk food. And they need to be in bed at regular time. School starts soon and they need to get back to routines."

"This is the only snack. We're watching a movie. Then everyone will go to bed. I know how to do this."

Tess felt stupid for saying it. It was her nerves making her dumb. She never had to tell her mom anything. Her mom went to the living room and handed Andrew the bowl. Then she came back to stand near Tess.

"Are you all right?"

Tess swallowed. "Yeah. I'm out of practice."

Her mom crossed her arms.

"I've barely dated. I don't know if I should ask Miles in or wait until we know what we're doing or what." She looked at Helen but didn't expect advice from her mom. Tess had never known her mom to date. "Why didn't you date when I was a kid?"

"Who says I didn't?"

"But I never met anyone."

"No one was important enough to introduce to you. I dated quite a bit early on. Don't you remember spending nights at Grandma's house?"

Tess nodded.

"I dated then. But after a whole lot of dating, I learned I didn't need a man to be happy. I began making friends." She touched Tess's arm. "But if I found a man worthy, I would've brought him home."

"How do I know?" Tess whispered.

"Go with your gut. How do you feel about this man?"

"I like him a lot."

"But?"

"But I don't like the idea of introducing him to the kids if we're temporary." And how could they be anything but temporary? Miles wasn't looking to settle down. Even if he were, he wouldn't choose a woman eight years his senior with a ready-made family. He would want to start his own and Tess couldn't give him that.

Huh. Go figure. One quick conversation with her mom and she was able to figure things out. "Thanks, Mom."

"For what?"

"Everything you do. I won't be too late."

"If I get tired, I'll go to sleep. You just worry about having a good time. We have things handled here."

Her phone buzzed with a text. Miles was outside.

"Okay, guys. I'm leaving in a few minutes. Be good for Grandma. I'll see you all in the morning." She moved through the room giving each of them a kiss good night.

Zoe tsked. "What kind of guy doesn't come to the door to pick up his date?"

Tess suddenly discovered the downside to watching romcoms with her daughter. Her own comments were coming back to bite her.

"He will come to the door, just not through it. But don't get any ideas. When you start dating, I expect a full introduction."

"So it's do as I say not as I do?"

"You got it." Tess patted her on the head.

The doorbell rang. Billy perked up and leaned over to see. Tess shook her head at her nosey kids and answered the door.

Miles stood on the porch with a bouquet of flowers. Tess's heart dipped. He handed her the flowers and kissed her cheek. "Hi."

"Hi," she said. "Let me run these inside."

The door opened behind her and Zoe stood there, hand out to accept the bouquet.

Tess glared at her. "It's not nice to spy on people."

"I'll take care of these for you. Be glad I beat Billy and Andrew to the door. Have fun." She nudged Tess and wiggled her fingers at Miles but said nothing. Then she slid back through the door and locked up.

"I take it that was Zoe."

"Of course."

He flicked a thumb over her shoulder. "I think we have an audience."

Sure enough, all three kids and her mother had their faces pressed against the front window.

"Shall we?" Miles asked. He bent an elbow for her to take his arm.

"Thank you."

"I haven't even done anything yet."

"You're here and not pressuring me to meet them even though they're so damn nosey they're staring at you."

"I told you we'll do this at our pace." He opened the car door for her.

"It wasn't *my* idea to go on a date tonight."

"Well, your pace within reason. If I left it completely up to you, I'd be nothing more than a midafternoon booty call."

Tess laughed as she sat and he closed her into his car. He rounded the hood and Tess couldn't get over how good he looked. Almost every time she'd seen him, he wore a suit, but she didn't tire of it. He had some scruff along his jaw as if he was too busy to shave this morning. His sunglasses shaded his warm brown eyes, but when he looked at her as he climbed in, she knew those eyes were filled with heat.

Heat and desire she could handle. Sharing time for now wasn't a problem. As long as she remembered all the reasons why this wouldn't be permanent, she'd be fine.

Chapter 10

Miles had such a good time on his first real date with Tess that it didn't even bother him to drop her off and only get a kiss good night. She'd finally started opening up to him. They'd had only one more regular date, but they spoke every night, and she even let him come over and sit in her backyard with her late another night. Today, he'd told Sabrina he was working from home. Tess was meeting him at his condo, and he didn't want to rush their time together.

Since they'd started dating, they hadn't

had sex, so he tried not to read too much into her coming over now. It had only been a couple of weeks since he'd seen Tess naked, but he suddenly couldn't wait for her to arrive. She texted when she pulled into the parking garage, so he went down to meet her.

Maybe he should give her a key. Then again, that might spook her. He waited at the door for her, and she squinted at him as she neared. "Is it super casual day at work?" she asked.

He was wearing basketball shorts and nothing else. Laughing, he said, "Sabrina would never let me get away with this. I'm working from home today."

As soon as she was within reach, he pulled her into his arms and kissed her. They stood in the doorway making out, relearning each other's taste.

When he pulled away, Tess looked dazed. Good. Just the way he wanted her.

"Hello," she said, quietly drawing out the word.

"Missed you," he responded, pulling her into the hall and toward the elevator.

"I missed you, too," she said when they were riding up to his place. She stroked her fingers across his bare chest. "I have some good news."

"Yeah?"

"My client canceled on me for this afternoon. He has a doctor's appointment, so I'm not needed."

He closed his eyes to focus on her words. The elevator dinged for them to get off. "Does that mean you don't have to rush out?"

"Not until it's time to get the kids."

"So how long?"

"Hours," she whispered as he tugged her into his condo.

"Excellent."

She kissed his throat and then his pecs. His dick rose to the occasion. He yanked at

the baggy scrubs shirt that hid her curvy body
and slipped it over her head along with the T-
shirt underneath.

Kneeling in front of him, she slid his
shorts off until they pooled at his ankles. She
looked up with a wicked little grin and licked
his tip. Swirling her tongue over him brought
a groan from deep in his chest. She leaned
forward, taking him in her warm, wet mouth.
One hand gripped him at the base and the
other hand reached around and grabbed
his ass.

He pulled the band out of her hair to
thread his fingers into the wavy locks all the
way to the scalp and hold on. She sucked and
licked and massaged his balls until he was
losing his mind. She felt so good, yet he
wanted more. He wanted to be inside her.

With tremendous effort, he slid from her
mouth and pulled her to standing. Her lips
were puffy and sexy as all hell. Even as she
looked at him, she stroked him from base to

tip in the same rhythm she'd used with her mouth. He stepped forward, pushing until the backs of her legs hit his couch.

Then, in one swift movement, he yanked her pants down and shoved her onto the couch. He knelt and spread her legs wide. She was already wet. He loved that making him feel good made her hot. Lowering his head, he kissed her inner thigh and nipped at the tendon that joined her thigh to her hip. She rubbed his head, nudging him forward.

"What do you want?"

"Lick me."

He took one long stroke of his tongue over her, and she moaned when he backed off.

"Miles."

"Yes, Tess."

"Stop playing. I've been thinking about this for days."

He massaged her legs, working his thumbs deep on her inner thigh. "Only days?"

She tossed her head from side to side. "Longer."

He smiled. "That's what I thought." Another swipe of his tongue. "Every time I saw you, I thought about stripping you naked and making you come." He lapped at her again, swirling his tongue on her clit. At her moan, his dick thickened. "Do you want me to make you come?"

"God, yes."

"What are you going to do for me?"

"What do you want?"

Miles stroked his fingers over her before sliding one deep inside her. Her breath caught. Her eyes fluttered closed as her hips tilted up to greet him and his hungry mouth. A second finger joined the first. He got her worked up until her hips were thrusting, chasing his tongue and his fingers.

He stilled, and her eyes flew open. She panted, and her gasping breath had her chest heaving.

"I want more, Tess."

"More what? I was blowing you and you pulled away."

He pushed his fingers deep. Her eyes rolled back.

"More of you."

"Take it, Miles. Take what you want."

That was what he wanted to hear. Sure, it was underhanded and a little unfair, but he'd hold her to it. He sucked her clit hard until her thighs trembled. He quickly sheathed himself with a condom and replaced his fingers with his throbbing cock. He sank deep, and they both sighed.

He rocked into her twice and then couldn't hold back. She was wild with need and took him with her. Their teasing lovemaking turned into slapping flesh, harsh curses, and tender bites. At one point, they slid from the couch and fucked on the floor, unconcerned about comfort. They lay spent and panting on the small rug in front of the couch. He still covered her with his body, using his last bit of strength to hold himself from crushing her.

"What...the...hell...was...that?" she gasped out.

He had no idea. It had started with him wanting leverage to get more from her, but it had turned into a desperate need he couldn't explain. "Making sure you couldn't argue that you owe me." His speech was slurred so it almost sounded like he'd said own me. It wasn't far from the truth.

"Owe you what? You came as hard as I did."

He rolled off, disposed of the condom, and flopped beside her. "You said I could take anything I wanted."

"I think you did." She turned and traced lines on his abdomen.

"I missed the fuck out of this. But I mean more of you. I love dating you. Going out places. But you're still keeping me from the biggest part of your life." He stilled her hand on his heated body. "You should probably pull on clothes if we're going to keep talking."

"Why?" The wariness in her voice stabbed into his chest.

He rose, tossed her shirt at her, and stepped into his shorts. "Because you told me a long time ago you wouldn't talk about your kids when we're naked."

She pulled the shirt over her head. "What do my kids have to do with this?"

"They have to do with everything in your life."

She fumbled with her pants, which he'd left in a tangled heap next to the couch. "And?"

"I want to meet them."

She froze and tripped as she tried to get her leg into her pants. He caught her and brought her to his lap. Once her pants were over her legs, she stood and pulled them all the way up. "We talked about this."

"Yeah, but they know about me now. And I feel like I know them because of everything you've shared."

"I can't, Miles."

"Why not?"

She sat beside him on the couch, clasping her hands between her knees. "My most important job in life is to protect them."

"I would never hurt your kids."

"You wouldn't mean to. But this, between us, is still new. They're not even used to me dating. What happens if they like you and we don't work out? Then you go back to your party life and my kids are hurt."

He sat for a moment and dissected her words. What was she really afraid of? That he'd leave her? She had a point. He wasn't ready to promise forever.

"So what? You keep a huge part of yourself separate from them. Shouldn't they know you as a real person? Not as some self-sacrificing woman? Even if I meet them and we don't last, would it ruin them in the long run? Or would I become simply part of their life experience? Like a friend who moved away."

She sank back on the couch and scratched her head. "You ask a lot of questions."

"I deserve some answers."

Nodding, she said, "You probably do, but I don't have any right now. This is all new for me. I've never given much thought to how to navigate these waters."

He sighed. He might not have won this battle, but he'd taken another piece of territory. "I want to be part of your whole life."

"Why?" He shrugged. He had no freaking clue. It just felt right. "It's the next logical step in a relationship, right?"

"Let me think about it, okay?"

"Yeah." He didn't like it, but he knew when to back off. He'd just have to show her that meeting the kids wasn't a big deal. He smiled and leaned in for a kiss. "Hungry?"

"I could eat."

"Go out or stay in?"

"Stay in. I like having you to myself."

"Excellent thought."

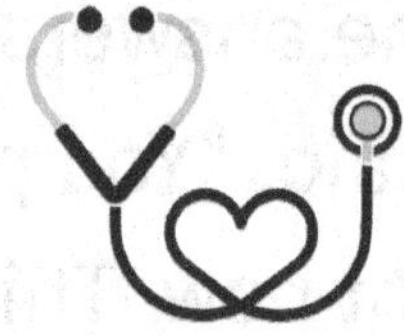

Tess and Zoe left Helen and the boys the following Saturday and went to the spa. Although Tess tried to do something special with each of her kids, she and Zoe rarely got a ton of alone time. This spa day was a treat. Unfortunately, she felt bad that Miles had splurged on the certificate and then was disappointed she couldn't go out with him Saturday night.

He had a fancy banquet to go to and had asked her to be his date, but she and Zoe wouldn't be back in time. He hadn't sounded irritated, but Tess still felt bad.

As they pulled up to the posh resort, Zoe's eyes widened. "Wow. We can afford this?"

"We?" Tess echoed.

"You."

"Not in this lifetime. I have a gift certificate."

They stepped from the van and Tess embarrassingly handed over her car keys. These guys were used to parking luxury cars. They'd probably have a good laugh about her later.

"Where'd you get it?"

"It was a *gift*. Hence the name, gift certificate."

"Oh." Zoe nodded. "Your boyfriend gave it to you."

"He's—" Tess stopped. She'd almost said Miles wasn't her boyfriend, but what else would she call him?

"He's what, Mom?"

"Yes, it was from Miles."

"Miles. Huh."

"What?" she asked as they walked through the door to the spa.

"You've never mentioned his name. You just say you have a date. Like it's a mystery who you're going out with. But we all know it's him."

"Does it bother you?"

"You dating? No."

At the reception desk, Tess gave their name and handed the woman the certificate. They were then led to a changing room where they changed out of their clothes and into a plush robe.

"Think they'd notice if I left in this?"

"I'm sure they would." They sat in chairs waiting for their treatments to begin. Tess had signed them up for manis and pedis and new hair dos.

After choosing their nail color, Zoe sat back and elbowed Tess. You should take a selfie and send it to Miles. Let him know you're getting pretty for him."

"This is about hanging out with you, not getting pretty for him."

Zoe huffed. "Then send a pic to say thank you. Give me your phone."

"Why would I have my phone with me here?"

Zoe rolled her eyes. "You never go anywhere without it in case Grandma needs to reach you."

She held out her hand expectantly.

Tess pulled it from the pocket in the robe. She opened the phone and said, "Let's take one together."

Zoe leaned close and Tess snapped a shot. Zoe made a face, though. "You're terrible at this. Give me."

She took the phone and snapped a bunch of pictures. Then she scrolled through and handed the phone back to Tess. "This one."

Tess stared at it. Both she and Zoe were

smiling wide on the brink of laughter. They looked happy.

Zoe nudged her again. "Send it. It'll show him the gift is being put to good use."

Without thinking more about it, Tess tapped on the phone and texted the picture to Miles with a quick message thanking him.

He responded quickly.

> She's almost as beautiful as her mom.

Tess swallowed the rapidly forming lump in her throat. Miles knew exactly what to say to make her melt.

The nail techs began working on their feet and Zoe talked about the upcoming school year and starting high school. Tess let her daughter ramble, grateful for the chance to just listen. When their toes were finished and their hands were soaking, Tess asked, "How do you feel about meeting Miles?"

Zoe shrugged.

In Tess's experience, a noncommittal answer from a teenager wasn't a good sign. She sighed. Zoe was old enough for a real conversation, as much as Tess hated to admit it, so Tess spoke the truth. "He's been wanting to meet you guys and I told him no."

"Why?"

"I told him I don't want to bring men into your lives until...I don't know...I know he's not going anywhere."

"No. Why does he want to meet us?" Zoe asked without lifting her head, her focus locked on the paint being brushed on her nails.

"He wants to meet you because you're the most important part of my life."

"So you've told him about us?"

"Yeah. I talk about you to him."

"Personal stuff?"

Tess stared at Zoe and thought about how small things could mortify a teenage girl.

"Nothing I wouldn't say to Trevor or Owen or Gabe."

Zoe nodded.

"I would never intentionally embarrass you. You know that, right?"

Zoe laughed. "Every mom says that, but you're all embarrassing. It's like your job."

They got quiet again for a few minutes. "I guess if you want us to meet him, it would be okay."

"What do you want?"

"I don't know. I like that you're dating. I like that he makes you happy. But I remember when Dad wanted us to meet Margaret. God. He was so desperate for us to like her. He was like pushing her on us."

Tess wouldn't forget either. William had already decided to have Margaret move in with him before he'd introduced the kids. Such a fiasco. To suddenly have a stranger living in your home. Tess couldn't imagine. That had been one hell of a fight they'd had.

"That was a little different because he'd fallen in love with Margaret and she moved in. With Miles...I don't know. We're not anywhere near that serious. I don't want to push anyone on you. That's why I'm asking. What about Billy and Andrew?"

"They want to meet him."

"How do you know?"

"Because every time you go out with Miles they ask when they get to meet him."

"They've never said anything to me."

"I told them not to."

"Why?"

"Because your dates with Miles are just for you."

The lump returned to Tess throat. How the hell had her daughter grown up so much? "You're an amazing kid. You know that?"

"Yeah. I know." Zoe held up her finished hand and studied the color. "I guess it might be nice to invite Miles over for dinner. He sprang for this awesome day after all. All I ever got from Margaret were some really horrible muffins."

"What?"

"Don't you remember? She made some awful bran nut raisin gross things that tasted like dust. And Dad kept raving about how much he loved them." Zoe proceeded to make some gagging sounds, sending them both into a fit of laughter.

Tess couldn't have asked for a better day to spend with her daughter. They laughed so hard they cried. They talked beauty tips and boys. By the time they were driving home— with an extremely expensive robe for Zoe— Tess knew she owed Miles more than dinner.

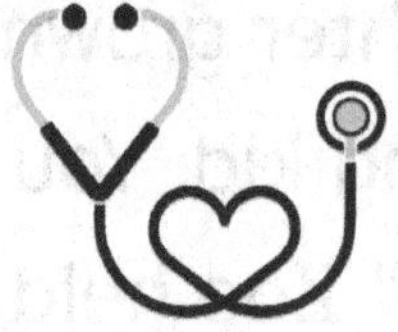

Monday morning, Tess was running late for coffee at Sunny's, so she was the last to arrive. When she sat at the table, everyone stopped talking. Turning over the coffee cup, she asked, "What?"

Evelyn leaned forward. "We're waiting for an update."

"About?" Tess smiled.

Nina copied Evelyn's pose, arms crossed on the table. "Miles. We want details."

"Things are going well. We've been dating. The kids know about him. This weekend Zoe and I used the spa gift certificate Miles gave me. Girl time was great and we talked about Miles being in my life." The waitress stopped by and filled her cup, so she took a sip before continuing. All eyes remained on her. "I'm thinking about inviting him over for dinner to meet the kids."

"Wow," Trevor said. "Big move."

"Right?" Tess said. "He asked, and I've just been flopping about it."

"What's the big deal?" Nina asked.

"I don't want to introduce random guys into the kids' lives."

"More than that," Trevor added, "by bringing him home, you're admitting he's important. Someone you care about."

She wasn't even sure she was ready to admit that to herself.

"You do, don't you?" Evelyn asked. "Care about him?"

"Yeah, I think so. But it's complicated."

"Always will be," Trevor said.

Gabe leaned back, one arm resting on the back of Nina's chair. "He looks good on paper, Tess. No red flags."

"You didn't."

"Of course I did. And now that you're talking about bringing him into your home, I'm glad I did."

She didn't want to care what Gabe had found. She wanted to believe that what she knew about Miles was all she needed to know, but curiosity pulled at her. "So he's good?" "He's no altar boy. By the standards of the Prescott family, he's...not a joke, really, but he's not taken too seriously. That said, it doesn't seem to bother him. He's not like his siblings."

"Oh my God. Did you investigate the whole family?"

"I didn't investigate them, but he works for his family. How could I ignore them?"

"It's not healthy," Nina said.

"Sure it is."

"No, it's not. Part of falling in love with someone is learning who he is. You take all the fun out of the mystery," Nina insisted.

Gabe set his coffee down and twisted to fully face Nina. "What if the mystery is a bad thing? What if the guy is a functional alcoholic? You'd fall for him, and it would be too late by the time you figured it out. He'd ruin you."

It was low for Gabe to strike the one thing he knew would tear Nina apart, but Nina sniffed. "I think I'm pretty good at seeing an alcoholic for who he is. Most aren't as good at hiding it as they like to think."

"But you see my point." When Nina didn't answer, Gabe tugged the ends of her wavy black hair.

When she looked at him, her walls were fully in place, but she nodded. "Not everything is bad."

"You're right. I'd rather be safe than sorry. It's a healthy habit for me because it keeps me sane."

"Enough of Stalky McStalkerson talk," Evelyn interrupted. "I wanna hear about the sex. Is it great?"

Tess's cheeks heated. "I'm not talking about it."

"What about the rest of you?" Nina asked. "We should all have updates."

Evelyn and Owen glanced at each other but didn't respond.

Trevor hunkered down over his coffee, not making eye contact with anyone, and mumbled, "I talked to Lisa."

Everyone fell silent. They all knew he hated that he'd destroyed his marriage.

Trevor shook his head. "We talked for a long time. But she won't take another chance on me. She's in a good place and thinks working toward any kind of reconciliation with me would be a step backward. She wants us both to move on."

Tess reached over and rubbed a hand on Trevor's back. "I'm so sorry."

"It's probably for the best. After talking to her and my sponsor, I realized I was trying to hold on to something that hadn't worked. She's what I know, what's comfortable. It's time to move on."

He straightened and raised his cup. "Who's next?"

No one else added to the conversation.

"You're pitiful," Nina said. "I at least did speed dating. It totally sucked, but I tried."

"But the trying didn't work," Gabe pointed out.

"So what are you gonna do? Stop trying and sit in your cave all alone for the rest of your life?"

Tess laughed, because a cave was how they all pretty much imagined Gabe's house. They'd never been there, mostly because he never invited them. Given that he worked from home doing some kind of computer security stuff, they all pictured him in a dark room surrounded by monitors.

"My cave is pretty comfy."

Nina poked at him. "You need to try. Venture out. Look around. You might find a perfectly nice woman right here in Sunny's."

Gabe looked up and around the diner. The clientele tended to skew older at this establishment. He smiled and shook his head.

Following his gaze, Nina sighed. "Okay, bad example. But think about other places you go."

"I don't."

"What do you mean, you don't?" Nina asked.

"I don't go anywhere else."

"You must," Tess said. "What about groceries?"

"Delivery."

"Meeting with clients?" Trevor asked.

"Virtual conference room." Gabe shifted again to face Evelyn and Owen and waited for their questions.

"I got nothing," Owen said.

"Maybe it's time to go somewhere, Gabe," Evelyn said. "Nina has a point. Keeping to yourself is one thing, but this is a little extreme."

"I'll think about it."

Tess didn't know what had made Nina start to push them all, but she was glad.

Eleanor walked into Miles's office and slapped another pile of folders on his desk.

"What the hell?" he asked his secretary.

"Your sister has too much time on her hands," she responded.

Without flipping through the stack, he picked up the phone and dialed Sabrina's extension.

"Hello."

"You said you wanted me to make this foundation happen."

"I'm fine, Miles. How are you today?"

"Seriously? You're going to give me a

lesson in manners when every time I turn around, you're dumping more files on me?"

"I'm trying to help. You need a board of directors."

"I'm aware, Sabrina. I haven't screwed anything up. You haven't given me enough room to. If that's your greatest fear, maybe you should oversee everything yourself."

"I don't have time. I have a company to run."

"Yet you find time to keep sending me information."

She laughed. "I delegated."

"Like you already delegated this project to me. Back off. You either trust me or you don't."

Her sigh was heavy and irritated. "I do trust you. But if we're going to establish this and have it ready to unveil for the anniversary, we need to get moving."

"Throwing a hundred candidates at me

won't make it happen faster. If anything, it wastes time. Let me do things my way."

Silence met him for a long moment. "Okay," she said quietly.

Her response caught him off-guard. Sabrina never capitulated.

"Miles?"

"I'm here. I'm just trying to figure out if you're pranking me."

Her laugh was low and a little maniacal. "Pranks aren't my style. I do trust you. I sent the files because I thought they'd help. Toss them out if you want. Yell if you need anything." Then she hung up without a goodbye.

He'd point out her lack of manners later. Instead of dumping the files in the trash, which was his immediate instinct, he paused. Sabrina might be bossy, but she knew what she was doing. Her instincts were dead on. If she thought the people in this stack were worth looking at, he'd check them out.

An hour later, he had a list of people he felt would be the best candidates to help develop and run the foundation. Damn, he hated when his sister was right. He was about to pick up the phone again to thank her when his cell buzzed with a text from Tess.

Have time to meet for coffee this afternoon?

He'd had to cancel their lunch earlier in the week, so he was glad she'd texted.

What time?

My schedule is flexible. I can come to you.

That would be great.

He thought about when she'd have to get the kids and suggested two p.m.

Sounds good. Tell me
where.

He spun his chair and looked out the
window as if he could see the coffee shop on
the corner. He texted the address and
checked the time. A little over an hour and
he'd see Tess.

He was amazed at how quickly she'd
become an integral part of his life. He had no
idea why everyone had led him to believe that
a serious relationship was hard. He and Tess
worked pretty effortlessly. As long as they
remained flexible about what their
relationship should look like, things would
continue to run smoothly.

Sabrina had been telling him for years
that when he least expected it, someone
would come into his life and change
everything. He'd laughed her off.

He really hated when Sabrina was right.

Not wanting to hear the smug tone of her

voice when he thanked her, he chose to send an email full of emojis to make her crazy. He included the list of candidates, along with his notes on why he thought they were a good choice, so she would know he hadn't been slacking. He didn't mention her being right about his love life as well.

One "I told you so" was enough to last a long time when it was coming from Sabrina's mouth. He finished reading through the files and answered some emails and before he knew it, it was time to head downstairs.

He waved to Eleanor. "I'm going out for coffee. I'll be back within the hour."

"My coffee is unsatisfactory?"

"Eleanor, my love, your coffee is extraordinary. This is a meeting."

"You have nothing on your schedule."

"It just came up."

She cocked her head and twirled a pen in her hand. "How am I expected to maintain your schedule if you add appointments without informing me?"

"I'm sorry." He leaned in close and dropped his voice. "I'm meeting my girlfriend."

"Your—" Her eyes shot wide, and she fought a smile. "Very well then. I'll see you when you return."

One of the things he liked best about Eleanor was that she was nosey but managed not to pry. She would have questions when he came back, but he hadn't yet decided if he'd answer them. He was testing the waters, trying out the word "girlfriend" as part of his vocabulary.

When he got to the coffee shop, he looked for Tess but didn't see her, so he got in line and ordered for both of them. While he waited for the coffee, Tess walked in. She strode straight to him and took his hand. "Sorry I'm late. I forgot how long it can take to find parking."

"No problem." He kissed her cheek, knowing if he went for her lips, it might lead to something indecent.

The barista called his name and smiled as she handed over the cups.

"To what do I owe the pleasure of making you trek downtown?" he asked.

"Isn't it enough that I wanted to see you?" He scooted his chair closer and laid a hand on her thigh. "It's definitely enough."

She placed her hand on his. "I also wanted to talk."

"Good talk or bad talk?"

"Good." She inhaled deeply and set her cup down. Suddenly, this didn't feel like a good talk.

"If you still want to come over to meet my kids, it's okay."

He turned his hand over and laced his fingers with hers on her lap. A quick stab of panic hit him. He'd been pushing so hard to be included in her whole life, but the reality of hanging out with kids worried him.

"Have you changed your mind?" Looking at the doubt in her eyes made him shove his thoughts aside.

"No. I want to meet them."

She licked her lips. "I'm nervous. I've never brought a date home, so this feels very significant."

"It doesn't have to be." It wasn't like he was asking to be their dad.

"Yeah, it does. By bringing you into our home, I'm admitting you're important in my life."

The panic returned. They hadn't spoken much about where they were going. For a while, he thought she might never want more. Now she did, and part of him was reconsidering, but he wanted to put her at ease. "Change is scary, but we'll keep it simple."

I'm a good uncle. I know kids and how to have fun with them. Simple.

"I was thinking you could come over for dinner one night."

"Name the day, and I'll be there."

"There are ground rules, though."

"Rules?"

"No PDA. The kids know we're dating, but they don't need to see us making out."

He huffed a dramatic sigh. "I suppose I can keep my hands to myself for one evening."

"And you can't buy them anything."

That was a strange request. "No playing Santa. Got it. Can I ask why?"

"It'll feel phony, and kids can spot phony. Plus, you're generous. I doubt you know how to give a small gift."

"I only brought flowers on our first date. Nothing extravagant."

"True. But you also paid for an expensive day at the spa. While Zoe and I had a fabulous time, I don't want them to get into the habit of thinking they should receive gifts just for being there."

"Done." Although he didn't see what the big deal was. Kids liked presents.

"What does your schedule look like? What day works for you?"

"I told you I don't care."

"I know you have *things*." She waved her hand at the word "things" and then pulled out her phone and started scrolling through. "It looks like the kids' schedules are clear Friday."

"What time?"

"Five thirty? Is that too early for you?"

It was early for dinner, but he could make it happen. "I'll be there. Can I bring something? A bottle of wine? Dessert?"

"Just bring yourself." She leaned over and kissed him. Her soft lips parted slightly against his.

"I want them to like me." In his gut, he

knew if he couldn't win her kids over, he'd lose her. She'd never said it or even hinted at it, but he knew. She was fiercely protective of them, so he couldn't screw this up.

"They will. I'm worried they might like you too much." She took her hand away from his face and picked up her coffee again. "So how's work?"

"You don't want to hear about my job. Tell me more about the kids so I'm prepared for dinner." He spent the next half hour asking questions so he'd be well-armed.

Chapter 11

Friday afternoon, as she checked the roast in the oven, Tess's stomach churned. Pot roast and mashed potatoes. This was not the kind of meal Miles was used to. He was accustomed to linen tablecloths and multiple courses. *What am I doing?*

She grabbed her phone and called Angie.

"Hey, girl. Aren't you supposed to be getting ready to introduce your man to the kids?"

"I think I screwed up."

"I doubt it."

"I made pot roast."

"So what? I've had your pot roast. It's damn good. If that man has a problem with a hunk of tasty red meat, he can answer to me. What do you think he expects, caviar?"

Tess rubbed her forehead. "I don't know. I suddenly panicked that he would never eat pot roast."

"So the pot roast is your kids."

"What?"

"You're worried about pot roast, but your real concern is your kids. It'll be fine. It's a meal. You're not moving him into your bedroom."

"What if they hate him? Or worse, if he hates them?"

"Your kids are great. He'll love them. They might not love him at first, but they'll probably like him. And if they don't, point out how filthy rich he is."

Tess laughed. Angie was definitely good

at talking her down. "Thanks, but I don't want to advertise that."

"Use what you've got. I bet he does."

"Do you really think pot roast is okay?"

"Look. This is your life. He needs to see all of it. The real. Because if he can't handle it, now's the time to get out."

"You're right. I've gotta go and finish dinner. He'll be here soon. Wish me luck."

"You don't need luck. He's lucky to have you."

Angie made excellent points, but the worry continued. What if he could handle it? What if her life didn't scare him off? She couldn't imagine this was the life he'd ever imagined for himself. She'd never allowed herself to envision someone else in her life as a partner. Worse, the nagging voice deep down still asked, *"What if he can't handle it? Are you willing to walk away?"*

While she prepped the rest of dinner, she turned those thoughts over in her head.

What had started as a great sexual relationship was becoming more, and that scared her.

When the doorbell rang, Andrew raced to answer. Tess came up behind him as he swung open the front door. Miles stood on the front porch, wearing jeans and a T-shirt instead of the suit she'd expected. She'd assumed he'd come straight from the office.

Miles opened the screen door and looked at Andrew. "Hi. I'm Miles." He extended his hand to shake.

Andrew took his hand. "I'm Andrew."

"Andrew, huh? Not Andy or Drew?"

"Nope. Just Andrew."

"All right, then, Andrew. May I come in?"

"Sure." Andrew turned. "Can we eat now?"

"Tell your brother and sister to wash their hands. Then, yes, we'll eat."

He ran up the stairs, yelling at his siblings. Miles came in and handed her a bouquet of flowers from the bag he held. He glanced to where Andrew had run off and then leaned forward and kissed her cheek.

"You said no PDA, but since no one is here to see, I'm safe."

She smiled at the fact that although he played by her rules, he looked for loopholes. "You're not wearing a suit."

He looked down at his clothes. "I'm sorry. Was I supposed to?"

"No. I figured you'd come straight from work."

"I went home to change. I thought the suit might be too stiff and formal."

She closed the door and turned back to him. "They're used to suits. Their dad wears one every day."

"Then I'm extra glad I took the time to change."

"What's in the bag?"

"I know you said not to bring anything, but my mother always taught me not to come to someone's house empty-handed."

Thundering footsteps behind them told her the kids were there. She took Miles's hand and pulled him into the living room.

"Miles, I'd like you to meet my kids." She pointed to each and introduced them.

The kids stood there and sized him up in a way she hadn't seen them do in a long time. The first time they'd met Trevor was probably the last time she'd watched this phenomenon, and Trevor had never been anything other than a good friend.

Suddenly, she was at a loss for words. She had no idea how this was supposed to go.

"Dinner smells good," Miles said.

"Shoot. Dinner. Make yourself comfortable. I have to get the food."

She heard Zoe snicker as she left the room. She hoped they would take it easy on Miles.

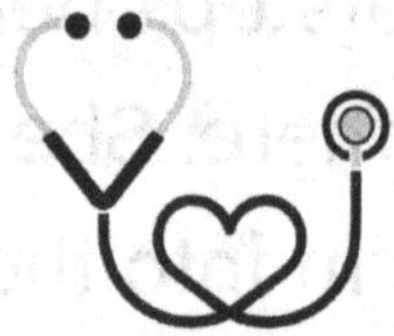

Miles stood in the living room, holding on to the bag with a book for Zoe and a video game for the boys, along with the cake he'd brought for dessert. Of course he'd broken the rules. He couldn't help it. He wanted her kids to like him. If he had to bribe them, he'd take that chance.

"What's in the bag?" Billy asked.

Miles leaned back so he could see where Tess was. Still out of sight. "I brought dessert and gifts, but I wasn't supposed to, so now I don't know what to do."

His humility seemed to work. Zoe stepped forward. "Give me the dessert. I'll take it into the kitchen and let Mom know. Unless you bought us something crazy like a car, she won't care."

"You sure about that?"

She nodded and took the cake he pulled from the bag. He kept the plastic closed at the top so the boys couldn't see what he had.

"Here's the deal, guys. I wasn't sure what to get you, so I guessed. This is something you have to share, and you can't do anything with it until your mom says it's okay."

Billy crossed his arms. "What is it?"

Miles pulled the game out. "A video game. It just released this week, so I didn't think you'd have it yet."

Billy looked at the title. "Yeah!" he yelled.

"I thought I was gonna have to wait for my birthday for this. Thanks."

Andrew took the box from Miles. "Miles said we have to share, so you have to play with me."

Oh God. What had he started? "You can't fight over the game. Your mom will never let me hear the end of it if you do."

Billy laughed. "Don't worry. We share a room, so it's not like I could hide it."

When Zoe came back, Tess followed with a stern face. She had never looked as much like a mom as she did in that moment. He shrugged. "Nothing extravagant."

She eyed the video game Andrew held, Billy reading over his shoulder. Miles pulled the book from the bag.

"I hope you don't have this. Your mom mentioned you're a big fan of the author."

"Oh my God! It's the new Sasha Belfrey book. How did you get it? It doesn't even come out until next month."

"Oh." He feared he'd really stepped in it now. He rubbed the back of his neck and debated. But he knew Tess would want the truth. "I went to college with Sasha. When your mom said you loved the author, I emailed Sasha to see if she'd send me an autographed copy. I didn't know this wasn't out yet."

Zoe's eyes just about popped out of her head. "You *know* Sasha?"

He nodded. She squealed and almost started hyperventilating when she opened the book and read the personalization.

Tess shook her head. "Gifts down. Dinner is ready."

When they made no effort to move, Tess snatched the game and the book, receiving groans in return. "Go," she said, pointing to the dining room.

She set the items on the end table before facing him.

"The book cost me nothing. The video game is one I wanted to try anyway. This way, I can play and leave it here."

She crossed her arms. "As far as gifts go, they're pretty perfect. It was very nice of you. But don't make a habit of it. They'll totally take advantage."

Habit? That implied long-term. *We're actually doing this.* He swallowed against the stab of anxiety and shrugged. He'd let the kids take advantage if it gave him any leverage.

She took his hand, led him to the dining room, and pointed to a chair. "Have a seat."

"Smells delicious."

"Hope you like it."

"I rarely get a home-cooked meal, so I'm happy to eat." He sat in the chair next to Tess and across from Zoe.

Tess took plates from the kids and loaded them with food. With the exception of forks clanging against plates, they were quiet.

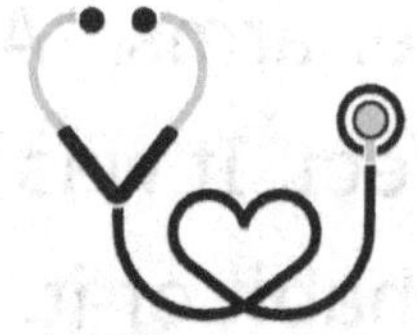

As Tess took her seat and watched Miles fill his plate with food, a ball of dread filled her stomach. The kids stopped talking. They ate and stared at her and Miles. She didn't know what they were waiting for, but it was unnerving.

Miles leaned over, and in a loud stage whisper, asked, "Are they always this quiet?"

She laughed. "I wish. This is kind of creepy." She looked at Billy and Andrew, who were suddenly fascinated with their mashed potatoes.

Miles took a bite and moaned. "This is so good." He glanced at the boys. "You guys get to eat like this all the time?" They shrugged, and he sighed.

Tess tried not to cringe. Maybe it was too early for this. Maybe they weren't ready for her to be dating.

"So, Andrew, I hear you play baseball."

"Yeah."

"What position?"

"Usually outfield."

"Did your mom tell you I used to play? In high school and college. Shortstop."

That caught Andrew's attention and he

finally looked up. "Do you know anyone famous?"

"Ball player?" Miles asked. When Andrew nodded, Miles said, "Sorry, no."

"Could you teach me to bat better?"

Miles slid a look to her before answering. "If your mom says it's okay."

"Not tonight."

That simple conversation opened the floodgates. All three kids chimed in with questions about who else Miles knew that might be famous, what he did for a living, and whether he had any kids.

Tess gave him credit. If he was nervous, it didn't show. He answered every question they lobbed and still managed to clear his plate and have seconds.

As soon as the boys finished, they jumped up. "Can we go play the game Miles gave us?"

"Miles brought dessert."

"We're not hungry. We wanna play."

"Go ahead."

"You coming, Miles?" Everything in Tess settled with their invitation.

Miles smiled. "I'm going to help your mom clean up first."

"Zoe and I have it."

"I can help."

Zoe stood. "It's my turn for dishes."

"Go play," Tess said as she took his plate.

The boys took off, and she yelled after them, "No fighting or Miles takes the game home with him."

He squeezed her hand and followed the boys.

"He's okay," Zoe said as they wrapped the leftovers.

"You think?"

"Even without the bribes." She rinsed a plate and slid it into the dishwasher. "I mean, I totally love my present and I'm not giving it back, but even if he hadn't brought anything, he still seems okay."

"Why do you say that?"

"He tried. Unless you told him what to buy us, he must pay attention. He remembered what author I like. I bet Dad wouldn't have a clue."

Shit. She didn't need the kids to make those kinds of comparisons. "Your dad pays attention."

Zoe snorted.

"It's not a competition."

"I know. I love Dad. And Miles wants to make a good impression. It's not like I'm going to start calling Miles Dad. But Miles tried."

They finished cleaning up, and she packed some leftovers for Miles. Zoe had disappeared with her phone and new book. Tess was sure she was bragging to all her friends.

After pouring herself a glass of wine, she leaned against the counter and absorbed the quiet of the house. This was when she normally snuck into the laundry room to talk to Miles. She finished her wine in peace and then went to see how he was doing with the boys.

She stood in the hall and listened to the conversation before making herself known.

"I can't believe your mom lets you have video games in your room. I'd never sleep."

Thanks, Miles. Like I need you putting those thoughts in their heads.

"She'd know," Billy said. "It's like she's got super hearing or something. And if she catches us, she'll take the whole system and give it away."

"Ouch. Brutal."

"No, no, no, no," Andrew yelled.

"Come here," Miles said.

She eased forward and peered through the open door. Andrew was sitting on Miles's crossed legs. Miles had his arms wrapped around her son, and they both had their hands on the controller.

"Take that," Miles said.

"Oh," Billy groaned.

Andrew fell into a peal of laughter. Miles dropped the controller and tickled him. Tess's heart lurched. In one swift moment, she was both happy and disappointed.

Miles would want this for himself one day. He'd want his own sons to play with. What was she supposed to do? Break up with him now? The day after she'd introduced him to the kids and they'd gotten along great?

She swallowed the ball of confusion in her throat until she thought she could speak. "Hey, guys. Sounds like you're having fun, but it's time to get ready for bed."

"Aww," both boys moaned.

"Even on a Friday night?" Miles chimed in.

"Yes," she answered, even though she wanted to break her own rules for a change to prolong the night.

Miles stretched his legs out in front of him before pushing up from the floor. "It's time for me to go home anyway." He pointed at Andrew and Billy. "But I expect a rematch."

"When?" Billy asked.

"We'll check with your mom." He ruffled their hair. "See you later."

As he walked by, he brushed his hand against hers. The contact was minute but intimate. Their gazes caught, and a charge ran between them.

No, I'm not ready to walk away from this.

Suddenly, Zoe was there. "Go walk Miles out, Mom. I'll make sure they brush their teeth." Without waiting for a response, she pushed past them into the boys' room. "Let's go. Time to brush."

Tess swallowed a laugh at how much Zoe sounded like her.

"Who made you boss?" Billy asked.

"Mom's busy. I'm the oldest."

Tess took the hint and followed Miles down the stairs. "I have a container of leftovers for you. I thought you might like a bonus home-cooked meal."

"I would never say no to a free meal."

She grabbed the container off the counter and met him in the living room.

"So, Zoe's pretty intuitive, huh?"

"Until recently, I hadn't realized how much."

"I'm glad she took over bedtime stuff so you could walk me out. Maybe I'll even sneak a good-night kiss."

Her heart fluttered with his flirtation. "Maybe I'll let you."

He took her hand as they walked out the front door and stood on the porch.

"Did we adequately scare you off?"

"That was supposed to scare me?"

She smiled. As nights went, it had been tame. "It rarely goes that smoothly. They were on their best behavior."

"I had a great time tonight. I'm glad we did this."

"You are?"

Miles stepped closer, pushing her against the brick wall. "I told you I want to be a part of your whole life. I know every night isn't dinner and video games. But sometimes it is."

She wanted to talk to him about the future, about what he wanted and how she couldn't give him his own kids, but the thoughts died in the back of her head. They weren't in a position to be talking babies.

He stroked a finger down her cheek. "What are you thinking?"

"Nothing."

"Liar. I totally lost you there."

"Do you want kids?" she blurted.

He blinked rapidly. Obviously, not the question he'd been expecting.

"I don't know. Maybe." Backing away, his gaze searched hers, but she didn't know what he was looking for.

"You were great with the boys. You'd make

a great dad. But I'm done with that part of my life. I don't want to do the whole babies and diapers and daycare thing again." She laid her hand flat on his chest. "Even if I wanted to, it's not possible. I had my tubes tied after I had Andrew."

"Okay."

"That's it? Okay?"

"What do you want me to say, Tess? It's not like I have some lifelong plan of having two point five kids and a house in the 'burbs. So you can't have more kids. Okay. There's nothing I can do about that."

"You can find someone who can before we get in too deep." As soon as the words left her mouth, the air in her lungs froze. She hated needing to do the right thing. She didn't want this to end yet.

Miles leaned close again. "Already too late."

He proceeded to kiss her until she completely forgot the conversation at hand.

All that mattered was his body hard against hers and his mouth making her greedy.

When he finally pulled away, she had a hard time focusing.

"Good night. Tell the kids I had fun. Talk to you tomorrow." Then he walked to his car, leaving her standing there more confused than ever.

For the next two weeks, Miles worked with his head down, doing everything he could to build the foundation that would be his father's legacy. In addition, he continued to work with the same charities they'd donated to for years. He and Tess had been able to meet for lunch and even go on some more real dates.

She'd let Zoe babysit the first time and no

one had died, so she'd said they could do it again. Things were going so well that on their last date, he'd talked about planning a family outing for Labor Day. It would be the last weekend of the summer for the kids, and he wanted to do something special.

He got her to agree. Barely. They hadn't spoken about the future or kids or where they were headed since that night on her porch. He hadn't come up with any answers. All he knew was that he loved being with Tess, and she came as a package deal with three kids.

Knowing that led him to be sitting in Sabrina's office with his sister and his mom. They'd just finished talking about some details for the James Prescott Foundation and Miles figured it was as good a time as any to bring up Tess.

He cleared his suddenly dry throat. "As long as you're both here, there's something I want to talk to you about."

Sabrina smiled and tossed her pen on her

desk as she leaned back to give him her undivided attention. Both Sabina and his mom stared at him.

"For Monday, I'm thinking about taking the boat out."

"You're not coming to the barbecue?"

"Just a couple of hours. Then I'll be at the party. But I'd like to bring some guests."

Sabrina smirked, so he turned to look at his mom.

"Of course. Since when do you ask to bring friends?"

He rubbed his jaw. "Well, this isn't just some friends. I'd like to bring Tess."

"About time," Sabrina said.

"Tess?" his mom asked.

"Uh...Theresa. You met her at the St. Mark's gala. We've been seeing each other."

"Who else?" Sabrina asked.

"She has three kids."

Sabrina's look was full of skepticism. "You're dating a woman with three kids?"

He nodded.

"And you've met them?"

He locked his jaw but nodded again.

"Wow," Sabrina said. "I thought that was a deal breaker for you."

"Kids?"

"Yeah. Ready-made family."

"I never gave it much thought before."

His mom reached over and touched his hand. "Is it serious?"

"I think so. I mean, we're taking it kind of slow. We dated for over a month before she let me meet her kids. We're not rushing toward anything though."

"So no wedding bells in the near future?" Sabrina asked.

"No." While the lack of relationship conversation with Tess meant he didn't have to make any decisions, it also meant he didn't know what she wanted either. Was she looking to get married again? He couldn't imagine her living with someone without being married. She seemed traditional in that sense.

"I look forward to seeing her again." His mom stood. "I'll see you both Monday."

Miles went back to his office and tried to concentrate on work, but Tess invaded his thoughts. It didn't help that every time he turned his attention to the foundation, his phone bleeped with a text from her. Tess hated the idea of him creating a plan without her knowledge. She *really* hated surprises.

His phone rang. "Hello, Tess."

"Okay. I know I'm being a pain in the ass, but I'm working for the next two days. I have to plan ahead for Monday."

"What do you need?"

"I have three kids. You don't just drop everything and wander off with kids. They require things. Like what do I have them wear? What am I going to feed them? And how many meals should I arrange or pack?

Are we going to be outside? Will we need sunscreen?"

He laughed. It shouldn't have been funny, but she was so stressed about a simple outing that he couldn't help it. "I give up. I'll tell you where we're going, but let the kids have the surprise."

"Yes. Okay." He could almost hear her inner control freak practically sigh in relief.

"We're going to spend the day on the lake on my family's boat."

Tess dropped into silence. Her lack of response began to worry him. He hadn't thought about it being a problem. He knew Zoe was a swimmer, so water shouldn't be an issue.

"Something wrong?"

"You said your family's boat?"

"Yep."

"Will your family be there?"

Ahh. Now he understood her concern. "Not on the boat, no. My family has a huge barbecue in the afternoon, so I thought we could go."

"With your whole family?"

"Yeah. The kids will have a blast. My nieces and nephews and friends' kids will be there."

"So this is a huge *family* event."

"Huge, yes, but it's not a family thing per se. My family hosts, but we have employees and their families and neighbors and friends. You don't have to worry about being surrounded by Prescotts."

"You want me and my kids to meet your family?"

"Of course."

"But—"

"My sister has been nagging me about meeting you. It's only fair. I survived the first meeting with your kids. It's your turn."

"We're really doing this, huh?"

"Doing what?"

"Being a couple."

"Is this just dawning on you now? We've been dating for almost two months."

"It was easy for it to be fun when it was just the two of us. Bringing family in and doing couplish things makes it feel real. And serious."

"I seriously enjoy being with you."

"Me, too. See you Monday."

"Won't we talk later?"

"I'm on at the hospital, but I'll call when I get a break."

"Talk to you later."

When they disconnected, he stared out his office window and considered whether he could sneak over to Tess's house after she got off work.

Chapter 12

Monday morning, Tess packed sandwiches and drinks into a cooler. Then she checked to make sure the kids had swimsuits and a change of clothes for later. Regardless of how many questions she'd asked Miles about what they should wear to the party, he insisted it didn't matter. Somehow, she thought he was wrong.

She'd met his mother. She'd seen how he dressed most days. What if their idea of a barbecue was formal dining outdoors? That would be a disaster with her kids.

Miles had tried to reassure her, but she wasn't feeling at ease. On her third check of everything, the doorbell rang. Miles agreed that it made more sense for them to take her car because they would fit more comfortably, so he was meeting at her house.

Billy ran to let him while Tess recounted the number of sandwiches and snacks in the bag.

Miles came into the kitchen where she was packing and kissed her cheek. He looked at the cooler and bags and said, "We're only going to be on the boat for a few hours."

"I know. But it'll be lunchtime. And being out in the sun makes it easy to dehydrate, so I have extra drinks. That bag has towels and sunscreen." She looked up at him. "I want to be prepared.

He shrugged and grabbed the cooler. Tess yelled to get the kids moving. Outside, Miles slid the cooler into the van and she handed him the two bags. "Keys?" he asked.

"For what?"

"So I can drive."

"You want to drive my mom mobile?"

"My masculinity isn't threatened by your van." He leaned over and whispered in her ear, "I like to be in charge of *all* the driving."

She felt her cheeks heat but handed him the keys.

The kids settled in the back and the trip to the lake was relatively quiet. Miles led them to the slip and Tess couldn't believe what she saw. When he said the family boat, she imagined a pontoon boat or something similar. What Miles pointed to was nothing short of a yacht.

Then she wanted to slap her head. She'd known Miles had money. His family was wealthy. Why hadn't she thought ahead to this?

Andrew looked at the boat and said, "Wow. Are you rich?"

Tess groaned.

Miles laughed. "My family is. This belongs to all of us."

"You mean you have to share?"

Miles nodded as he hefted the cooler on deck. "My dad bought this when I was about your age. My brother and sister are a lot older, so they got to use it more. But now that we're all grown up, we share."

He lifted Andrew onto the boat and waved the rest of them aboard.

Zoe turned to Tess and whispered, "He's really rich, isn't he?"

Tess didn't want to lie, but she didn't want this to be a big deal either. "Does it matter?"

"I know it shouldn't, but it's pretty cool."

Once they were all on the boat, Tess coated everyone with sunscreen while Miles prepared to leave the dock. He walked by and dropped a pile of life vests.

"What are those for?" Billy asked.

"You need to have life vests on."

Zoe shot a dirty look at the orange vests. "I know how to swim. I don't need one."

"Doesn't matter. Rules are that all minors have to wear them."

Tess breathed a sigh of relief. She'd thought she'd have to fight with the kids on this.

"Mom, would you tell him." Zoe pointed to where Miles had walked off.

"I don't think he makes the rules, honey. How about if you put it on, but I won't make you tie it?"

She turned her attention to Billy and Andrew and made sure they were fastened. The kids walked around and explored the boat while she set up towels and found a place for lunch. The boat was beautiful and spacious.

Zoe was lying on a towel in the sun and Billy was reading a book on the bench in the shade. She went to find Andrew. She found him with Miles, who was steering the boat.

Once on the open water, he let Andrew take the wheel.

He looked so damn good with her son in front of him, teaching him. He spoke in low tones and although she couldn't make out what he said, Andrew was eating it up. Tess watched them together for a few minutes and tried not to let her imagination run away. This was what she'd imagined for her life as a family. One where both parents worked and played and acted as partners.

But Miles wasn't a parent. At least not for her kids.

She needed to remember that. Enjoy the moment. Don't stress about the future or unknowns.

Not exactly her strong suit, but if she was going to do this dating-relationship thing, she needed to accept she couldn't control every outcome.

Miles caught her eye and smiled. He kept

one hand loosely on the wheel and let Andrew steer.

"You want to try?"

"No thanks. It looks like you boys have it covered."

"Go sit and relax. We'll go out until we're free and then the kids can swim."

She nodded, but the thought of letting the kids jump off a boat unnerved her.

Miles spent the day amazed by Tess. She kept a constant watch on all three kids. It was like she had a weird sixth sense and always knew when someone was going to need something even before they asked. Miles didn't know how she wasn't totally exhausted. As he pulled back into the slip, she was below packing up the remainder of their stuff. He wondered if she ever took a break. He'd thought today would be a fun outing for them, but now he had doubts.

He'd seen Tess smile, so she hadn't hated the day. She had worried when he suggested the kids jump off the back of the boat to cool off. He went in with them while she stood watch. That was how Tess handled life—she took care of everyone.

He cut the engine and went to help her grab the bags and cooler. The kids were sprawled all over the deck. When he went below, Tess was rolling towels and shoving them in a bag.

"What can I help with?"

"I got it. We just need to carry it all back to the car."

He flipped the lid on the cooler. "They demolished the food you brought."

"Swimming and sun equals constant hunger."

"Are you still okay with going to my

parents' house?" He stumbled as he said parents. Although his dad had been dead for more than a year, he still thought of it as his mom and dad's house.

Tess looked down at her clothes. "I wish I'd brought something else. We won't have time for me to go home to change."

"You look fine."

"I don't want to look *fine* when I meet your family." She ran a hand over her ponytail, which was barely restraining her hair. "And the kids. They're an even bigger mess."

"They're going to run around and get sweaty and messy at the party. Trust me. I'm not changing."

Tess rolled her eyes. He stepped closer and held her shoulders. "This is you. It's who you are. I don't expect you to change for my family. I've seen you in scrubs and a fancy gown and jeans. It doesn't matter what you wear. I like you in anything." He lowered his lips to her ear and whispered, "Or nothing."

Tess laid her forehead on his shoulder. "You make this hard."

He chuckled. "That's what he said."

"You're such a goof." She laughed.

"My family will be thrilled I'm bringing you to the party. They'll love you."

"What time does the party start?"

"About two hours ago."

She shoved away from him. "Are you serious? We're late for a party with your whole family?"

"We're not late. People drop in whenever they want." He checked the time on his phone. "Food will probably be ready in an hour or two, but then they'll make more later. It's an ongoing kind of thing."

She looked panicked. "We're going to make a horrible first impression."

"You'll be fine. Let's go."

"If your family hates me, it'll be your fault."

He shrugged. "I don't care what they think of you. This is my life."

He lifted the cooler and walked up the steps while calling to the kids, "Let's go. Time for a party."

They grabbed their stuff and followed behind him quietly. Miles was pretty sure they'd had a good time, but their silence was unnerving. "Are they okay? They're really quiet."

"They're exhausted. Wait until they get their second wind."

He closed up, and they piled in the car. Within five minutes, the kids were in various stages of dozing off, so he took advantage of the moment and held Tess's hand.

"Did you have a good time today?" he asked her.

"Yeah. The kids had a blast. They've never been on a yacht before. Well, neither have I. When you said the family's boat, that's not quite what I imagined."

"I meant did *you* have fun?"

"I said yeah."

"You didn't look like you relaxed at all. I wanted you to have a day off."

She laid her hand over their interlocked ones. "There is no such thing as a day off for me. I'm a mom. I don't mind doing the things I do. My pleasure comes from seeing them have a good time. You gave them a great experience. That matters more to me than taking a nap and missing out."

He wanted to understand. Her words made sense, but she should be able to have more, have it all. "You still need to take time for you."

"I do."

He didn't believe her for a second. As he pulled off Lake Shore Drive to head toward his childhood home, he released Tess's hand. "You should probably wake them. We'll be there soon."

Tess looked around. "Crap. I know I should've asked this before, but you grew up in a mansion, didn't you?"

He had never given it much thought. "I suppose by some standards it might be considered a mansion. The house isn't castle-size or anything. There are only four bedrooms."

Tess laughed. "Only four."

"You have three."

"And they're all small."

"Does it matter where I grew up?"

"Not really. You won't get it. I grew up lower middle class, like barely clinging to middle class. We lived in an apartment my whole childhood. When I was able to have a house for my kids, that was huge. But they look at our house and compare it to the one William bought for himself and his new wife. I can't compete. They're kids. They don't understand what things cost."

"Do you want to skip the party?"

"No. I'm just feeling uncomfortable in my skin right now. I'll get over it." Then she reached around like some kind of contortionist and woke the kids. Andrew groaned at her to leave him alone.

She shook his leg. "Come on, buddy. We're almost at Miles's party. He said there are going to be a bunch of kids there for you to play with."

He kicked out, not really at her, but more of a flailing leg.

"This is where I grew up," Miles said as they turned a corner. He pointed at the park. "That's where I used to play baseball." He pointed at a large old house. "That was where my first girlfriend lived."

"Hey, Miles," Zoe called from the back seat. "Don't you know you're not supposed to talk about ex-girlfriends in front of your new one?"

He looked at her in the rearview mirror. "Only if your new girlfriend is insecure, which mine absolutely is not." He winked at Tess. "And this is home."

Andrew groaned again. "I don't feel good, Mom."

Tess twisted in her seat. "What's wrong?" She took one look at him and jumped from the car. She flung the sliding door open, and before Miles could even process what was going on, she had Andrew out of his seat.

The boy hurled all over the grass.

"Ew. Gross," Zoe called as she climbed out.

"Is he okay?" Miles asked, keeping a safe distance.

"Probably just too much sun." She went to the back of the van, pulled out a bottle of water, and put it up to Andrew's lips. "Take some small sips and see if it helps."

"Should we take him home?" He realized the significance of *we* and *home* but hoped no one would read too much into them. He wasn't ready to consider why they so easily slipped from his mouth.

"No way," Billy said. "We're already here."

Tess looked at Miles and then at the kids. She pressed the back of her hand to Andrew's head. "What do you think? You want to rest a little while and see if you feel better?"

He nodded and then hung around her neck. Tess struggled to stand with her son in her arms.

Miles rushed to her side. "Let me take him."

"I don't think he'll go for that."

He touched Andrew's shoulder. "Can I carry you inside? I'll take you to my old bedroom."

Andrew nodded again and leaned over for Miles to take him. Holding him as Tess had, on a hip, was awkward as hell, so he shifted all of Andrew's weight to the front and started toward the house. He couldn't see over his shoulder, so he hoped Tess followed.

As he let them in the house and trudged

up the stairs to his bedroom, he couldn't help but think about how much work kids were. He'd played and hung out with Tess's kids and always had a good time, but today he'd seen parenting, and it wasn't pretty.

He remembered why he didn't have any of his own kids.

Tess was torn. Being at the party to meet Miles's family was important to him, and she wanted the kids to have a good time. But her baby was sick. This was her primary job. She followed Miles into the house and tried not to let the shock get to her.

He might not call this a mansion, but she would definitely classify it as such. They stepped into a foyer that led to an open-concept living room and beyond that, a huge kitchen filled with stainless steel appliances. Miles headed up the stairs, so she continued on.

Behind her, Zoe and Billy murmured their opinions, but Tess figured they were as in awe as she was. Miles pushed into a room and laid Andrew on the bed. When he turned, he looked surprised to see her and the kids.

"You didn't have to come up. I can handle laying Andrew down."

"I want to make sure he's okay. And uh... we don't know anyone. Can you take Billy and Zoe down and maybe introduce them to people? I'll join you in a couple of minutes." While Zoe might be adventurous enough to head out, she knew Billy wouldn't.

"Oh, sure." He turned to the kids. "Let's go see who's here. I know there's some good junk food around, too."

Tess shook her head. He'd lowered his

voice as if he was sharing a secret, but he'd said it loud enough for her to hear. She moved to the edge of the bed and touched Andrew's head. "How you doing, buddy?"

"Tired."

"Is your stomach still upset?"

He shook his head.

"Why don't you take a nap, and then if you're up to it later, we can enjoy the party?" She brushed his hair off his forehead. His skin was pink from the day in the sun even though she'd slathered him with sunscreen. She'd thought she'd given them all enough water to stay hydrated, but maybe she'd miscalculated. "Want to try another sip of water?"

He shook his head again.

She put the bottle on the nightstand. "I'll leave it here in case you change your mind."

She stood, and he said, "Are you leaving?"

"No. Just going to look out the window to

see if I can spot Zoe and Billy." She took a slow walk around the room, checking out the trophies and medals lying on the dresser and bookcase. No pictures on any shelf, which seemed odd since she'd seen pictures in his condo. Maybe he'd taken them all from here.

Tess scanned the titles on the bookshelf. Mostly required reading kind of books, except for the long line of fantasy novels and computer gaming books. Miles was a nerd. She chuckled to herself.

"Spying?"

His voice from the doorway startled her.

"Of course. Did you think you were going to bring me into your childhood bedroom and I wouldn't snoop?"

"There still might be a *Playboy* under the mattress," he whispered.

"Not the kind of information I need."

He took her hand. "Ready to come downstairs?"

She looked at Andrew. "I don't think he wants me to leave. He's in a strange place."

"Give me your phone."

"Why?"

He held out his hand, and she gave it to him. "Does he know how to use it?"

"Of course."

"Passcode?"

Then she realized his plan. "He knows it."

Miles arched a brow. "But I don't. Keeping secrets?"

"No secrets. It's not like I know your passcode." Were they at the point where they should share those details? "It's my birthday."

Miles knelt beside the bed. "Hey, Andrew." When her boy opened his eyes, Miles put her phone in his hand. "Call my phone when you wake up if you want to come out to the party and we'll come get you. Okay?"

"Or call if you feel worse, and we'll go home," Tess added.

"Call if you need anything."

"'Kay. Night." Then he rolled over with the phone tucked in his little hand.

Miles stood. "Problem solved. Let's go get you a drink."

"I thought I was here to meet your family. Are you telling me I'll need a drink to get through this?"

"You've met my mom, so that's no problem. Sabrina is pushy. She'll ask a ton of questions. Bradley is a dick. He probably won't say much of anything." He pulled her from the room. "I want you to relax a little."

"Where are Zoe and Billy?"

"Last I saw, Zoe was playing strip poker with a room full of guys, and Billy was doing shots at the bar."

She nudged his shoulder. "Funny."

"I introduced Zoe to a neighbor's daughter who is about the same age, and Billy found my nephews, who were all talking about video games."

"It's not that I don't trust you. I worry about them. I can't imagine that will ever change."

At the bottom of the stairs, Miles stopped and faced her. "I think you're a great mom. But I feel like you don't trust me. I would never do anything to hurt your kids."

Tess didn't know how to explain herself. It had nothing to do with Miles. She was like this with pretty much everyone. "You barely know my kids. I don't think you'd do anything to intentionally hurt them, but you're not a parent. You won't think like one. It's not a flaw, just a reality."

He pressed a closed-mouth kiss to her lips. "Ready to meet everyone?"

"As ready as I'm gonna get." Tess tried not to be nervous. The problem was, she hadn't had to meet a boyfriend's family since she'd started dating William. This was far worse than first-date jitters.

"They'll love you."

"Sure." She looked down at her clothes again. She probably smelled like puke. *This is such a bad idea.*

Miles led her through the house, giving her a brief tour as they made their way toward a wall of glass that led out to a beautiful brick patio. Tess surveyed the guests. Never in her life had she wanted to punch someone as much as she wanted to hit Miles right now.

Everyone was dressed beautifully in designer—although casual—clothes. She looked like a schlub. Never in her life had she wanted to punch someone as much as she wanted to hit Miles right now. She didn't think she'd given anything away, but Miles stopped again.

"What's wrong?"

She gritted her teeth. "What's wrong?" she asked with a clenched jaw. "I'm completely underdressed for this party. Look around.

Can't you see the difference between how I look and how they do?"

He didn't even glance at the crowd. Instead, he lowered himself so they were eye to eye. "I don't care what the label says. Having money doesn't make me a snob."

He didn't understand. He couldn't. He'd grown up like this, so he had no way of knowing how this would make her feel, so she couldn't hold it against him.

"I care about you," he added. "If they don't like it, they can fuck off."

She couldn't help but smile. He was so sure of himself and his feelings. In the back of her mind, though, this was a pulsing reminder of why they wouldn't work long-term. She couldn't live her life feeling like an outsider. Mustering up some bravado, she threw back her shoulders. "Then let's do this."

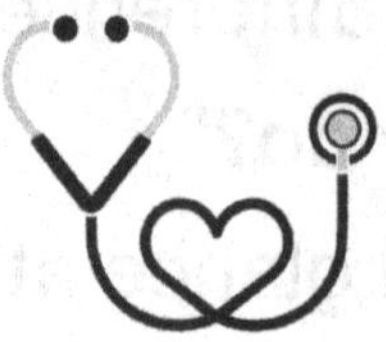

After the bumpy start they'd had to their afternoon, Miles was thrilled at how things had changed. Andrew had woken up from his nap and called him. He'd had dinner and began running around as if he'd never lost his lunch on the lawn. Zoe and Billy barely stopped to check in with Tess, which bothered her more than he thought it should.

But mostly, he loved that Tess relaxed enough to have a good time. She had a couple of glasses of wine and really hit it off with Sabrina, which was no surprise since they were two independent, career-minded moms. Sabrina took no time at all to lure Tess away from his side and they spent hours talking.

Unfortunately, he knew it was too good to last. Tess gave him a look that said the fun was over. She crossed the lawn in bare feet, having kicked off her sandals shortly after she'd been hit with a stray water balloon. He was caught in a sad mix of emotions. He loved the sight of her coming to him, but her attention was still split. Even with her eyes on him, she was cataloging the location of each of her kids.

"Something wrong?"

"No, but it's time for us to be going. First day of school tomorrow."

"The sun hasn't even set yet."

She laughed. "I can't use that as a guide. They all have to take showers and make sure their bags are packed so I don't maim anyone during the mass panic tomorrow morning." She took his hand. "If you want to stay and enjoy yourself, that's fine. You don't have to come with us. I'm sure you can get a ride from someone."

The offer was tempting, and in truth, had she been any other date, he probably would've taken her up on it, which led to more confusion. As much as he was glad he didn't have to check on the kids to make sure they were okay, he enjoyed being part of their family, even if it was only a small part.

"I'll drive you."

"We came in my car. I can drive. I don't want to take you from your family."

"We came together, we'll leave together. Plus, if I wait until the kids are in bed, I might get a kiss good night."

"Are you sure?"

"About the kiss? Absolutely." He put his arm around her shoulder.

She smiled and said, "I'm going to run to the bathroom. Then I'll round them all up." She glanced around, much like she had when she first stepped into the yard. "They look like they're having a blast. Thank you for inviting us."

"Any time."

She disappeared into the house and he

chatted with a few neighbors while he waited for her return. A few minutes later, he felt like he was being watched, and when he looked over his shoulder, he saw Tess standing at the picture window, staring out at the yard. He made his way into the house.

She remained in the same position. He came up behind her and wrapped his arms around her waist. He lowered his mouth to her neck. "I don't think I'll ever be able to see you in front of a window like this and not think about the first time I had you. Watching our reflections in the glass. He nipped her earlobe.

Her breath hitched and she arched her back, pushing her ass against him. He growled and tightened his grip on her. "I'd take you right here if we were alone."

"But we're not." Her voice was breathy and it made him hard to know he had this effect on her.

"We could be."

She chuckled.

"The bedrooms upstairs all have locks. Just you and me."

She sighed and relaxed in his arms. "As great as that sounds, we're not alone. And I do have to get the kids home."

"When will I get you alone again?"

Turning in his arms, she kissed his cheek. "First week of school is crazy. Nighttime dates are out of the question."

"What about next weekend?"

"I have the kids."

"You have them today."

"It's Monday. William had them Friday and Saturday while I worked. Next weekend is mine."

He tried not to be frustrated by this. She'd been nothing but honest in discussing her life. But dammit, he wanted more of her.

"You can stay here. I'll be fine getting home."

"We came together, we go together." He

forced himself to take her hand gently instead of scooping her up and taking her to a bedroom.

Outside, Tess called the kids. Twenty minutes later, he began regretting the move to go with them. Andrew whined that he didn't get to have enough fun. Zoe was surly, and Billy wouldn't stop talking about the video game cheats he'd learned. Once they were all buckled in the van, Miles thought for sure he could breathe easy, but he had no such luck.

It was like they'd all consumed energy drinks. They shouted over each other to get Tess's attention. Somehow, she managed to follow each of the conversations. She was either a really good actress or she truly had mastered the ability to have multiple conversations at once. To him, it was headache-inducing.

He drove to her house as fast as he could. By the time they arrived, the kids had settled down and guilt tugged at him for being irritable. He parked the car and helped unload everything from their day. The kids trudged up the stairs, and Miles recognized the exhaustion in their movements.

Tess was nothing short of pure efficiency. She hustled Andrew into the shower while Zoe and Billy made sure their bags were packed. Then she questioned what everyone wanted for lunch tomorrow. He felt completely in the way and unneeded, but he was also compelled to stay and watch. This was a side of Tess he'd known existed but hadn't witnessed.

She'd amazed him this morning and he was in complete awe right now. She did this every day. Every week. Nonstop. No wonder she constantly told him she didn't have free time. And why she'd told him early on she didn't have room in her life for an overgrown kid.

It also made him understand how much

she needed a break, whether she realized it or not. Going at this pace forever would eventually ruin her.

Andrew appeared in front of her, clean from his shower. "Peanut butter for lunch. Lucky Charms for breakfast. *Harry Potter* for bed."

"Go upstairs and brush your teeth. Then we can read."

"Already brushed. Hurry up." Then he took off up the stairs.

"Can I read to him?" he asked before considering what he was doing.

Tess stared at him as if just remembering he was there. "You don't have to do that, Miles. You've already done so much today. More than you ever signed on for."

He pulled her into a hug. "I signed on to be with you. Besides, I've never read *Harry Potter*."

She gasped, and put a hand over her heart. "You poor thing. You have no idea what you've missed out on." She relaxed into a smile. "Thank you for offering. If he puts up a stink, holler, and I'll come rescue you."

"I won't need a rescue."

"Okay. I'll open some wine and maybe we can hang out for a little bit."

He lowered his voice again. "Can we make out?"

"Maybe."

Chapter 13

The week ran Tess ragged. She and Miles had barely connected for a quick cup of coffee. Their nighttime chats had been interrupted by a number of things ranging from ridiculous first week of school assignments and special requests for school supplies or, in Miles's case, late meetings in the office.

When he called the following Monday and asked her to be his date for some event, she turned him down. She couldn't imagine dressing up and smiling all night. Plus, she didn't have anything to wear. She didn't want to admit it to Miles. With her next paycheck, maybe she could squeeze some extra money to buy a new dress or two. She didn't care if Miles said her dress didn't matter, she knew better.

He'd sounded disappointed but didn't pressure her to change her mind. All day at work on Wednesday, she'd caught snippets of rumors about budget cuts by the end of the year. It was one more stressor she didn't need. The PICU was a small department that cost a lot of money. Caring for the smallest and most ill patients was expensive.

If her department lost money, she would probably have to look for a new job. She shook the thoughts off. No need to borrow trouble.

She'd already gotten a text from William saying he'd have the kids home right after dinner. Luckily, it had been a quiet day with patients, so she shouldn't be late. Knowing William, he probably hadn't asked the kids if they had homework, which meant it was a task still relegated to her to-do list.

She took a swig of her cold coffee and wrapped up the charting she had to do for her shift.

Angie plopped onto the chair beside her. "How are things going?"

"Good. Kids are back in school and while I couldn't wait for that to happen, now I can't remember why. The freaking homework is a killer."

"And Miles?"

"What about him?" She dropped her nasty coffee in the trash.

"Are you still dating?"

"Yeah. Things are good there, too, I guess."

"You're not sure?"

"It's hard with the kids' schedules and he's working on a huge project for work. We don't get to spend much time together. I met his family on Labor Day."

"Oooo… Exciting." Angie twirled on the chair. "Details."

"His family was really nice. I hit it off with his sister, Sabrina. The kids had a blast. We spent the morning on his family's yacht." She smiled at Angie when her friend's eyes turned to platters.

"Yeah. He invited us to go out on the boat for a few hours. Then he drives us to a mansion in Kenilworth and is all like, 'it's home.' As if it's some ranch house on the North side."

Tess shook her head at the memory. Miles was never snobby about having money, which would've spelled doom for them a long time ago. But he was almost clueless about it.

"So you're really into each other, huh?"

Tess lifted a shoulder. "We're having a good time. I have no idea where it's going or if it's going." She checked the time. "I have to head home. William will be there soon with the kids."

"God forbid you should be late."

Angie's snarky comment crawled under her skin. She knew Angie was right, but this was the way things were with them. "I keep things simple. I find that when I expect very little from William, I'm rarely upset. The kids have a good time with him. They have dinner together and he usually buys them some expensive thing to express his love. That's fine."

"No one is going to erect a sainthood statue in your honor. I say let him have it."

"There's nothing to say. And I'm not looking for sainthood. I'm okay with the way my life is going. See you this weekend?"

"I'm on on Saturday, so see you then. I want better details about Miles."

"We'll see."

As she headed to the train, her phone vibrated with a text from Miles.

Dinner?

On my way home now. Kids
ate with William, and they'll
be home soon.

                              Dinner for two?

If you want to eat while
listening to me argue about
homework.

                     Can I hold your hand?

I think I'll need my hand
to eat.

She leaned against the bench to wait for
her train.

But I'll let you ogle me
while I help do math
worksheets and sign
assignment notebooks.

Sexy. Make-out session
after kids are asleep?

I don't know if I'll be awake
much longer than they are.

Close enough to agreeing.
See you soon.

She tucked her phone back in her purse and waited for the train. Her life was always so full of taking care of things that she rarely had time to step back and think. Miles had a way of making her think, but it wasn't always good.

They hadn't revisited their conversation about where they were going and what he wanted. She felt like he was avoiding it because he'd come to the same conclusion she had. They couldn't last. He would want to have his own family. He didn't want to see it because they were enjoying what they had going.

But even she could recognize how one-sided it was. Sure, Miles received as many orgasms as he gave, but in every other aspect, their relationship revolved around her. As much as she enjoyed it, she knew how resentful a lopsided relationship could make a person feel. On the train ride home, she thought of ways to turn the tide and make things more equitable.

Bottom line, Miles had to want to bring her into his life. Other than doing fun things like going out on the boat. Hell, even that had been more about her and the kids than it had been about her participating in his life.

She decided she'd try tonight. After the kids were settled, she'd ask about work and his father's foundation. The project was consuming a lot of his time, but he never really spoke about it, other than to say he had a meeting.

When the train jostled at her stop, she got off and walked home. As she neared her house, she saw Miles sitting on the front porch looking pretty damn unhappy. Then she realized why. William was there with the kids.

"Hey," she said, trying to sound cheerful.

"When you said the kids had eaten with your ex, I didn't make the connection that he would be here."

She took a deep breath. "Do I even want to know?"

"I rang the bell, expecting one of the kids to answer. When a grown man opened the door, I was surprised."

"And?"

"I told him I was here to see you, and he told me you weren't here yet and closed the door on me."

She shook her head. William was an ass. "Can you wait out here for like five more minutes?"

"Sure." He looked disappointed, but his presence in the house would only make things worse.

"I'm home," she called as she went inside.

Andrew and Billy sat at the dining room table, doing homework, she hoped. As she neared, she realized that no, they weren't. They were playing on tablets. "What are those?"

"Aren't they cool? Dad got them for us. He says this way we can FaceTime him while he's away."

"Away?" *What the ever-loving hell?* Her fury bubbled up faster than she could control.

William came from around the corner, where she sincerely hoped he'd been in the bathroom and not her bedroom. William didn't always respect boundaries. "We need to talk." She moved past him straight to the kitchen, assuming he would follow.

Behind her, she heard Billy say, "Ooo... that's her mad voice."

"What do you want, Tess? I have plans."

She spun and waved her hands. "Plans. You always have plans. So do I. He happens to be sitting on the front porch because you slammed the door on him."

"What would you have me do when some strange man comes knocking? Invite him in?"

"Yes. That's the courteous thing to do. You didn't have to hang out with him, but to leave him outside was ridiculous."

"I'm here with the kids. It's my time—"

She almost lost it. "Yes, *your* time. You could take them to *your* house and spend hours with them. Instead, you feed them and dump them off at your earliest convenience."

"Convenient. Need I remind you that I take Wednesdays as a favor to you?"

"They're your children. It's not like I'm out partying while you slave away caring for our kids. I'm at work. And even if I were out partying, it shouldn't matter. Those kids are your responsibility, too."

He bristled at her tirade. "I've always provided well for our children."

"Yes, provided." She held up her hands. They'd been having this same conversation and argument for years. "It doesn't matter. From now on, all I'm asking is that you not be rude to my guests."

"You mean your boyfriend." He crossed his arms.

She matched his stance. "*Whoever* happens to be here."

"Are we done?"

"Yes." As he turned to leave the room, she remembered the tablets. "Wait. I thought we agreed no more buying expensive gifts *just because*."

William turned back. "The tablets weren't very expensive. And kids need the most up-to-date technology. It's how to be successful."

I'm so sure the games are all about being successful. "The boys said something about you going away?"

"Yes. Margaret and I have a vacation

planned. We're leaving Saturday and we'll be gone two weeks. I want to be able to talk with them and see them."

Tess ground her teeth. "So you're cutting this weekend short, and you'll miss next Wednesday and your next weekend. Am I hearing that right?"

"Yes. But we'll be able to talk using the tablets, so you don't have to worry about using your phone."

As if the phone were her biggest problem. William was trying to buy the kids' love, using money to make up for not being there. "Well, thanks for all the warning so I can make plans around work."

"I'm sure your mother will help. She always does."

"That's not the point."

He didn't get it. He never would. She waved him off before her anger got the better of her. "I'll talk to you whenever you get back." She walked past him to get Miles from the porch. What she'd thought would be a simple conversation had lasted much longer than she'd planned. She hoped Miles hadn't left.

She heard William saying goodbye to the boys as she opened the front door. Miles was sitting on the top stair. "I'm so sorry. I completely understand if you don't want to stay. As much as I'd like to say it won't happen again, I can't guarantee it."

Miles stood and smiled at her. "I don't scare off that easily. Unfortunately, dinner is probably on the cold side now."

"I'm like the worst girlfriend ever." The tension from her argument with William still sat in her shoulders and guilt for everything with Miles made her stomach ache.

Miles set the bag of food down and pulled her into a hug. "I happen to think you're a pretty good girlfriend. Your ex sucks, but you're not so bad."

The door behind them opened, and Tess

stiffened. She had zero reason to feel guilty, but having William see her in Miles's arms made something twist inside her. Instinct had her wanting to pull away, so she forced herself to stay put. On the rare occasion Tess was in the same room with William and Margaret, they made no attempt to hide their affection for each other. Tess sure as heck shouldn't have to do that in her own house.

"Tess," William said with a nod.

She guessed that was his version of goodbye. Or fuck off. Or whatever.

"Is it safe to go in now?" Miles asked.

"If you still want to." She stepped back but left her hands on his waist, enjoying the brief physical connection. "I told you my life was messy. You're the first man William has ever seen me with. He obviously didn't handle it well."

"It could've been worse. He could've punched me in the face to try to claim his territory."

She burst out laughing. "He has no claim here, but even if he thought he did, he would never risk his precious hands."

Miles looked confused.

"He's a surgeon."

"Ahh."

She tugged him toward the door. "Let's go warm up the food and you can witness the arguing and fighting over homework that is the perfect end to a long day."

They walked into the house together and Tess was glad Miles didn't frighten easily.

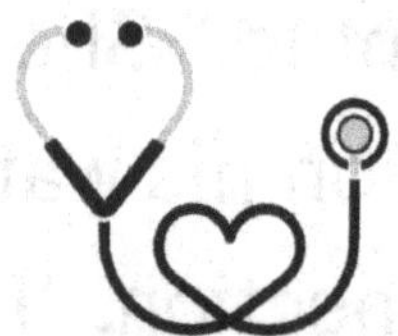

After a warmed-up dinner, Miles sat at the dining room table and watched Tess work magic. He didn't care that she made jokes about yelling and fighting over homework. He was amazed she completed homework with

Andrew. The boy obviously hated math, but Tess had endless patience with him.

Billy worked silently on some worksheet, pausing on occasion to tell Tess or him about another feature of the tablet that made it awesome. Miles got the distinct impression the tablet was a point of contention for her, and Billy was trying to turn the tide. Miles gathered they were gifts from their father, but other than that, he couldn't figure out why she'd be mad about them.

Then Billy let it slip that he and Andrew had spent their dinnertime telling their father about the day on the lake and the party at Miles's house. When she heard that, Tess's head shot up from where she'd been looking at third grade math.

Miles swallowed a chuckle. That one sentence from Billy told Miles all he needed to know. William was staking a claim, but it was more about the kids than Tess. Billy didn't seem to recognize the effect of his words. He slid his homework into a folder and pulled out another paper.

"I want to join STEM club. I need you to sign the permission slip."

Tess took the paper. Before reading it, she pointed to the page Andrew was working on. "You forgot to carry." Then she looked at the pink paper. "When does it meet? Thursdays? That should be okay. Is there a fee?" She scanned the page and then took the pencil she had tucked in her hair and signed.

"Mr. Ross didn't say anything about a fee. But it's really cool. We meet every week and do a bunch of different projects. He said we can enter some competitions as a team."

Miles saw that Tess tried to be engaged and listen to Billy, but Andrew growled at his homework again.

"Hey," Miles said to Billy. "Can you help me take your mom's dish into the kitchen and show me where stuff is? You can tell me all about the club. I used to do Science Olympiad when I was your age."

"I thought you played baseball," Andrew said.

"I did both. I played Little League. Then in middle school, I did Science Olympiad. In high school, I had to pick one and I went with baseball. My dad hated that."

"Really?" Billy's eyes got wide. "Why?"

"My dad was a huge science nerd. He loved helping out with the team. He knew nothing about baseball, so he couldn't help." He leaned closer to Billy. "Sometimes it's nice to do something your parents don't get."

Billy smiled.

Miles stood and grabbed his plate. Billy took Tess's from where she had it shoved to the side and went toward the kitchen, chattering as he walked. "I asked Mr. Ross about Science Olympiad, but he said that since we're a new club, we couldn't do Science Olympiad. It's too complicated to start now, but if we get enough interest, maybe next year."

Over Andrew's head, Tess mouthed, "Thank you."

Miles winked at her. For the next fifteen minutes, he moved like a snail through the kitchen, cleaning dishes and packing up leftovers. He hoped he wouldn't have to keep Billy busy too much longer. The boy had a million questions about what kinds of projects he had done and if he still had any of them.

He was lucky if he could remember what he ate for breakfast, so a project he'd done more than twenty years ago was low on his list of important things to remember. "I can ask my mom. You know how moms are. They save everything."

Billy laughed. "Right? What's with that? It's weird." He ran over to the side of the refrigerator and pulled a paper from under magnets. "I made this in kindergarten, and she still has it. It's just my name."

"It was the first time you wrote your name by yourself. I was proud of you," Tess said from the doorway.

Billy rehung the paper with a sheepish look.

"Homework is finally done, so you guys can watch TV or play games for a half hour."

"Can we play on the tablets?"

Tess sighed. "That's fine."

He took off running into the other room and yelled for his brother.

Tess remained in the doorway, leaning against the frame, arms crossed. "Thanks."

"For what?"

"Cleaning up. Talking to Billy to keep him in here so I could help Andrew with homework."

"No big deal."

"It means more than I can explain."

Miles tossed the towel on the counter and

crossed the room. "Hey, I'm not going to turn down brownie points you're handing out so generously, but if that's all it takes to make your life a little easier, think nothing of it." He stroked his thumb across her jaw.

She leaned into his touch, and he realized how tired she looked. He kissed her gently. "Everything okay?"

"Just feeling stressed. The beginning of the year is hard because we have to build new routines. And then William." She gave another sigh, this time with her eyes closed. When her gaze met his again, she said, "Plus, he's going out of town on Saturday, and he'll be gone for two weeks."

Sounded damn good to Miles. "How is that bad?"

"It's his weekend. And he'll miss next Wednesday. And probably his next weekend. More for me to juggle. To top it all off, all day at work people kept whispering rumors about budget cuts for our department."

"What can I do to help?"

"Nothing." She pushed off the wall and out of his reach. "I have to start a load of laundry. Then we can sit and talk or watch TV for a while."

He watched her go through backpacks and pick up stray items from the living room. Then she yelled up to Zoe who tossed clothes and towels down the stairs. Tess gathered the pile, which completely filled her arms by the time she was done.

"Two minutes," she said, pushing her way through the kitchen. "Go relax."

Instead, he followed her. With her elbow, she flipped a switch and a light flickered on. As she shoved the clothes into the washer, Miles came up behind her. "How much laundry do you do in a week?"

She chuckled. "More than I care to think about."

She measured detergent, poured, and then pressed buttons. When the machine started, Miles stepped closer, allowing his hands to roam down her sides. He kissed her neck. "So this is the infamous laundry room?"

"Infamous?"

"Isn't this where you hide out to talk to me?" He continued to touch, caress, and rub against her as he spoke.

She licked her lips and nodded.

Gripping her hips tightly, he turned her to face him. He began kissing her in earnest, tasting lips that until that moment he didn't truly comprehend how much he'd missed. Grinding his hips to hers made her breath hitch before she moaned into his mouth. Miles slipped a hand between them and stroked her through her jeans.

Her hips bucked, and she met his hand twice before squeezing his shoulder. "Stop, Miles. We can't."

"Sure we can."

"No. My kids are home."

"They're busy with games. We can be

fast." He kissed her neck, and her pulse pounded against his tongue. She wanted this. More, she needed it.

"Let me make you feel good."

She whimpered, and he thought he had her, but she pushed him away.

"I want to, but no. My kids are home. I can't have sex with them here."

He closed his eyes tightly for a minute. "You've had sex with them in the house before. You managed to get pregnant three times."

"That was different. It was their father. We were married."

"Do you think your ex refrains from sex when the kids spend the weekend there?"

"I don't know. I don't ask. But they're married."

"So it's only okay to have sex if you're married?" He rubbed a hand over his face.

"Obviously, I don't expect marriage in order to have sex. But these are my kids."

She reached out and rested a hand on his chest.

He wanted to understand but couldn't. It wasn't like he was trying to take her on the dining room table. The kids were nowhere to be seen.

"Please don't be angry." Her voice almost broke him. Like she couldn't handle one more emotional hit.

He placed his hand on top of hers. "I'm not mad."

Irritated? Yes. Disappointed? Definitely. But he couldn't be angry at her. He blew out a breath.

"Want to have some wine? Watch TV?" she offered hopefully.

"In a minute. If you don't want the kids to know what almost happened here, we need to wait for the evidence to go away."

She chuckled in that low, sexy way she had, which didn't help.

"Since I don't get to have you naked tonight, how about this weekend?"

She shook her head sadly. "I'm working, and I have to figure out what to do with the kids since William is going away."

"I can hang out with them for a while if you want."

"That's sweet, but I can't. I trust you, but the kids don't really know you yet. I wouldn't be comfortable leaving you with them."

The hand beneath his turned over, and she interlocked their fingers. "It's not about you. I knew Trevor, Owen, Evelyn, Nina, and Gabe for more than a year before they even met the kids. Even longer before I asked any of them to babysit."

"Who are all those people?"

Tess pulled him from the room. "They're my friends. We met in a divorce support group."

He followed her into the living room and

consumed every small bit of detail she offered about her life. As frustrated as he was that he couldn't have sex with her, spending more time understanding Tess wasn't a waste of his time.

Tess worked all day and into the night on Friday. She took every hour she could in case she needed to call in sick while William was out of town. The thought still grated on her. She was so tired of him using his money as a substitute for his time and energy. And it was pretty evident—at least with Zoe—the kids were growing tired of it, too. At eleven o'clock, she was leaving the hospital when her phone buzzed.

Only two people would text her this late— William and Miles. So she fished out her phone while she headed to the front. She was so tired, she wished she'd driven to work instead of taking the El.

When are you off work?

Miles had impeccable timing. It was like he had a sixth sense for when she might be free.

Leaving now.

Good.

Do you want me to come over?

She walked through the lobby as she texted and waited for an answer. The glass doors whooshed open, and the cool night breeze swept across her.

"I was actually thinking I could come over."

His voice startled her. He was leaning against his car in the drop-off area. She hadn't realized how much she wanted to see him.

"What are you doing here?"

He reached out and tugged her waistband until their bodies were flush. "I missed you. And I knew the kids were supposed to be with their dad, so you'd be free."

"I am," she said with a smile.

"Excellent. I can't wait to get you naked."

She sighed as he kissed her.

"Can I drive you home?"

"Uh...you want to go to my house?"

"If it's okay. You always come to my place. I know you have to work tomorrow, so if we're at your house, we can maximize our time together."

She hugged him tightly. "You're too good to me."

He opened the door, and she slid into the car. On the drive to her house, Miles asked about her day and the kids. As tired as she was, she realized he was doing it again. Putting every ounce of focus on her.

"How are things going for you at work?" she asked.

"Okay. We've run into a few tangles with paperwork and stuff, but we're moving forward. Any word about the budget rumors?"

"More of the same. Tell me about things with the foundation."

He glanced at her from the corner of his eye. "What do you want to know?"

"What are you doing? What are your plans?"

"I spend most of my day on the phone and in meetings. When I'm not doing that, I'm staring at spreadsheets. Trust me, you don't want to talk about my day."

She twisted in her seat to fully face him. "Then tell me about your family. Or your friends. Something."

"Did I do something wrong?"

She was tired and cranky, and he didn't deserve her snapping at him, so she softened her voice before speaking again. "No, but you always ask about my day and listen to me bitch and complain."

"That's what being in a relationship is."

She grunted. "You don't tell me about your day. Your problems. Your ups and downs."

Miles changed lanes as they neared the highway exit for her house and then took her hand. "I'm not keeping secrets. My job would bore you. And I don't need your help with anything."

Something about the way he said it made her bristle. "Do you think I need your help? I've been getting along just fine on my own for years." A bitter chuckle slipped past her lips. "Long before my divorce if we're being honest. I don't share my life and problems with you because I'm looking for you to rescue me."

He pulled into a spot a few houses down

from hers. He took a deep breath as he cut the engine. "I wasn't implying you need my help. But you fix everyone's lives. I don't want you to see me as someone else to take care of. I want our time together to be a reprieve for you."

Well, damn. His words deflated all her bluster. "I'm sorry."

"For what?"

"I want us to be equals and so far, you've been doing all the giving and I've been taking."

He wagged his eyebrows. "You've given me plenty."

"I'm trying to be serious." Swatting at him, she smiled.

He sobered and leaned across the car until their noses were almost touching. "I seriously like you. If I need to vent, I promise you'll be my first stop. But my life is pretty even keel."

"Okay."

"Does that mean we can go in and get naked now?"

"Yes."

"And I can spend the night?"

She hadn't thought about him sleeping in her bed.

"The kids aren't there."

"I know. It's just…a big step."

"Not that big. I want to spend the night wrapped around you without you sneaking off because you have to take care of people. I want to sleep with you and have breakfast with you."

She wanted all that, too, but would it set a precedent? She knew she wasn't ready to have him spend the night when the kids were there, and part of her believed sleeping with Miles would be every bit as addictive as having sex with him. "Okay. But only tonight. It won't happen when the kids are here."

"You got it." He turned and jumped out of the car.

Tess barely got the door open before he was reaching in and taking her purse and her hand. "In a hurry?"

"I told you I want to maximize our time together."

They walked into her house and Tess felt different. She'd never had a man here. She hadn't shared her bed with anyone since the divorce. Nerves tumbled through her, which she tried to bat away as silly. She and Miles had been together for months now. They'd had plenty of sex. Sleeping shouldn't be a big deal.

She kicked off her shoes and pulled her hair from the ponytail in the hallway.

"I love that look."

"Huh?" she asked.

"Watching you let your hair down. It falls in these crazy waves." He shoved his fingers into the mass and massaged her scalp.

Tess moaned and then giggled. "I must

sound so easy if rubbing my head makes me moan."

"I enjoy knowing all the ways to make you moan."

Chapter 14

The following morning, Tess stretched, or at least attempted to. Her body was trapped beneath an arm and a leg. Hairy ones. She knew she needed to get up for work but snuggled closer to Miles for a few more minutes. They'd made love slowly last night, enjoying the quiet of the dark early morning hours.

She felt all warm and gooey inside waking beside Miles. Closing her eyes, she reveled in being held, having someone care about her and put her first. It went beyond the physical. The orgasms were great—phenomenal, really—but the simple touch of his hand on her hip, simultaneously possessive and supportive, undid her. She wanted more. More of this, more of him.

He tightened his arm on her waist, pulling her deeper into the curve of his body.

"I have to get up."

"No."

"Yes."

"I'm taking you hostage. No work today."

"Sorry, my captor. If you get up now, I'll make you breakfast."

He nuzzled her neck. "I'd rather starve and have an extra fifteen minutes of this."

"You make an excellent case, but I need a shower and food. If I don't eat now, coffee might be my only fuel for the rest of the day."

"They can't make you work without a lunch break. There are labor laws, you know."

He was so cute. "My lunch pales in importance to helping a sick kid. Some shifts are crazy busy. Others are quiet. There's no way to know which I'm walking into."

"Responsible people like you make the rest of us look bad."

She rolled away from him and glanced back as she walked to her dresser. "From where I stand, you look pretty damn good."

"Then get back in bed."

"Don't tempt me." Ignoring the desire to crawl back in bed, she went to the bathroom to shower. Moments later, Miles came into the bathroom and peed.

"Can I join you, or is that too much of a temptation?"

"You're always too much of a temptation. But water conservation is important." She nudged the door so he could step in.

"Damn. That's hot," he said as he held his palms under the spray.

"I thought you liked things hot." She tilted her head back and rinsed the shampoo. He skated his hands over her breasts. "I can handle the heat just fine."

She twined her arms around his neck and kissed him. "As much as I'd like to stay here and play, I have to leave you now."

"You suck."

"Uh-huh." She smiled and kissed his cheek before slipping out of the shower, drying off, and wrapping her hair in a towel.

By the time Miles came downstairs wearing yesterday's clothes, Tess was dressed, drinking her first cup of coffee, and had eggs and toast made. "I take it you're not much of a morning person."

"Not when I was up half the night enjoying myself." He accepted a cup of coffee. "Speaking of enjoying myself, I'm meeting up with friends tonight. You should join us. I want to introduce them to the hot woman I nabbed."

Tess laughed. "While being your trophy sounds great, I can't. I'm working all day and into the evening. Then I have to get back here. William is leaving for vacation today. My mom is going to take care of the kids until I get off."

"Can't she babysit while we go out?"

Tess thought about it for a minute. "I can't ask her to do that. I already dumped today and tomorrow on her last minute. Plus, I'll be dragging by the time I get home. I won't be much fun."

His expression sank. She hated disappointing him, but she knew if she went to a bar tonight, she'd be ready to go home after one drink. "Go have fun with your friends."

"Can I come over later?"

"After going out? It'll be too late. I'll be asleep."

"Unguarded and undressed."

She laughed again. "Wrong. Totally dressed. Kids will be here."

He gave her another look of disappointment, so she added, "Come over for dinner tomorrow."

"Sure."

He inhaled his food and left. Then she went to work and tried not to think about Miles and how she'd managed to let him down.

As long as her day was, in some ways it felt longer because the floor was quiet. Angie was working, which usually made time go by faster. Tonight, though, time stood still. She'd played more games of Go Fish and Uno and read more stories than she'd done with her own kids in quite a while.

After she'd tucked in a young boy and said good night to his grandma, who was staying with him for the night, Tess plopped on a swivel chair beside Angie and swirled back and forth in half-circles, thinking about what Angie had told her earlier about budget cuts being imminent. She considered going over the nurse manager's head to see if there was a way to secure her job. Or maybe she should put feelers out for a position at a different hospital. The kids were older now. A regular full-time position might be the way to go.

"You've been holding out," Angie said.

"About?" Tess asked, stopping mid-spin.

"Your man is not only hot, he's a party animal." Angie turned her phone to face Tess. It was a picture of Miles surrounded by a bunch of people. She handed the phone back. "Why do you have a picture of Miles on your phone?"

"Remember when we first looked him up on social media? I started following him. He's been real quiet lately, but he's blowing things up tonight."

Tess had no idea if that was supposed to be good or bad. Miles looked like he was having fun, which was what Tess had told him to do. And she was tired. Going to a bar was the last thing she wanted to do.

"Uh-oh," Angie said.

"What?"

When Angie didn't answer, Tess took the phone from her. Another picture, this one of some woman kissing Miles's cheek while he smiled at the camera. A jealous poke stabbed her. If it had meant anything, Miles never would've posted it on social media where she might see it. Logically, she knew that. She didn't think he'd cheat. But she was still bothered by another woman's lips on his face. "We're not supposed to be on our phones."

She handed the phone back and stood and stretched. "I'm going on break. You want a coffee?"

"Sure."

She knew it was petty and jealous, but she wanted to hear his voice, to reassure herself, so she left the PICU and called Miles. It rang and rang, and before she got to the coffee shop, his voice was asking her to leave a message. She disconnected and sent a text telling him she hoped he was having fun and that he should call when he got a chance.

By the time she'd finished working her shift and gotten home, the call still hadn't come.

Miles sat at the table and finished his glass of whiskey. He felt the vibration of his phone, and he fished it from his pocket. He'd missed a call and a text from Tess a while ago. She was probably already in bed, so there was no point in calling and trying to convince her to come meet him. Tony yelled from the bar to ask if he wanted another drink, and Miles held up his empty glass.

Pam bumped his shoulder with hers. "No phones. We haven't seen you in forever."

"My girlfriend. I'll talk to her later."

"Girlfriend? You didn't say anything about a girlfriend."

He hadn't? He shrugged, because he didn't have a reason for not mentioning Tess.

"Where is she? Why didn't she come tonight?"

"She was working. Then she had to get home to her kids."

"Whose kids?" Tony asked as he set drinks in front of everyone.

Pam leaned closer to Tony. "Miles has a girlfriend. And she has kids. Like plural."

Tony chuckled. "Are any of them yours?"

"No, smartass."

"I want to hear all about her. What's her name? How long have you been dating? How serious is it?" Pam asked.

Miles took a drink and let the alcohol warm his throat. "Her name is Tess. We've been going out a couple months, give or take." He let the last question fall, because he wasn't sure how to answer.

"You screwed all the childless women in the city, so you've moved on to the mommies?" Tony asked.

Yeah, Tony was about as funny as he'd been in college. "I met her at a work thing. We hit it off. She's divorced and has three kids."

Pam tapped her lips with her long red nail. "Hmm... Have you met them?"

"Who?"

"The kids."

"Yeah."

"Has she met your family?"

Is this an interrogation? This was why he hadn't said anything about Tess. "Yeah. They all came over for our Labor Day barbecue."

"They?" Tony asked. "Damn. You move fast. Did you buy her a ring and write your vows yet?"

The mention of a ring and vows made Miles's heart thump. He and Tess had only been dating a little while. "What are you talking about?"

Pam shook her head. "Please tell me you're not really that clueless."

Miles stared at his glass of whiskey. *A simple conversation shouldn't have me this confused.* Then he remembered Pam rarely kept things simple.

"Miles, baby, a mother is nothing to screw with. If you're doing the whole family thing—and I do mean whole family—this is the real deal for her. If you're not on board, you better set sail."

"It's not like that with Tess. We're having a good time and seeing where things go. She's not rushing me into anything." He drained his glass again.

"You sure?" Tony asked. "She might be looking at you as a nice meal ticket."

"What? No." Of that much, he was

absolutely sure. "In fact, Tess hates when I spend money on her or the kids. She does things on her own."

"Suspicious." Not surprising that Tony would take that stance since he was a lawyer. "If things progress any further, give me a call. You should have a prenup ready to go long before anything else."

Prenup? Damn. Were his friends trying to kill him? Although he'd been enjoying his time with Tess and the kids, he was far from thinking about marriage. His gut churned, because although he wasn't there yet, he couldn't answer for Tess.

Pam cackled, startling him. "We better stop, Tony. He looks like he might pass out."

"I'm fine," Miles muttered. "I thought we were out to party tonight. Don't the two of you have anything better to talk about than my love life?" He tossed some bills on the table. "Let's get out of here and find a better party."

Anything to get his mind off the weight of the conversation.

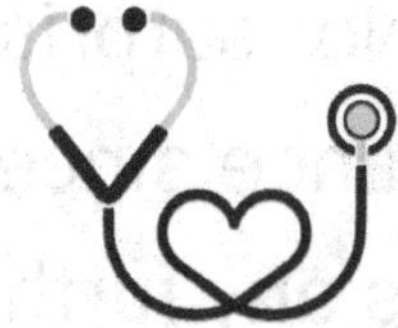

On Sunday, Tess worked a short shift at the hospital and then spent her afternoon running errands. She still hadn't heard from Miles. He'd said he'd come over for dinner, so she worked on the assumption he would call or just show up. It took a lot of restraint to not call or text him all day. More than that, it felt weird. They talked every single day. Although it had only been a little over twenty-four hours since she'd seen him, it felt longer.

He usually sent her a text in the morning, or she called on her way to work. Maybe she should've called him, but she didn't want to be the needy, possessive girlfriend. She wouldn't like herself that way. And it wasn't who she really was.

As she carried groceries into the house, she yelled for Zoe. Her mom came from the kitchen.

"Need some help?"

"That's what kids are for."

Zoe bounded down the steps.

"Go get the rest of the groceries." Tess looked at Billy and Andrew sprawled on the couch with their tablets. "Boys, start putting food away."

They grumbled but managed to get moving without another reminder.

Tess moved straight to the coffee maker and poured herself a cup. One thing she could always count on with her mom was a constant flow of fresh coffee. "Any problems today?"

"Of course not. The kids are great. Those tablets are a menace though. The boys turn into zombies with them."

"Gifts from William," Tess said as she took a gulp of coffee. "I'm hoping the novelty will wear off soon. You want to stay for dinner?"

"I get an invitation?"

"You never need a formal invitation."

"The kids mentioned that the man you've been seeing sometimes comes over for dinner."

Ahhh. Mom's looking for information.

"Miles is supposed to come over for dinner. You are welcome to stay if you'd like."

Zoe came in hauling more bags and set them on the kitchen floor. "That's it."

"Okay. Thanks."

Billy said, "That's not fair. She only had to make one trip. Now we have to put all of this away." He pointed to the piles of food.

"And you have help." Tess pointed to Andrew. "Leave the strawberries and watermelon on the counter and I'll take care of them in a little bit."

Then she took her coffee and went to the dining room with her mom following.

"So tell me about Miles," her mom said as soon as they were seated. "It must be serious if you let him meet the kids."

Tess thought about that a moment. "More serious than a fling, but we're not talking about forever. We're letting things run their course."

"What does that mean?"

Tess sighed. "He's a few years younger than me. Never been married. No kids. At some point he might want all that and it won't be with me."

"So then why start at all?"

"Because I'm tired of my life spinning in circles. This at least feels like forward movement."

Her mom shook her head and stared at her cup. Tess knew the drill. Her mother would sit there and judge, but she never offered advice or comments unless Tess asked. It was a dual-edged sword. Part of her didn't care. She was enjoying her time with Miles and it had been a long, lonely few years. But she also knew if she didn't let her mom vent, the opinions would fester into something uglier and ultimately put a strain on their relationship.

"Go ahead, Mom."

"I understand you're young and you have needs, Tess. I was young once, too. But introducing him to the kids? I never brought a man home to you."

"Why not?" Tess always wondered but never had the guts to ask. She never knew if her mom had any kind of social life when she was younger.

"I didn't want to bring someone into your life who might abandon you like your father had. I wanted to spare you any hurt I could."

"I appreciate that, Mom. But you also never let me see you be in a relationship. I never got to see you happy."

"But you also never saw me miserable either."

Her mom had a point, but William hadn't abandoned their kids. He might not be the most involved parent in the universe, but he was there. "I think the kids are old enough to handle things. Being with Miles makes me happy."

"And what happens when he decides to move on?"

The hot coffee sloshed around in Tess's stomach. She'd been telling herself from the beginning that Miles would leave someday, but she hated thinking about it. "Then he moves on and I lick my wounds alone, like I did when William and I split."

"But that was your choice."

"It wasn't an easy one to make. But I did it and survived. So did the kids." She finished her coffee and stood. Her feet protested and her back ached. Sitting down to chat hadn't been a smart move.

"So, are you staying for dinner?"

"What are you having?"

"I think I'm going to throw some burgers on the grill." Her mom didn't eat much red meat, so she said, "I might have some chicken I can toss on, too."

"No, a burger would be fine." She rose to follow Tess back into the kitchen. "Just please tell me the kids aren't allowed to have the electronics at the table."

"Of course not. Dinner time is family time. It gives us all a chance to catch up. I'm going to fire up the grill."

"What can I do?"

"Make a salad?"

"Sure."

Tess stood over the grill and turned the conversation with her mother over in her head. The burgers sizzled and smoke curled around her. She'd made a burger for Miles too even though he still hadn't called and she wasn't sure if he was coming. She must've checked her phone fifteen times in the last twenty minutes. He knew they ate early, so she was pretty sure he could guess what time to show.

She growled at herself. Since when did she let a man dictate how her night would go? This was family time before the craziness of the week took over. The more she thought about how Miles had spent his weekend and how hers looked, the more her mom's words weighed on her. Those same haunting thoughts about how mismatched she and Miles were came back to poke at her.

Billy and Andrew came out and ran down the stairs. She smiled. Her mom must've chased them outside. They tossed a ball back and forth.

"What'd you guys do all day?"

"Played on our tablets. Dad called and we talked to him," Billy answered.

"You have homework to do?"

"Nope."

"How about you, Andrew?"

"Not on Fridays."

Tess tried not to let him see her sigh of relief. "How about we go get ice cream after dinner?"

"Yes!" they both answered.

"You have to eat your dinner and that includes salad. And we're walking."

"Okay," they said eagerly.

"Good. Go wash up. Dinner is almost ready."

They ran back in and she slid the burgers onto the platter she'd brought outside. See? She could have a good night hanging out with her kids just like she always had. Miles could have his partying all night.

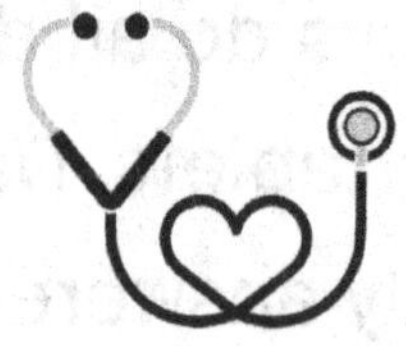

Miles sat up and looked at his phone. Fuck. He was supposed to have dinner at Tess's house. He'd thought he'd nap on the couch for an hour, but it had been four. He rubbed his eyes again and pushed off the cushions. He walked stiffly to the bathroom, splashed water on his face, and looked at his reflection in the mirror. He looked as horrible as he felt.

Grabbing his keys, he headed out the door. He thought about calling, but since he hadn't returned her call last night, he needed to face her. He drove as quickly as he could to her house. A few lights were on, but no one answered when he knocked. Damn. He wondered how pissed she was.

She hadn't mentioned any other plans for tonight. The kids didn't have practice on Sundays and her car was parked at the corner. He thought about looking in the front window to see if maybe she was just ignoring him, but that was too stalkery. He rang the bell again and waited.

Nothing.

Taking a seat on the top step, he pulled out his phone and stared at it. Just as he debated what to say, he heard voices down the block. Tess and the kids were nearing the house. He stood and leaned against the rail. Andrew saw him first and yelled for him.

They all looked happy, each licking an ice cream cone.

"Hey," he said and stepped down to the sidewalk toward them.

"I didn't know you were coming," Andrew said. "You shoulda come earlier so you could have ice cream, too."

"I wish I had," Miles said, looking at Tess.

She handed Zoe her keys. "You guys run ahead. We'll catch up."

Zoe looked at her and then at Miles, knowing something was up but not asking. Thank God. He didn't want to have to explain to a teenager as well as her mother why he was an ass.

The kids took off, and he and Tess walked. She said nothing. He knew it was a mom tactic; his own mother had used silence to get a confession out of him more than once. They walked side by side until they stood in front of her house.

He didn't even try to fight it with Tess. "I'm so sorry. I meant to be here for dinner. I lay on the couch and conked out."

"Late night, huh?" Her voice held no emotion.

"Yeah. I met up with a couple of friends. We hit a few bars, and then Tony wanted to drive to the Brat Stop. It was far from the wisest choice I've made in a while."

"The Brat Stop? You drove all the way to Wisconsin after midnight?"

"How did you know how late it was?"

She bit her lip. "Angie saw some pictures you posted on social media."

Miles's thoughts scrambled. What had he

posted? "Pam likes to snap pictures all the time."

"Pam?"

"My friend." He reached for Tess's arm to make her stop. "That's all she is," he reassured. "Tony, Pam, and I met in college. We hung out a lot back then, and we get together a few times a year to catch up."

"Okay."

He had no idea how to interpret that one word. "Are we okay?"

She shrugged, which wasn't any better.

"I'm not lying about Pam. If you want, we can call her right now. She'll tell you the same thing."

Tess blew out a breath. "I'm not accusing you of cheating. I'm frustrated. You didn't return my call or text last night. You said you were going to come over for dinner, and you blew me off. Blew *us* off."

"I'm sorry. I hadn't planned on sleeping that long. I was just beat."

"I get it. You can do whatever you want. It's the lack of communication that's the problem." She turned and sat on the concrete step.

Miles joined her, not liking the fact they were talking outside instead of being in the house. Although he wasn't sure he wanted the answer, he asked, "What are you thinking?"

"I think we're in different places in life, Miles. You stayed out most of the night partying. My partying days are long over. There's no way you can convince me that driving to the Brat Stop at one in the morning was a good idea."

"I'll make sure to leave that off the list of possible dates."

"This isn't a joke." She licked her lips. "I've already been through a marriage with someone who routinely ignored my needs. I'm not looking to be the center of your world, but I also don't want to be an afterthought. I deserve better."

"You're right."

She twisted the napkin that had been wrapped around her ice cream cone and looked up at him with eyes shining with hurt and confusion.

"I'm sorry I didn't call you back and that I missed dinner." He took her hand.

She sighed. "Miles, this isn't—"

He had a bad feeling about what she was about to say. "People fight and they fuck up. This is the first time I've done this. What's this really about?"

"I've tried talking about this before and you dismissed it. We're in different places. I have to put my family first. That's not what you're looking for."

"I'm not asking you to change. I don't need you to come out and party. Although it might be nice if you could join me sometimes. I know you and the kids are a package deal. Have I done anything to give you the impression I have a problem with that?"

She angled her head, bit the inside of her cheek, and slowly shook her head.

"I like being with you and the kids. Sometimes we need adult time. But I don't think me missing a dinner should make you doubt me. Doubt us."

"It's not just the dinner. I don't think you're hearing me." She filled her lungs and her chest rose.

Miles half-expected her to start yelling, but he couldn't imagine what that would look like because she was always so even-tempered.

"What do you want, Miles?"

"What do you mean?"

"What do you want for your life? Where do you want to be next year? In five years? What's your plan?"

He opened his mouth and quickly shut it. He suddenly realized how he answered would determine what happened next. The thing was, he didn't have a plan.

"You see? That's it. I have to have a plan. I can't just float by. I'm not mad." She smiled. "I was. I was pissed you went out and posted pictures with friends at a bar at midnight while I was working. Then I felt petty and small because it made me mad." She stroked her fingers across his knuckles. "And you're right. Missing one dinner isn't a big deal in and of itself. But I think it's a symptom of the bigger issue."

Everything she said made sense. He couldn't argue. But his gut clenched, and he wanted to rage against it. He didn't want to walk away from her.

"Before you decide we're over, can I step back and think about what you've said?"

Her eyes widened as if he'd caught her off-guard with the request. "What do you mean?"

"I mean don't run off and find a new

boyfriend. Don't assume we don't have a future. I need to sort some things in my head."

"So you want me to sit around and wait for you?"

"Not forever. Just a little while."

"Why? You obviously have the same misgivings I do."

"That's where you're wrong. I don't. I've listened to everything you said, and I'm taking you seriously. I don't have answers for you right now. You're hinting we're done, but my gut—my heart—says hell no."

"Considering you're my first boyfriend in decades, I don't think you need to worry about me finding another one soon."

"You weren't looking. I'm asking you not to. Because, believe me, when you look, they're gonna flock to you."

She laughed, and he wanted to pull her into his arms and keep her forever. But he knew he needed to figure out his life first.

"Can I call you later?"

"Uh… I thought you needed to think. Won't that cloud your head?"

He smiled. "I like the way you cloud my head." Then he kissed her cheek. "I'll call you before bed."

He walked away and tried to convince himself it was the right move. Tess deserved someone who would put her and her kids first, and he needed to decide if he was that person. If not…he needed to let her go.

Chapter 15

Tess was on autopilot. She hadn't seen Miles since Sunday night, but he continued to text or call her every day. By some implied agreement, they hadn't discussed what she'd asked of him. He hadn't mentioned coming to any kind of conclusion, and she tried to hold on to the fact that he hadn't disappeared as a good sign.

But something about their conversations felt different. They were shorter, more like a check-in instead of a getting-to-know-you. Maybe they were past the getting-acquainted talks. Miles still flirted, but it was somehow cautious. He asked about her work and the kids, but he didn't tell her much about his work. When she prompted him with questions, he always answered, but his responses were superficial.

All of it had her tied up in knots. Added to that, she'd begun reworking her resume and looking at available jobs, so being overwhelmed had become a constant state for her.

As she completed her nightly cleanup of the living room, she had the strongest urge to dump the damn tablets William had bought into the trash. She tried not to be bitter that he was still on vacation—child-free of course —while she continued to work her ass off and worry about her job. Instead of caving in to her impulse, she took a deep breath, went to the kitchen, and poured herself a glass of wine.

With her phone and wine in hand, she sat

on the front porch. The beginning of fall had arrived with the nighttime temperature dipping, but right now, just the barest chill was in the air. In between convincing herself it was a good idea for Miles to ask for some time and then wishing they could rewind the clock to last Friday, Tess found herself checking into Miles's social media. He hadn't posted anything since Saturday night. Was that because she'd admitted she'd seen his pictures? Or had he just been busy with work?

No one had told her dating as an adult was every bit as torturous as it had been as a teen. Her friends had been very supportive, offering comments ranging from, "If he can't get his head out of his ass, he's not good enough for you," to, "It's smart that he's not trying to rush into anything too serious."

She sipped her wine and closed her eyes. The sounds of her neighborhood eased her tension. All in all, she had a good life.

Movement nearby had her eyes popping open. Miles stood in front of her. She almost lost her grip on her glass as she tried to figure out if she was hallucinating.

She blinked, and he smiled at her.

"Hi," he said.

"Hi." She set her glass down. "What are you doing here?"

Her heart raced. She'd missed him so much over the last week that she wanted to drink him in more than she wanted the wine.

"I hope it's okay I just showed up." He rubbed his hands on his jeans and pointed to the step beside her.

She nodded and shifted over. As he sat, she gulped the remainder of her wine, a little niggle of fear warning that she might need the liquid courage to accept his goodbye.

He stared at her for a full minute. At first, she had a hard time maintaining eye contact, but when she forced herself to, his eyes said so much. He was as tormented as she was.

Unfortunately, that didn't give her a clue as to how the rest of her night would go.

"God, I missed you."

His admission brought a wobbly smile to her lips. "I missed you, too." Then she broke their connection with a laugh and a shake of her head. "How silly are we? It's been a week."

"A week too long. I never should have left last Sunday."

Her heart surged and filled with happiness, but she held it in check. Just because he wanted to be here didn't mean he belonged here. She'd known he wanted to be with her all along. Of that she had no doubt. "I shouldn't have tried to pressure you."

"Yeah, you should have." He moved her empty glass farther back and took her hand. "I get it, Tess. You have kids—a family—and they come first. I needed time to think because I didn't know how to answer your questions. But I think I have some answers now."

Tess waited, afraid to interrupt.

"I want to run my family's foundation. When I started this mess, it was mostly because my brother had pissed me off. But the more I try to figure it out and build something that would make my dad proud, the more I find it's what I want to do. At least for now. In the future, I might want to move on to something else, but I'll always be able to take care of myself."

"I never meant to imply you couldn't. I know you can support yourself."

"But all of your questions were valid. Until you asked, I was going through the motions. I did the bare minimum of what was expected of me and didn't have any real drive." He stroked her hand. "It was important for me to figure out that part because it's important to you. I want to be with you, Tess. I like who I am with you. I know you have responsibilities, and I'll never be the center of your world, but maybe we can take a break together. Make our own universe for a little while."

"You still want to be with me?"

"Why the hell wouldn't I? You're a hell of a catch."

"But—"

"There is no but. I'm in. Baseball practice, swim meets, dinner at a crazy early hour... I want it all. We'll figure it out together." He leaned forward and captured her mouth with his.

The kiss was filled with longing. His scent surrounded her, and her whole body relaxed more with that one kiss than with her whole glass of wine.

He pulled away gently and rested his forehead against hers.

"It's not easy," she said.

"What?"

"Being in my life."

"But it's worth it." He pulled back a little

more but kept his hands in her hair, on her neck. "I thought about the whole kid thing, too. I never considered whether I wanted any, other than to see kids and say, no way. I like kids—my sister's, yours—but I never looked at them and said, I want that."

"You might change your mind, Miles. You have plenty of time."

He shook his head. "The first time I came to your house...I remember wanting to be invited in. I want to be in your life."

Tears formed, and Tess swallowed hard. She wasn't sure she believed him, but she wanted to. What single guy would want to sign on for this?

Miles stroked her cheek. "So what do you say? Are you in?"

She nodded, because even if this turned out to be a mistake, it was one she was willing to make. Every relationship had doubts; they would figure it out.

Miles was pretty damn happy with his life. For all of Tess's reservations about his involvement in her life, he thought he'd proven her wrong on all counts. Of course, she hadn't been lying about her life not being easy, but he'd already seen that. For the last few weeks, he'd been at her house most evenings, even though she wouldn't let him spend the night when the kids were there.

He'd been to Zoe's swim meets with them—talk about a never-ending day—but he understood the joy of cheering on a kid. He washed dishes while Tess wrangled homework so they could relax and hang out together afterward. He was becoming part of their family.

It was a good place to be.

Now, if only setting up the Prescott Foundation would run as smoothly. The paperwork had been filed, but he still needed to come up with a board of directors. He hadn't thought that establishing the board would be his most difficult job. He was trying to find the best people in their fields who would volunteer.

Both Sabrina and their mom insisted the foundation's money not be used for salaries. He understood their perspective, but tapping successful people to add something else to their already overflowing plates was a bigger task than he'd expected. So far, he'd received a whole lot of verbal support, followed quickly by, "I wish I could help, but..."

He'd discussed everything with Sabrina, and she'd agreed he couldn't be the only paid employee. He needed help, and he knew who would be perfect.

After dinner at Tess's, he sat at the dining room table scrolling through emails while Tess helped Andrew finish his math homework. Not one email was a positive response regarding volunteers. Plus, he still hadn't heard from Toya Brigham, the woman he needed to bring on as grant administrator for the foundation.

Sabrina would have a fit if she knew he hadn't extended a job offer to anyone other than Toya. He'd known Toya for as long as he'd held his position. She was the kind of woman who could out-network anyone. He wanted her for the job. She'd be a perfect fit. But first, he needed to get a meeting with her.

Billy came in for the third time to ask Tess if she was done. When she told him she needed five more minutes, he looked at Miles.

"Not supposed to have electronics at the table," Andrew whispered.

Miles set the phone down. Tess laid a hand on Andrew's arm. "Children do not need to correct adults. Miles can do whatever he wants since he's a grown-up."

"Sorry. I had a couple of emails to look at for work."

"Problem?" Tess asked as she tapped the paper to draw Andrew's attention back to the worksheet.

"No." She didn't need to hear about his struggles with work.

Billy stood behind Tess, tapping her chair. She took a deep breath and closed her eyes. "I said five minutes. Standing there annoying me won't make the time go faster."

"Something I can help with?" Miles asked.

Tess's eyes fluttered open and she offered him a relieved smile. "Billy needs to come up with an idea for a STEM club project."

"I can handle that." Miles stood, and Tess mouthed, "Thank you."

He pocketed his phone and followed Billy to his room. "So what kind of project is this?"

"I can do any kind of project I want. It's

kind of like a science fair. The kids whose projects get the highest scores get to be on the competition team. First competition is next month." Billy turned and stared up at him with serious eyes. "I want to be on the team."

The sincerity on the boy's face hit Miles hard. "Then let's figure out a winning project."

They spent the next hour combing through old articles on the school's website to see what had won in the past. Ultimately, they decided a tech-based project won more often than anything else. Miles thought back to his own science projects.

"What about building and programming a robot to do a simple task? You can use the coding skills you learned this summer to program it."

Billy scrunched his face. "What am I supposed to build it out of? We had kits in camp this summer, but they're expensive.

Mom said maybe for Christmas. I don't know how to start from scratch."

Miles's immediate reaction was to offer to buy a damn kit. But he knew how Tess felt about him buying things for the kids. He didn't understand. It wasn't like he wanted to buy them useless things. This was educational. "We'll figure it out. The materials don't matter much. You could make the body out of a cereal box if you wanted."

Billy's face fell, and Miles knew the idea was stupid. What kid wanted a cereal-box robot? Yeah, he came from privilege and had never had to worry about something like this, but neither did Billy. At least not as long as Miles was around. "We can make a trip to the home improvement store or maybe a junkyard and find cheap parts."

"Really?"

"Sure. What purpose do you think your robot should have?"

"I want it to do something useful." He

thought for a couple of minutes. "Do you think we could make it get me something from the fridge?"

"We can do whatever you want."

Billy already had a notebook out and began sketching a design and making a list of materials he'd need to make the robot. Miles watched, unsure if he was supposed to offer input.

The boy looked up with a smile. "Thanks, Miles. When can we go look for stuff?"

"We better check with your mom. You know how she is with her color-coded calendar."

They both laughed, and when he got downstairs, he found Tess in the kitchen loading the dishwasher. He came up behind her and wrapped his arms around her waist. Her hair was still up in the ponytail she always wore while working, which gave him full access to her neck. He kissed her, and she shivered.

"Thanks for helping with Billy. Did you guys figure out a project?"

"He's going to build a robot. I told him I'd take him shopping for parts."

She turned quickly in his arms. "Miles—"

He pressed a kiss to her lips. "Parts, Tess. He already told me the kits are expensive. Are you really going to tell me I can't take him to buy some junk?"

She sighed, and he knew he'd won. "I told you I'm all in here, but I never know what I'm doing."

"You're doing fine."

"But I don't notice things. Like tonight, when Billy came in and interrupted you three times. Why didn't you just ask me to help him the first time he came in?"

She licked her lips and dodged his gaze. "Because... they're not your kids."

"I know." His response was sharper than intended, but he didn't need the constant reminder, either.

She patted his chest. "I mean, they're not your responsibility. You obviously had something on your mind, which was why you were on your phone. I didn't want to pressure you into doing something you didn't have time for or didn't want to do."

"If I didn't have time, I wouldn't be here. And even if I don't want to, I'd do it anyway. We're supposed to be a team, right?"

"So tomorrow you'll take math homework with Andrew?" she asked with a grin.

His utter fear must've shown on his face, because she burst out laughing. "Just kidding. I wouldn't wish that on anyone." She twined her arms around his neck and kissed him. "Thank you."

"Not that I won't totally take any kisses you offer, but for what?"

"For helping. For being here. For kissing me like I'm the sexiest woman on the planet."

He shifted and pressed her against the

counter, kissing her again, because to him, she was the sexiest woman on the planet.

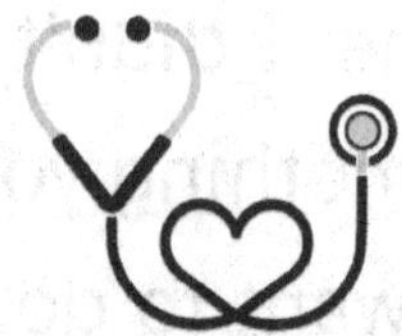

Two days later, Tess sat at the dining room table and crunched the numbers of the budget. After a serious conversation with her supervisors, they'd admitted there were going to be cuts. Her job was in jeopardy, and she couldn't figure out what to do. No matter how she looked at it, home healthcare wouldn't be enough for her and the kids to live on. She wore her worry like a wet winter coat. She'd begun applying for other nursing positions and sending out resumes, but no one had called to even set up an interview.

Panic filled her chest, and she swallowed it down. She had time. It wasn't like the administration had handed out pink slips.

And when they did, she would be able to collect unemployment, so that would help.

She'd be okay. They'd be okay. She took a sip of her coffee, and a different kind of worry settled in. Her house was quiet. No noise emanated from anywhere.

But the kids were home.

She set down her cup and went to search them out. It was kind of like when they were little. Any time her house fell silent, she knew they were up to no good. Now that they were older, she didn't have the same concerns, but things were unusually quiet. And Miles was here. He was supposed to be helping Billy with his robot.

She peered in Zoe's room. Her daughter looked up from the computer screen and waved. "Just checking in."

Moving on to the boys' room, she began to hear noise. She stopped in the doorway and watched. Andrew was sitting on the floor in front of the TV playing a video game with headphones on. Every now and then, he'd let out a little yip. Miles and Billy were bent over the old computer on the desk, talking about coding. At least that was what she assumed. Nothing they said made any sense to her.

As if he sensed her staring, Miles looked up. His grin was broad, and in that moment, she realized she'd fallen in love with him.

Andrew suddenly jumped up and yelled, "Miles. Miles! Did you see? I did it. It worked just like you said it would."

"Awesome." Miles glanced at the TV and gave him a high five.

Billy shook his head and pointed at the computer screen. "Like this?"

Miles rubbed a hand over his head. "Crap. I don't know. Coding was never my thing." He narrowed his eyes at the screen. "It'd be easier to test this if we had the robot built."

"I'll take him this week to get stuff," Tess said.

"I thought Miles was gonna take me," Billy said.

Both of them looked at her like she'd told them they were grounded for a month. She rolled her eyes. "If Miles wants to take you, that's fine. When is this thing due?"

"We're supposed to bring them in on Thursday to present them after school."

Miles laid a hand on Billy's shoulder. "I know someone who could give you coding tips."

"No cheating," Tess warned.

"I said tips. I wasn't suggesting we find someone to do it for him." He turned back to Billy. "My sister knows everything. She doesn't code anymore, but she knows the right people in the company who could help."

"Company?"

"My family owns a software company. They live and breathe computer programs. We could probably even do a STEM club field trip."

"Miles—" The look he gave her made her reconsider interfering.

"Really? Awesome!"

"Download your work to a flash drive and give it to me. I'll have our experts look at it. They'll probably be able to glance at it and know if it'll work."

"This is going to be the best robot they've ever seen."

Tess smiled, because it had been a long time since she'd seen Billy this excited about anything. Miles straightened and fist bumped Billy before coming to her.

"Time to get ready for bed," she called.

"Aww," both boys responded.

"Fifteen minutes."

She and Miles went downstairs. "I think you just made his list of top five people for all time."

"I didn't do anything. He was coding, and I more or less just watched."

"You're supportive. And you get the geeky science side to him."

"He's a cool kid."

"Yeah, he is." At the bottom of the stairs, she wrapped a hand around the back of his neck and pulled his mouth to hers. She kissed him with the newfound knowledge that she loved him. Even though she couldn't say the words yet, she felt it.

"Wow. You keep kissing me like that, and you'll be on my top five list."

"I'm not already on that list?" He gripped her hips and held her to him and his growing hard-on. "Of course you are. I was trying to sound tough. You completely unhinge me with every touch."

"The feeling is mutual. Do you have to run off? Or can you stay a while?"

"Hmm...depends. Am I gonna get lucky?"

"I think we both are." The words slipped out as the idea struck.

He jerked back. "Seriously? The kids are here."

She liked surprising him. Going up on tiptoe, she whispered in his ear, "You can't spend the night in my bed, but if we're quiet, I'll let you fuck me senseless."

"Fuck." He groaned. "Are you trying to kill me?"

"Go get the bottle of wine and meet me in my room. Ten minutes. I'll speed read to Andrew tonight."

She stepped back to go upstairs, and he leaned against the wall to watch her walk away. While they'd been having sex since they met, this was new. Maybe she could have him start spending the night sometimes even if the kids were here. He was part of all of their lives now. He'd proven to all of them that he wanted to be there.

Miles needed a full minute to regain his senses. For weeks he'd been part of Tess's family, and they'd kind of fallen into a routine. While he was allowed to kiss her or touch her innocently at her house, the only time they'd had sex there was when the kids were with their dad. He'd almost forgotten about the woman Tess could be when she wanted to.

Pushing off the wall, he walked toward the kitchen to get the wine she requested. On the way, he passed the papers she'd left on the dining room table. He paused to look. He knew financials when he saw them. Picking up a sheet, he studied the numbers.

Was this what she was living on?

He scanned the other pages and realized she was figuring out what her finances would look like if she lost her job. He knew she'd been worried, and they'd talked about her looking for another job. This made him wonder if she'd gotten word.

No way would he let her kill herself to try to make ends meet. That was ridiculous given his means. But he knew she would never want to take his money, even if it was just temporary. Sometimes her stubbornness did not serve her well.

He folded the paper, tucked it into his pocket, and continued on to the kitchen. After retrieving the wine and glasses, he went to Tess's room, set the wine on the bedside table, and turned on the lamp. He took a deep breath to settle his nerves. He'd never had to monitor what he said or how loud he got while having sex. At least not since sneaking around as a teenager. Tess said they needed to be quiet.

How quiet?

The woman was damn near silent every time they fucked. He wasn't sure if he could be that quiet. He looked around and wished she had a TV to at least disguise their sounds. Maybe she'd let him install one so they could worry less.

He sat on the edge of the bed, poured the wine, and waited. Sometimes Andrew would rook her into reading extra chapters. A few minutes later, though, she strode through the door with a wicked smile on her face.

God, he loved that look. It was one she saved just for him.

She closed the door behind her, and the snick of the lock sounded through the room. He rose and handed her a glass of wine. "You sure about this?"

Without taking a sip, she set the glass back down. "Absolutely. Aren't you?"

"I'm totally on board for having sex with you right now, but it's the whole being quiet thing that concerns me."

She chuckled. "Don't worry. If you get too loud, I'll stuff a sock in your mouth."

"Funny." He pulled her close and kissed her. Every time they were alone together reinforced how he felt about her.

He loved her.

He loved who they were together.

Tess began tugging at his shirt. "As much as I love the whole seduction scene, I never know how much time I'll have alone. Let's go."

He pulled her shirt over her head and kissed her neck while unclasping her bra. "Maybe we should take this down to the laundry room. We know we'll have privacy there."

Her laugh was husky as he cupped her breasts and licked her nipples. He kissed his way down her body, removing her pants as he went. Moments later, they tumbled into bed, Tess in his arms, laughing and sighing in pleasure.

Yeah, he definitely wanted more of this.

Chapter 16

Tess couldn't catch her breath. She lay on top of Miles with her heart crashing against her ribs. She didn't know if it was the realization she'd fallen in love with him or if the pressure of being quiet made them refocus, or if something else had shifted between them, but her entire body buzzed. Miles had rocked her world every time they were together, but this was different.

"You okay?" he whispered.

"No. Can't move."

"Then my work here is done." He stroked her back, and she knew she'd fall asleep right here if she didn't get up now.

She pressed her lips to his chest and levered herself off. For a moment, she just looked at him. Was this her life now? Secret sex while her kids were in their rooms? At what point should she stop acting like their relationship was temporary and might end?

He tucked her hair behind her ear. "What are you thinking?"

"That you're really pretty," she said with a smile.

He slapped her ass. "No man wants to be called pretty."

"I only speak the truth." She climbed off the bed.

"Where are you going?" He pushed up on his elbows and watched her pull her clothes back on.

"I love lounging around in bed with you,

but I'm not ready for the kids to find you here. Let's take the wine downstairs, and we can talk or watch TV or something."

"I like the *or something*. Let's stay here and do more of that."

She gave him her best mom look. "Not happening. Get dressed." She tossed his clothes at him and gathered the glasses and bottle of wine.

"Why did you have me bring that here if you weren't going to drink it?"

She shrugged. "I thought I would, but then I saw you and just wanted to get you naked."

With the glasses in one hand and the bottle hugged close to her body, she eased the door open to check if the coast was clear. With a quick look over her shoulder to make sure Miles was putting clothes on, she left the room.

She waited for him on the couch with the

TV on but didn't bother to flip through the channels. A few minutes later, Miles plopped down and put an arm around her, pulling her to rest against him.

"Have I told you lately how much I love being rushed in the bedroom?"

"Take what you can get, Prescott."

He took the remote and flipped channels. He stroked his fingers up and down her arm, the rhythm soothing and relaxing her even more. She hadn't known that was possible.

"Hey, I was looking at your papers on the table."

"Hmm?" She thought for a minute and then remembered her lists.

"Have you heard something about your job?"

"No. I'm preparing for worst-case scenario."

"Your worst case looks pretty bleak."

She lifted a shoulder as if it wasn't a big

deal. She didn't need the reminder of how bleak it was.

"If things go south, I'll help."

She shifted to look up at him. "That's nice of you to offer, but I'm not your charity."

"I don't think of you as charity. I also can't sit by and watch you kill yourself working crazy hours so you can pay your bills and still be with your kids. That's ridiculous."

"It's my life, my responsibility."

"I understand, but I have the means to make your life easier."

Suddenly, it was like their first date together when he'd made her feel a little like Julia Roberts in *Pretty Woman*. She knew he didn't mean anything by the offer, so she took a deep breath before responding. "I know you're trying to be kind. But I can't rely on you financially, Miles. I did that for years in my marriage, and I regretted it. I don't want money to come between us."

"It wouldn't."

She swallowed a laugh. "That's easy for you to say now, but it would. You have money, and I don't. It absolutely would come between us."

"So I'm supposed to watch you suffer, knowing I could help? That's bullshit."

"It's the way it has to be."

"No, it isn't."

Now he was irritating her. "It does. At first, it'll be fine, but at some point, you'll start to feel like you're being used. You'll resent my inability to live the life you're used to."

He sat back, putting distance between them. "I don't give a fuck about money."

"That's because you have that luxury."

"Why are you doing this?"

"I'm not doing anything. I'm explaining to you why I won't let you help pay my bills."

"But you need help."

"No, I don't." She stood, and he followed. "I have my job. I can get another. Like I said, those numbers, my personal finances, are worst-case scenario."

He crossed his arms. "So if you hit worst case, you'll let me help?"

She growled. "No. I'll take care of myself."

"You don't have to do everything yourself."

"Yes, I do."

"Why?"

"Because you might leave!" The words burst from her. She wanted to suck them back in but realized how true they were.

Miles dropped his arms. "I thought we'd moved past that. I'm here, Tess. I'm fitting into your life. I'm not going anywhere because I love you."

She had already filled her lungs to prepare for a rebuttal, but his words stopped her. Her heart leaped into her throat. Her own declaration tried to escape, but she held it back. Her breaths came quickly, and she wanted to throw herself into his arms. And because she wanted it so badly, she locked her knees.

"If it were just you and me, it wouldn't be such a big deal. I have to think about the kids. I've brought you into their lives, but I can't allow them to get used to a different lifestyle. Things changed for them when William and I divorced. William routinely uses money to buy their love. He misses time with them and buys a gift instead. They're always gifts I can't compete with."

Miles stepped closer and took her hand. "I don't want to compete with you. I don't want to buy their love." He paused, then added with a smile, "Well, maybe if I had to..."

She closed her eyes and shook her head. Now was not the time for jokes. He cupped her jaw and waited for her to open her eyes.

"I'm not going anywhere. I've played by your rules one hundred percent, and I have no desire to compete with you or make you look like less in the eyes of your kids. I can help with money if you need it."

"I won't."

"Okay. Then I guess this is a silly argument."

She wanted to believe it was, but a niggling feeling poked at her deep down.

He kissed her temple. "It's getting late. I have an early morning meeting."

"Okay."

Miles continued to hold her face. "Can I take Billy shopping on Wednesday?"

"I'm working. I'll have William bring him here and ask my mom to wait with him until you get off work."

"Is that going to cause a problem with his dad?"

She huffed. "Not likely."

"If you say so. I should be able to pick him up around four-thirty or five."

"Talk to you tomorrow?"

"Absolutely."

His comment reassured her, so the sting of their argument lessened. He left, and she returned to her glass of wine and thought about how far into her life she could allow Miles. He was asking for full access and had even said he loved her.

After another glass of wine—or two—she picked up her phone and texted him.

I love you, too.

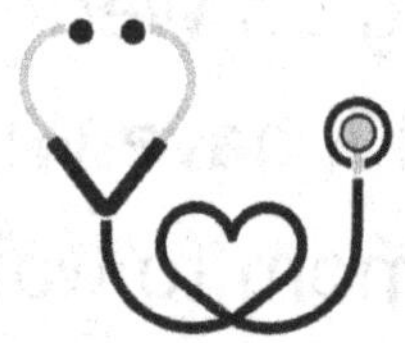

Miles went to work the following morning with a fresh mission. He might not be able to convince Tess to let him help her financially, but he could help secure her job. The first order of business for the James Prescott Foundation would be a sizeable endowment to the PICU department of St. Mark's. After leaving Tess's house last night, he'd stayed up developing the proposal.

Because when you loved a woman, you did whatever you could for her. Knowing she loved him had set his world right after they'd argued. He would've preferred hearing the words from her lips, maybe while they were naked, but a text was better than nothing.

He proposed the endowment to St. Mark's PICU to Sabrina via email. She thought it was a great idea. Although he presented the idea as something their father would have liked because St. Mark's gala had been his favorite, Sabrina warned against making it all about his girlfriend. He assured her it wasn't. Then he spoke to his contacts at the hospital to discuss the finer points of the endowment and what his family expected.

He had a few weeks until they revealed the foundation to the public, and he had most things in place—everything except the director of grants. He'd finally gotten a good email address for Toya and expected to hear from her soon. She'd switched jobs since he'd seen her last. He wouldn't say she was climbing the corporate ladder as much as she was always looking for her next big challenge.

As he bounced ideas back and forth, a new message hit his inbox.

Hi, Miles! It's great to hear from you. Sorry you had to work to track me down. I haven't updated my contacts recently because the last job I took didn't work out. The non-profit went belly-up less than a month after I joined. So much for my instincts. I know you said you wanted to meet with me this week, but that might not be possible. I have a job interview in New York. If all goes well, I'll be moving there. I'll let you know where I am when I land a new position. I'd love to catch up.

Toya

Miles couldn't believe his luck—both the good and bad. Toya was in between jobs, so now was the time to make an offer, but she was unavailable. He knew she'd get the job. Whoever was interviewing her would be foolish not to hire her. He checked his calendar. The only pressing matter for the next two days was his trip to take Billy shopping Wednesday night.

If Toya was unavailable to come to him, he'd go to her. He picked up his phone. "Eleanor, book me the next possible flight to New York. Get me a hotel room and reservations for tomorrow night at a great restaurant."

"Any preference as to where you'd like to go?"

Miles almost laughed. Every time he'd

been in New York in the past, he was partying with college friends. A fancy dinner had never been on his list of things to do. "Wherever Sabrina normally takes clients."

"Will do."

Miles emailed Toya and told her he'd be in New York tomorrow and asked her not to accept any job offer until after they'd spoken.

He spent the rest of his day juggling work so he could go to New York. He prepared a presentation to get Toya to sign on with him while he talked on the phone to Sabrina's event coordinator to discuss the foundation party. He wanted the endowment to St. Mark's to coincide with the celebration of the foundation being made public.

In line with the mission of the foundation, the celebration would be a family event, not a stuffy black-tie affair, because at the James Prescott Foundation, family came first. Miles was happy with the work he'd done and was sure his father would be proud to have his name associated with it.

He couldn't count the number of times he'd picked up his phone today to tell Tess everything but then stopped. By the time he had everything done and was leaving the office, it was after nine. He called her on his way home.

"Hey," she answered.

"How was your day?"

"Same as always. How was yours?"

"Exhausting." On days like this, he was grateful to have a driver. He leaned his head back on the seat and closed his eyes. "Very productive, though. I have to go to New York tomorrow to interview someone for the foundation."

"New York? Wow."

"I'll try to call you, but I might be tied up. I'm not sure how long the meeting will go."

"Good luck."

"Thanks."

Why is this conversation so painful? Talking with Tess is usually so smooth and natural.

"Should I just take Billy shopping for robot parts tomorrow?" she asked.

"No. I'll be back on Wednesday."

"But you might be tired. That's a lot of travel."

"I'll be fine." He rubbed his forehead. "Are we okay?" Silence hung in the air. He'd thought for sure after her text last night they were past the argument.

"I don't know. Are we?"

He sighed. "I love you, Tess. We're gonna fight, but it's up to us to make sure it doesn't ruin us."

"I wasn't sure you got my text last night. I was a little buzzed because I drank all the wine after you left."

"I got it." She'd been drunk? A thought struck him. "You meant it, right?"

"Yes," she whispered. "I shouldn't have

chickened out of saying it. You took me by surprise, and we were fighting, and...” Her sigh coasted over him.

“I don't know why it was a surprise. I kind of thought it was obvious. If it wasn't, I need to up my game.”

She laughed. “Trust me, your game is just fine.”

Dave pulled up in front of the condo, and Miles briefly considered having the car continue on to Tess's house, but he needed to pack for his trip. “Good. Now that we have that settled, tell me about your day for real.”

“Billy woke up talking about his robot and hasn't stopped since. I don't know if he did any actual work in school.”

“Shit. I have his program. If I email it to you, can you give it to him? Or does he have his own email?”

“Of course he has his own email. Otherwise, my inbox would be filled with video game crap every time he signs up for something. I'll text it to you, and you can send whatever you want."

"Just so you know, my guy said it's good. You might have the next computer billionaire on your hands."

"Not quite."

"He's only had one coding class. He's got a knack for it."

"Awesome. Then I can count on him to take care of me in retirement."

"I doubt you'll need him. You're pretty good at taking care of yourself."

"Is that a dig?"

He trudged through his condo, sat on his couch, and imagined being in Tess's living room with her in his arms. "Not at all. You always impress me, but when I looked at your list yesterday, I developed a new level of admiration."

"You have a way of making me feel like some kind of superhero."

"Not far from the truth. Have a great day tomorrow. I have to go pack for New York."

"Have a good trip."

"Will I get in trouble if I bring back souvenirs for the kids?"

"If you buy a little snow globe, no. If you spend a gazillion dollars on something crazy, yes."

"You have some silly rules, Ms. Howland, but I respect you. Snow globes it is."

She laughed as they disconnected, and Miles knew he needed to finish building the foundation so he could focus on building his relationship with Tess and her kids. They were every bit as much his future as the Prescott Foundation.

All day on Tuesday, Miles functioned at a mildly panicked level. Eleanor couldn't get him on a flight to New York until early afternoon. Normally, not a big deal, even with losing an hour to the time change. But by the time he got to his hotel, he was cutting it close to his dinner reservations, and he still hadn't heard from Toya.

He'd texted her as soon as he landed, but she hadn't responded. He knew she was in an interview and, depending on the circumstances and how badly the organization wanted her, it could take a while. They'd asked her to fly halfway across the country, so it wouldn't be a twenty-minute conversation.

Then, as luck would have it, when she did respond, she said she wouldn't be able to have dinner with him because her interview had gone well and they wanted to show her the town. She reassured him she wouldn't accept the offer without giving him a chance and then offered him a lunch date for Wednesday. She was the best person for the job, and he needed to hire her. So he agreed.

He called Eleanor to get her to reschedule his flight, then called Tess as he ate a lonely room service dinner.

"Aren't you supposed to be having a fancy high-powered dinner in New York?"

"Yeah, I am, but plans got moved. I'm eating dinner all alone, so I'm calling you to keep me company."

"What happened with the interview?"

He sighed. "The woman I came here to interview got tied up with another prospective employer. We're having lunch tomorrow instead."

"Ouch. It's not a good sign if she bumped you."

"In her defense, she already had this scheduled. I'm kind of poaching."

"Intriguing."

"Not really. Just business."

"Since you're going to be stuck there, should I try to take Billy shopping tonight?"

"No. We're eating lunch, and my plane takes off at three. I gain an hour coming back to Chicago. I might have to come straight to your house, but I'll be there."

"If you're sure…"

Her doubt had his back up. He wanted to do this. She'd just started trusting him to do things with the kids without her constant supervision. He didn't want to give this up. "I'm glad he got the code I sent. It was nice of him to text to thank me."

"He did?"

"Yeah. I didn't recognize the number, so it took a minute for me to respond."

She chuckled. "The phone is relatively new. We obviously still have to work on phone etiquette. They always need reminders that not everyone texts like their friends."

"He did fine."

"So I'll see you tomorrow?"

"I miss you already."

"Better watch out, Miles. People might start thinking you're all mushy. It's only been two days since we saw each other. And you even got lucky that night."

"I'll let the world know you make me horribly mushy if it means I get to spend more time with you."

"We like to have you around, so you're on."

He liked the sound of that. Tess had said *we*. She included the kids as part of the equation.

They said good night, and Miles crawled into bed with spreadsheets and reports. He had a good feeling about meeting with Toya. Then he'd get back to Chicago to be with Tess and her kids.

All of Miles's good feelings disappeared the next morning with a simple text at eleven a.m. Toya needed to push their lunch date but promised she'd have coffee with him in the afternoon. Shit, what if he couldn't make it back to Chicago on time? Tess was at work today, so he had to make it.

When he walked into the coffee shop to meet Toya, he calculated he'd have just enough time if he went straight to the airport. Toya was already there sipping a coffee. Damn, she wouldn't even let him buy her a drink? She stood when she saw him and gave him a hug.

"Hey, Toya. It's good to see you."

"It's good to see you, too. I'm really sorry about pushing you off, but the non-profit that flew me out here wanted to squeeze every bit of time out of me. I felt obligated to give them that since I'm here on their dime." She pointed to the chair across from her, and they took their seats.

"I understand. I'm also sure they offered you the position, but I think I can top it."

She smiled. "You have no idea what's on the table."

"They're a nonprofit, so I know I can beat the salary hands down."

"You know I'm not looking for a corporate job, Miles. I would never be happy working at Prescott Workspace."

"Neither would I."

He told her about the James Prescott Foundation. Two sentences in, and he had her rapt attention.

"So in addition to making more money and not having to leave the fabulous city of Chicago, you'd also have your hands on plenty of money to help distribute to worthy causes. You won't be begging for donations."

"Wow. I didn't see this coming. I was so caught up with being in New York for this other position, I didn't know what to expect from this meeting. I don't know what to say." She turned her coffee in a slow circle on the table.

"Say you'll take the job. I like the way you work, and I think we'll make a great team."

"You've definitely piqued my interest. Can I have a few days to think about it?"

"Of course. As long as you decide Prescott is where you want to be."

"I'm interested, but it's a big change from what I'm used to doing. I need to weigh the pros and cons."

"I can respect that." He pulled the folder from his bag. "Take this. It'll give you an overview of the foundation, and there's a contract in there as well. Let me know what points you might want to negotiate."

He stood and shook her hand. He knew that giving her the option to negotiate would sweeten the pot. He just hoped it would be enough to get her on board. Checking his watch, he flagged down a taxi to take him to the airport. Since he didn't have to check a bag, he should have plenty of time.

Unfortunately, the universe was working against him, and his flight was delayed. They didn't know when they would be moving. He tried to hold his frustration in check. "Do I have any option other than to wait?" he asked the ticket agent.

The woman shook her head. "The plane has a mechanical problem they're checking out. If they need to get a new plane, it'll be a while. Sorry."

Shit. *Shit, shit, shit.* He'd told Tess she could count on him, and he was going to blow it. Although he wanted to throw his phone against the wall, he knew he'd need it. Taking a deep breath, he focused on solving the problem instead of screaming. He could handle this.

Chapter 17

Tess had a crazy busy day at work. Three new patients were admitted, so all of their beds were full. She hadn't been able to check in on the kids or William. She hoped their afternoon had gone well. When she finally got a break, she checked her phone and saw three texts from Billy saying Miles wasn't there. The first came in at four thirty, so her son was simply being anxious. However, when she saw the time stamp of the other two, her stomach sank. Then she listened to the voicemail Billy left. He was completely distraught. Her breath caught in her throat.

Miles hadn't made it. Her heart hurt for Billy. This stupid robot meant so much to him. God, why had she entrusted this project to Miles? She dialed his number and it went straight to voicemail. She kept her jaw clenched, because if she loosened it even a fraction, the entire department would know exactly how upset she was.

"How could you, Miles? You said you wanted to do this with Billy. It might not seem like a big deal to you, but this is huge to him. I asked you so many times if I should take him because you were busy. All you had to do was say yes. Now it's freaking eight o'clock and too late." She disconnected before she said anything really ugly.

Just as she was about to call her mom to see if there was any way she'd could take Billy somewhere to maybe cobble something together, she was called back to work by alarms sounding in one of the rooms.

An hour later, she finally left the hospital. Exhaustion pulled at her as she walked to the train, but she surfed the internet on her phone to see if by some long shot, a store might be open for her to go to. When the train pulled up, another text came through. From Miles.

I have it handled. Sorry.

She couldn't even begin to think how he believed he had it handled. Service was spotty at best on the train, so she didn't bother trying to call him, but when she walked to her house from the station, she was surprised to see him sitting on her steps.

"Hey, babe."

"Don't *hey, babe* me. You've got a lot of nerve sitting here acting like nothing's wrong. You completely fucked this up for Billy. Don't you get that?"

"I got stuck in New York. I couldn't help it."

"But I gave you an out, Miles. Last night. And the night before. I could've taken him, or I could've asked my mom. Hell, he could've asked William this afternoon. But we were all counting on *you*."

He at least had the decency to hang his head. "I know. But I fixed it."

An uneasy feeling stole through her. "What do you mean?"

"When I was stuck in New York, I called all over and had a kit delivered. I know it wasn't what you wanted—"

He did *what*? Her muscles tightened, her blood racing. She turned and went into the house. Sure enough, a fancy little robot sat on the dining room table. She couldn't begin to consider what it cost. "That," she said, sure Miles had followed her in, "is how you *fixed* it?"

"Yeah. I researched a model that would

be easy for him to put together and program. Then I found a way to get it delivered here in plenty of time for him to assemble. Problem solved."

He sounded so damn proud of himself. Her anger doubled. Just as she'd feared from the beginning—he was no better than William. "This doesn't fix it, Miles. He's a kid. He was counting on you. Not your damn money. Buying expensive gifts doesn't make up for not being here. It sure as hell can't replace your word."

She was so angry she was shaking. *How did I let this happen? I knew better.* He reached out and touched her shoulder, but she flinched. "You need to go."

"Tess—"

"No. I can stomach a lot of things. Blowing me off, showing up late... I'm an adult. I might get mad, but I can understand. I won't stand for someone letting my kids down. That's a deal breaker."

He jerked back and studied her. "That's it? I screwed up once, so you're going to break up with me?"

He didn't get it. He wasn't a parent. Maybe he would never get it. Then she saw his own anger rise.

"Hell of a way to show how you love someone, Tess. I did the best I could. I'm not perfect, but I tried. I would never intentionally let the kids down."

"Intentional or not, you did. And your solution was to throw money at the problem. They've already had plenty of that in their lives. I can't change who their father is or how he lives, but I sure as hell can control who else treats them that way."

"You can't control everything. As long as you try to rule everyone's lives, you'll never have one of your own." He paused. "You don't know how to let someone in. You set the bar impossibly high and no one can meet it. No one's perfect. We all fuck up." He shook his head and left without another word. He didn't slam the door or yell. He just slipped away.

Tess dropped into a chair at the table. Her chest was tight and tears threatened. It had been a while since she'd had a fight like that. Over the years, she'd learned to dismiss most of what William did in an effort to maintain her sanity.

She couldn't live through that again. She wanted something better. Her kids deserved better.

But Miles's words hung around her neck, weighing her down. Hadn't William accused her of being a control freak? It had caused a rift between them during their marriage, and it hadn't gotten better with the divorce. She'd somehow managed to find two men who were too similar. She put her elbow on the table and rested her head on her hand. Maybe she was a magnet for that kind of guy.

Miles might've been right about that part. She didn't know how to let anyone in.

Miles was pissed. In one swift conversation, Tess had disassembled everything they'd been building. Sure, he'd known she'd be a little mad about the robot kit, but he'd saved what could've been a disaster. She was wrong. He knew exactly how important the robot was to Billy. That was why he'd scrambled to make sure the kid had what he needed.

Why couldn't she see that?

He understood her getting upset, but to break up with him over a damn robot? By the time he got home, his anger had turned into a slow burn. He'd give her time to cool off. Then she'd come to her senses and realize his intentions had been good. And if she didn't, that was definitely a sign they'd never had a chance.

All day at work on Thursday, he watched the clock, hoping to get an update from Billy about his robot and whether he'd earned one of the coveted spots on the competition team. Between wondering if the robot worked, to hoping Toya would call and accept his offer, to waiting for Tess to call so they could make up, he couldn't focus on a damn thing related to work.

At five thirty, he tossed papers in his bag and went home. No point in being at the office if he couldn't be productive. Billy should've finished with STEM club. Tess hadn't called to tell him how things went, but they'd be doing their early dinner and run-to-practice that they did every night.

He was figuring out what to have for dinner when his phone rang. Toya. "Hello?"

"Hi, Miles? It's Toya Brigham."

"How are you? Did you have a good flight back?"

"Not really. I hate flying. I'm calling because I have a few questions about the position you offered me. Is now a good time? I know it's after office hours, so we can make an appointment for tomorrow if you'd like."

He straightened on the couch and reached for a pad of paper and a pen. "Now's good. Shoot."

"I have to say, you put together a very attractive package. It would be hard to turn it down."

"That was what I was going for. But?"

"My only concern is the amount of interference from the Prescott family and the board of directors. I know you guys have always done things your own way, and you've told me stories about your siblings. I don't want to take a position as grant director only to find all my job entails is pushing papers and making spreadsheets."

"The salary is a little high for a glorified

paper pusher. You'll be my right hand. You'll do most of the work sorting through grant applications. As the foundation grows and we put more specific programs in place, you'll be an integral part of developing the application process." He tossed the paper back on the table. "As far as oversight goes, you'll have to prepare quarterly reports for the board. You'll work closely with me. The rest of my family will be hands-off."

"Okay."

"Any other questions?"

"No. That was all I needed to hear." She paused. "I'd like to accept the position."

Miles jumped up and fist pumped. Then he schooled his face as if she could see him. "Excellent. Welcome on board. When can you start?"

"As soon as you're ready for me."

They talked for the next hour or so, and Miles filled her in on the celebration they were planning. When he hung up, he emailed

Sabrina to let her know everything was in place. Then all he wanted to do was call Tess and take her out to celebrate. But since she hadn't called or texted, he figured she was still pissed.

He stared at his phone. She might not be ready to talk to him, but he needed to know how the robot fared, so he texted Billy.

How did you do at STEM?

With his phone in hand in case he got a response, he went to the kitchen to scrounge for food. He'd gotten used to eating at Tess's house. Even if he'd missed their early dinner, leftovers waited for him. His kitchen was pitifully empty.

His phone lit in his hand.

I got it!! I'm on the
competition team. My robot
came in second. Most kids
had kits, too, so it was
totally fair.

Congratulations! I can't
wait to hear all about it.

He paused and debated whether he
should use Billy as his own little informant.

Is your mom still mad?

Oh, yeah. I don't remember
the last time she was this
mad. She's trying to hide it
though. I told her that
without your robot, I
probably wouldn't have
gotten on the team, but it
didn't work.

Hey, man. Don't try to cover for me. She's right. I screwed up by not being there like I said I would. I'm glad you made the team.

Will you come to the competition?

We'll see.

He was thrilled for Billy, but it wasn't a good sign that Tess was still so mad that Billy was trying to talk her down. Giving up on dinner at home, he grabbed his keys and called his sister to let her know he was coming over for dinner. While Sabrina didn't cook, most days she had someone who prepared meals for them.

He hoped that in addition to a good meal, he'd also get advice on how to fix things with Tess.

An hour later, with a plate of prime rib and a glass of wine in front of him, Miles was grilled by Sabrina about trekking all the way into the suburbs for a meal.

"Can't I just want to spend time with my big sister?" he asked and cut into his slab of meat.

She snorted. And waited.

After swallowing, he explained what had happened over the last couple of days. Sabrina listened closely, sipping her wine. His sister had the best poker face known to man. He never knew what she was thinking.

"So today, before coming here, I texted Billy to see how it went. He made the team, by the way. Tess is still pissed. He doesn't remember the last time she was this mad."

Sabrina shook her head. "I warned you. She's a mom. The kids will always come first."

"I was putting Billy first."

"But you were doing it on your terms. With your money. From what you've said about

Tess and her ex, he uses his money to buy his way out of everything. It's a trigger for her. That will probably never change."

Miles set his fork down. He hadn't considered that. "So what do I do? I can't pretend I don't have money."

"You need to decide if this is what you really want. Are you planning on sticking it out for good?"

He stared at his big sister. "Yes. I want to have a life with them."

A sly smile slipped onto her face. "That right there is a good start. A life with *them*. Prove to Tess the kids are important to you. That you're willing to give of yourself and put in the time with them."

"I've been doing that."

"But this stunt with the robot set you back a few paces. Like playing Chutes and Ladders when you were a kid. Sure, you could climb that long ladder, but one wrong move and you're sliding all the way down."

He could do this. He knew exactly how to prove to Tess he wasn't going anywhere.

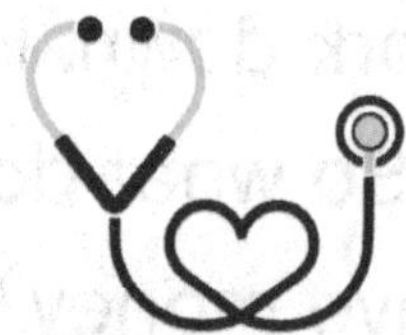

Ten days. It had been ten long days since Tess had told Miles to get out of her life, and she was miserable. The kids routinely asked where Miles was, and for the first time she could remember, she lied to them. She'd told them Miles was busy with work.

The lie was partly for her own benefit. She didn't want to believe they were really over, even though it had been her call. She pushed through the door of Sunny's and found Nina and Trevor at their usual table.

"Hey, what's wrong?" Trevor asked.

"I broke up with Miles."

"What?" Nina shrieked. Then she noticed

people looking and lowered her voice. "Things were going so well."

"They were. Until he told Billy he would take him shopping for robot parts for his STEM club project and then didn't show."

"Fuck," Trevor said quietly.

"Did he at least have a good reason?" Nina asked.

"He did. I guess. The thing is, I gave him an out. I offered to take Billy. I knew Miles was busy with work, but he insisted he could handle it."

"What happened with Billy?"

Tess took a sip of her coffee. "That's where things went really south. When he realized he wasn't going to make it, Miles ordered an expensive robot kit and had it delivered."

Nina and Trevor stared. They understood.

Evelyn and Owen came through the door and looked around the table. "What's going on?" Evelyn asked.

Trevor turned to them. "Miles screwed the pooch, and Tess broke up with him."

Nina gave them the run-down while Tess drank her coffee. Hearing her friend explain it didn't make it sound any better. Tess waffled between feeling completely justified in her response and feeling like she was a complete idiot.

"Well, he tried," Owen offered. "No Gabe today?"

Tess shrugged.

Trevor said, "He has a client meeting. Different time zone. He said he'd try to make it."

Evelyn dumped sugar into her coffee and then looked at Tess. "If this breakup was what you wanted, why do you look like hell?"

"Because I've done nothing for the last ten days but second-guess myself. I fell in love with him. I didn't plan on it, but we were so good together, and then I started to wonder if I overreacted."

Evelyn stirred her coffee. "You overreacted."

"That's not very supportive," Nina said.

Evelyn shrugged. "She doesn't need supportive. She needs honest."

"He called me a control freak with unrealistically high expectations."

Trevor, Evelyn, and Owen all laughed, and Tess gritted her teeth.

"What?" Nina asked.

"She does," Trevor said. "Miles nailed it. But he knows that about you and he loves you anyway."

His words sank in. *Oh crap. Trevor is right. Miles loves me.* "What do I do now? He hasn't called or texted since I asked him to leave. Maybe he's done."

Trevor lifted his cup. "You won't know unless you ask."

"So...what? I'm supposed to call him and say, 'My bad'?"

"For someone so smart, you sure are

dumb sometimes. Call and apologize," Nina said.

"Apologize? I didn't do anything wrong." She set her coffee down with a clank.

"You ignored everything he did right and focused on what he did wrong. He knew he screwed up and did what he could to fix it. You downplayed that like it was nothing," Evelyn said. She looked around the table. "I can't have another person in the kids' lives who thinks money is the answer to everything."

"Does he?" Trevor asked. "Or are you punishing him for the things William does?"

Tess wasn't even sure anymore. She was miserable, but she had no idea if getting back together with Miles would fix that. What was the likelihood he would continue to do this? That was a roller coaster she had no desire to ride.

Her friends gave her plenty to think about.

"So how's the dating scene going for you?" she asked Nina.

"If you decide things won't work with Miles, I can take you to a couple of hot spots to get your groove on."

The table erupted in laughter. She couldn't ask for anything more in a group of friends.

Throughout the course of her workday, she debated what to do about Miles. By the time she got the kids in bed, she still had no answers. Then, as she went through her mail, she found an envelope with a return address from the Prescott Foundation.

It was an invitation to a family fun day to mark the launch of the Prescott Foundation and a special benefit for St. Mark's PICU. Tears burned her eyes. Miles was making sure she had a job. She'd turned away his help, and instead of listening to her and letting her handle her life, he'd gone behind her back to secure her job.

She should be furious. But her heart swelled to the point of pain. Staring at her phone, she tried to form the appropriate words. Nothing came.

After more than a half hour of staring, she finally decided to take the chicken's way out and sent a text.

> Hi. Just got my invitation to the Prescott Foundation's first party and the benefit for St. Mark's. I'm at a loss for words. Thank you. Tess

She deleted and retyped her name three times. Of course he would know it was from her, but not including her name felt wrong. So she hit SEND. Then she busied herself with whatever tasks she could to keep her mind off the invitation and her phone. Not that it did a bit of good, because she checked the damn thing every five minutes, hoping for a response from Miles.

Miles stared at the screen of his phone. He'd hoped when Tess received the invitation, she'd call. A text wasn't quite the same, but at least she'd reached out. She'd left the door open, so he called.

It rang three times, and she answered it with, "Shit. Hold on," followed by some banging. Miles knew those sounds.

"Hello?" she said.

"Laundry again?"

She chuckled. "It's never-ending."

Then they fell into silence that crushed him. "I'm glad you got the invitation."

"You didn't have to do that, Miles."

"Do what?"

"I know you're giving the PICU money to save my job."

"Not everything is about you. As it

happens, I believe the PICU does amazing work, and St. Mark's was one of my dad's favorite benefits. If the endowment happens to ensure you don't get laid off, it's coincidence."

She laughed. "You're not a very good liar."

"Wasn't trying to be. How have you been?"

"Okay. You?"

Horrible. Miserable. Terribly lonely. "Fine."

"Good."

The conversation was more painful than he'd thought possible. The silence was suffocating. "I'm really sorry about what happened between us."

"So am I," she whispered.

Her admission gave him hope. He'd avoided talking to her because he wanted to prove to her he was serious about them and their future. The PICU endowment was only the first step.

"You were right about what you said," she continued. "I do have high expectations."

"That's not always a bad thing. I shouldn't have lashed out at you. I was frustrated about trouble with the foundation and getting stuck in New York, but I shouldn't have taken it out on you."

"You never told me you were having trouble. You never tell me much about anything."

"I didn't think you needed anything else to worry about."

"The whole sharing thing is supposed to go both ways." The machine behind her rumbled and there was another clang as the washer switched cycles. "We messed up pretty bad."

"No argument there. Are the kids doing okay?" He asked because she probably didn't expect him to, but he didn't need her to answer. He was getting regular reports from Billy. The kid's ability to keep a secret had surprised him.

"They're good." She sighed. Then more silence.

He didn't know what else to say. "I'll see you at the benefit then?"

"Of course."

She wasn't hanging up, but he had no idea what else she wanted.

"Billy made the team. His first competition is next week. He'd probably like to see you there."

"I'd love to." He wanted to tell her everything, but she needed to make the first move. An acknowledgment that they'd both screwed up was far from a declaration of love. "Send me the information."

"I'll text as soon as I hang up. See you next week."

"Sure."

"It was good talking to you," she said quietly.

"Like old times. Sneaking in a conversation in the laundry room."

"Yeah." But there was no humor in her voice. Not a hint of a laugh. "Bye."

She disconnected, and a moment later, he received a text giving him the competition information he already had.

As he crawled into bed that night, he swore to himself his plan would work and he'd win Tess back, but that promise felt pretty empty given the gloomy conversation they'd just suffered through.

Chapter 18

A week later, Tess stood outside the school trying not to tap her foot. She'd fussed with her hair and clothes in a way she'd never done for any school function, but the thought of seeing Miles again made her nervous. When she'd texted him the information, she'd told him to try to get here early because parking would be horrendous. She stood by the door watching cars pull into the lot, every car except his.

"You okay?" Zoe asked from where she sat next to Andrew on the steps.

"Yeah, why?"

"You're kinda jumpy. Plus, the thing starts in like two minutes. Are we waiting for Dad?"

"No. I don't think he's coming." She kept her answer intentionally vague. Tess took a deep breath and checked the time. Zoe was right. "Let's go in."

Tess hadn't told them Miles might come. She hadn't wanted to get their hopes up. Looked like she should've followed that thought for herself. Inside the auditorium, she walked down the main aisle, hoping to find four seats together without tipping off Zoe. As it turned out, the STEM club competition wasn't a huge draw, and there were plenty of seats.

She kept her phone in her hand in case Miles texted and wanted to sit with them. For all she knew, he was already here, sitting by himself. She looked around the room. The lights dimmed a little, and the assistant principal took the stage.

He introduced the five teams that were competing, and the first team came out and explained their project. Tess had no idea how any of this worked, but like with Zoe's swim meets, she figured she'd get the hang of it in time.

Since Billy's team was hosting, they went last. She listened to each team and watched their presentations. Some were pretty interesting, like the team who developed a new toilet paper product. The entire time, however, she gripped her phone and kept glancing around the room for any sign of Miles.

When Billy's team came out onto the stage with their robot—one that Tess had heard about nonstop since he'd made the team—Tess was filled with pride. Billy had found his place. He stood in front of the pack of kids and explained what the robot would do. Then he stepped back and another kid set the robot in motion.

When it was done, Andrew leaned over and whispered, "That was cool. Can he bring it home?"

"I'm pretty sure the robot belongs to the school."

They waited while the judges tabulated scores, and then the winning teams were announced. Billy's team took second place. A lump lodged in her throat, and she pulled out her phone and snapped a picture to send to William. It wasn't until after she took the picture that she noticed who was on the stage.

Her heart stopped.

Standing with the team and the coach was Miles, grinning like he'd won. His hand was on Billy's shoulder while they talked.

"Mom"—Zoe reached across Andrew to tap her leg "—Is that Miles?"

She nodded because she couldn't speak. She'd given up on him outside, sure he'd decided not to show up and suffer through any more uncomfortable conversation. She blinked rapidly to stave off the tears.

Yet here he was, coaching the STEM club.

The audience applauded the teams, and the house lights came up. People began filtering out into the hall to wait for their kids, but Tess sat frozen.

Andrew poked her arm. "Let's go, Mom. I wanna see Billy's medal."

"It'll take him a few minutes to come out. We'll meet him in the hall."

She stood and took Andrew's hand to help her stay focused. Why hadn't Billy said anything about Miles helping the team? She was thrilled to see Miles and to know he'd helped Billy made her happy in a way words couldn't express. At the same time, they'd kept this huge secret from her. Miles could've told her when they spoke last week, but he'd pretended to know nothing about the competition.

Her heart sank. They'd probably kept it from her because they figured she would ruin it. Miles's words from the night of their fight came back full force. She did like to be in control. She liked knowing what to expect. The kids needed stability in their lives. They should be able to count on an adult's word. But she should've recognized the lengths Miles had gone to make sure Billy had what he needed for his project.

As she stood in the hall with kids running out to meet parents, her nerves struck. Maybe Miles hadn't said anything because he was done with her. She'd told him to get out, and he had. He might not even come out to see her.

God, she hoped he would. If nothing else, she wanted to thank him for participating in STEM club with Billy.

Andrew bounced next to her, and Zoe wandered off after running into some friends.

Billy came through the door, and Tess waved at him. As he ran to her, his medal swung around in his fist.

"Did you see? We did it! Second place."

She pulled him to her with her free arm. "Yeah, I saw. You did a great job."

Andrew let go of her hand and tugged at the medal. Billy put it over his brother's head so he could wear it while inspecting it.

"I'm so proud of you. I've already texted Dad pictures. He'll be excited."

Billy rolled his eyes but didn't comment.

"Why didn't you tell me Miles was helping coach the team?"

Billy bit his lip and looked at the floor.

"You're not in trouble—although you probably should be for keeping a secret. I just want to know why you didn't tell me."

"Miles thought it would be better for it to be a secret until you weren't so mad."

"So he's been here the whole time, huh?"

Billy nodded. She took Andrew's hand

again and put her other arm around Billy. "Good to know. Let's go."

Billy shuffled his feet but didn't really move.

"Something wrong?"

"No...it's just..." He looked over his shoulder toward the door he'd exited.

Tess nudged him to get moving. The crowd was mostly gone now. There were only a few straggling families left. When the door opened again, Miles stepped out and turned toward her with a huge smile. Her heart lurched and her mouth went dry.

Billy snatched the medal from Andrew and handed it to Tess. "We're gonna go play on the playground. Okay, Mom?"

Without waiting for an answer, he took off out of the building. Tess shook her head. She'd been played.

Miles stepped close. "Hi."

"Hi," she said.

"Pretty awesome win, huh?"

"The win was great, but seeing you up on the stage with Billy was awesome." Her heart thundered in her ears. *Lord, I've missed looking at his face.* She wanted to reach out and touch him but didn't. "Can we talk?"

He chuckled. "I think that's the first time in my life someone has said that to me without it freaking me out." He tilted his head toward the front door. "Walk?"

She nodded. Outside, the sun was nearly gone, leaving the sky a purplish-blue. Tess sent Zoe a text to let her know they were at the playground. When the jungle gym was in sight, she faced Miles. "Why didn't you tell me you were coaching the STEM club?"

"Mostly because I wanted to prove to you I'm not going anywhere. This wasn't about putting on a show for you. If I'd called and told you, you would've thought I was doing it to fix things."

"Weren't you?"

"I wanted to make it up to Billy. I won't

say this wasn't about you at all, but it was mostly about Billy. Even if you'd left the auditorium today without looking at me, I'd still be here for him next week."

How could she have shoved him aside? She loved him so much. "I screwed up, and I was unfair to you. I'm sorry."

He blew out a long breath and stared across the street.

Tess had no idea how to interpret that, so she forged ahead. "I know we probably can't go back to what we had, but I'd like us to at least be friends. I miss talking to you."

"I can't be your friend."

She swallowed hard and nodded, even though he wasn't looking at her.

He took her hand and looked into her eyes. "I had a whole speech planned to beg you to take me back. Your apology kind of ruined it."

Her heart gave a quick thump. He wanted her to take him back? "I'm not looking for you to beg for anything. But we do need to talk. Really talk."

"Anything."

"I want us to be together. These last few weeks without you have been miserable. But I'm worried because what we had—that relationship—was unbalanced. You wanted to make my life easier, but you never wanted to lean on me for anything. You didn't even tell me when you were having trouble at work."

He stroked his thumb across her knuckles. "I didn't want to add to your stress."

"If we're going to be together, we need to be equal partners."

"Then you have to trust me to do my part with the kids. It doesn't matter that I'm not their dad. I don't need to be their dad. I'm your backup. Part of being backup means I'll use whatever resources I have available."

She groaned. He wanted to spend money on her kids.

"Before you start making grumpy noises, I

don't plan to buy them whatever they want, and I won't just throw money at things because it's easy, but you can't expect me to pretend I don't have money. I do. It's part of my lifestyle, and if we're together, that means you accept my lifestyle the way I've accepted yours."

It all sounded so reasonable when he said it. "I can try."

"So will I." He smiled and tugged her closer. "Can I kiss you now?"

"Please."

He slid his palm along her jaw as he lowered his mouth. He brushed his lips against hers, slipping his tongue along the seam of her mouth. She sighed with the rightness of it all.

He took his time relearning her. By the time their tongues touched, she was ready to climb all over him. It was magic and comfort all rolled into one.

That was until they heard, "Eww. Why are

you doing that in public? Little kids play here."

Miles pulled away, and they laughed at Zoe's admonishment.

"I guess you guys finally made up, huh?" Zoe asked.

"We did," Miles answered. Tess turned in his arms with a smile and looked at her kids.

"Good. We were getting tired of her being all sad. Try not to screw it up again."

Tess clenched her jaw. "Zoe—"

He stroked her arm. "It's okay. She's right. I'm not gonna screw up again. And I've got you guys to help me get it right."

"Hey, Mom," Billy called from the swings. "Can we go get ice cream?"

"Sure," she yelled back. She looked up at Miles over her shoulder. "Want to come for ice cream?"

"Can we hang out after?"

"We'll see." Tess was up for anything Miles wanted, because for the first time in weeks, she was happy again. She was glad she'd given them a second chance for love.

Next summer

Miles had no idea why Tess had refused to go to St. Mark's gala with him since they were together almost every day. He even had a drawer in her dresser for the nights he stayed when the kids weren't there. The kids knew he stayed over, but Tess still wasn't sure about him spending the night when they were there. It was unspoken that would happen in the future—their future.

He'd gotten the same suite at the Peninsula as last year, and he couldn't look at the picture window without imagining taking her up against it. He snapped a picture and texted it to Tess.

> Like the view?

Her response was quick.

> I don't remember much
> about the view last year. I
> was...preoccupied.

He was glad he'd sent a car to pick her up so she wouldn't have to drive, even though she'd tried to argue. It allowed for this playful texting.

> Aren't you going to send
> me a picture?

Moments later, he received a picture of her bare thigh and the hem of her shimmery blue dress. The woman was such a tease.

> You'll pay for that.

We'll see.

That phrase was one of her favorites. It

was a mom thing. He was slipping on his jacket when a knock sounded at the door. He opened it to see his mom there smiling.

"You're ready," she said.

"Don't be so shocked."

She huffed. "You're just in a hurry to go see Tess. Why isn't she here with you?"

"She said she wanted to make sure the kids were okay. She'll be here soon enough." He pulled the door closed and held out his arm for his mom to take. "How are you doing?"

"This year is easier than last. Attending with you helps."

As they stepped into the elevator, he realized that was probably the reason for Tess wanting to come alone. She knew how much his mother liked this benefit. He shook his head and smiled.

"What?" Mom asked.

"I think I figured out why Tess is meeting me here."

"Why?"

"So I'd be here with you now."

She patted his arm. "She's a good woman."

"Yes, she is." It was why he was thinking about asking her to marry him. He was just trying to figure out the right time and way. She wouldn't want anything showy.

They got to the ballroom, and Miles grabbed a glass of champagne for his mother and walked her to a table. She would hold council there as she did most years. People came to her to talk. Miles, on the other hand, preferred to mingle. He went to the bar to order a drink.

Sipping on his scotch, he leaned against the bar, so reminiscent of last summer when he'd dreaded coming here with his mother.

He knew the moment Tess entered the room. He felt her presence. They made brief eye contact, and she gave him a coy smile but didn't walk in his direction. Instead, she snagged a glass of champagne from a waiter and headed to the silent auction table. He waited to see how closely she would follow the events from last year.

She moved slowly at the tables. When she glanced back to him, he lifted his glass to her before draining it and then snuck up behind her as she placed a bid. "Still bidding on things you don't plan to win?" he whispered against her ear.

She started at his voice and shifted to face him. "I might win, but mostly I bid to get others to bid more. It's all for a good cause, you know."

"Any fancy French soaps? I could really use some."

She laughed, and he took her hand while she was distracted. "I don't like pretending we're strangers."

"I thought that was the kind of thing that keeps romance alive."

"Romance and lust is plenty alive in me. Thank you, by the way."

"For what?"

"It took until I was in the elevator with my mother to realize why you put me off."

She ducked her head but didn't say anything.

They made their way around all the tables, made a few bids, and then went to the dinner table where they found Angie. "You better hurry if you want to bid on the coffee basket. Tess thinks it's hers."

Tess gave him a gentle shove. "Hey. You're supposed to be on my side."

"Always," he said and kissed her.

"I'm glad you feel that way, because I have another reason for wanting to arrive separately."

"Yeah?"

She inhaled deeply, distracting him with the rise of the swell of her breasts in the low-cut dress. "I wanted tonight to be as special as it was last year when we first met."

She licked her lips before continuing. "This past year has been good. You've brought so much happiness into my life and the lives of the kids. We're all better for having met you."

"I feel the same. I love you."

Her eyes were wide, and it registered she was nervous about whatever she was about to say. "I love you, too, which is why I'm hoping you'll want to make an honest woman out of me." She pressed something in his palm, and he opened his hand to see a gold band.

"Miles Prescott, will you marry me?"

He stared at her, drinking in her beauty and vulnerability, as if there were any possibility he could refuse. He could deny this woman nothing. "I would love to marry you."

He slipped the ring on his finger and held her face to kiss her. "You couldn't even let me have that, could you? Always have to be in control."

"If I left it up to you, who knows how long we'd wait? I want us to start our life together now." She pulled him close. "Don't worry. When we get upstairs, I'll let you have all the control."

"Sounds like your best plan yet."

Also by Shannyn Schroeder

The O'Leary Family

More Than This (The O'Leary Family #1)

A Good Time (The O'Leary Family #2)

Something to Prove (The O'Leary Family #3)

Catch Your Breath (The O'Leary Family #4)

Just a Taste (The O'Leary Family #5)

Hold Me Close (The O'Leary Family #6)

The O'Malley Family

Under Your Skin (The O'Malley Family #1)

In Your Arms (The O'Malley Family #2)

Through Your Eyes (The O'Malley Family #3)

From Your Heart (The O'Malley Family #4)

The Doyle Family

In Too Deep (The Doyle Family #1)

In Fine Form (The Doyle Family #2)

Daring Divorcees Series

One Night with a Millionaire

My Best Friend's Ex

My Forever Plus-One

Stand Alones

Between Love and Loyalty

Meeting His Match

Hot & Nerdy

Her Best Shot

Her Perfect Game

Her Winning Formula

His Work of Art

His New Jam

His Dream Role

Sloane Steele's Books